"The gods wanted to curse her for her beauty."

Heat from his body engulfed her as he rose to stand behind her chair. His head was nothing but a breath away. She stopped reading and swallowed.

"Continue," he said, his deep voice caressing the wisps of hair that dangled by her ears.

"Can you not see the text yourself?" she asked, her voice breathy.

She met his glance and nearly forgot her name or where she was. Her mouth went dry. He looked as if he were prepared to devour her. Not in a lecherous fashion, but rather one she instinctively knew would be incredibly pleasurable. She grabbed a handful of the material at her thigh.

Oh for mercy's sake.

Without a second thought she leaned in and mashed her lips against his and held them there for a while. After sitting back she eyed his reaction.

"Miss Worthington, if you're going to kiss me, you must do so with more passion than that." He placed one hand beneath her chin.

Absently, she realized that his other hand was kneading the back of her neck. But his mouth demanded most of her attention as it moved elegantly, seductively across her own.

This was kissing...

Seduce Me

Robyn DeHart

FOREVER

NEW YORK   BOSTON

Book design by Giorgetta Bell McRee
Cover design by Claire Brown
Cover illustration by Alan Ayers

Forever
Hachette Book Group
237 Park Avenue
New York, NY 10017
Visit our Web site at www.HachetteBookGroup.com.

Forever is an imprint of Grand Central Publishing.
The Forever name and logo is a trademark of Hachette Book Group, Inc.

Printed in the United States of America

First Printing: August 2009

10 9 8 7 6 5 4 3 2 1

To my oldest and dearest friend, Amy White. We've grown up so much since those late nights on the sofa watching silly movies and laughing until we couldn't breathe, but our friendship has never faltered. And who knew crackers were so versatile. Thanks for always being there. No, this isn't Olivia and Simon, but I promise you'll love Esme and Fielding just as much.

And, as always, to my husband, Paul. Thank you for dealing with all my craziness, too many pizzas to count (not that you ever mind that!), and for always offering to make the scrambled eggs. You are my hero in every sense of the word.

Acknowledgments

No books are truly written alone, and this one was no exception. So to my critique partners, Emily and Hattie, you put up with more of my whining than any two people deserve. To my fantastic agent, Christina Hogrebe, who always gushes at the right moment and who, quite frankly, is a perfect matchmaker. Special thanks to everyone at Grand Central for the fantastic welcome, especially my brilliant editor Amy Pierpont, who gave me a new definition for revisions. Your insight is nothing short of astounding, and this book is better for it. Thank you for believing in me and this project. And I would be remiss not to mention Kelly Harms; though you've moved on to bigger things, I know my career would not be where it is today without your support and guidance, and for that I will always be grateful.

Seduce Me

Prologue

Sweat and sand mingled and dripped into his eyes, clouding his vision. Fielding Grey, the Viscount of Eldon, swiped an already damp rag across his mud-streaked face. There was never anything easy about crawling into a cave or digging up a tomb. Or excavating a temple, which was what he was doing now.

The grit and grime didn't matter. Nor did the object he sought. All that mattered right now, as Fielding squeezed himself into a small antechamber lit only by the lantern in his hand, was the huge sum of money his client would pay him once he found what was left of the Great Library of Alexandria.

The royal library had once been the largest in the world, housing such treasures as Aristotle's private collection. By royal mandate, Ptolemy II had stormed ships to confiscate any books or scrolls on board to add to the library. Legend had it that the library was destroyed by Julius Caesar's command, but most claimed warning had come in time to relocate the vast collection.

More than sixteen months of research had finally led Fielding here: the Temple of Isis on a small island off the coast of Egypt and not far from Alexandria.

He jumped to the ground of the antechamber, the sound of his feet slamming onto the stone floor echoing through the room. The two Egyptian men he'd paid to assist him entered next carrying more lanterns. The new light shone about the stone room, illuminating hieroglyphics. The colored drawings depicted several versions of Isis nursing Horus, as well as a full-grown Horus.

Fielding walked the length of one wall, running his hand against the cool stone. There would be a lever or a loose stone, something that would take them into the next hidden chamber. But he felt only smooth brick beneath his palm. He knew he needed to go down as deep as possible. The remains of the library would be hidden there; in particular the rumored secret writings of Socrates, a prized possession in Aristotle's collection. These writings were what the man who'd hired him was specifically interested in.

A six-inch black scorpion scuttled over his boot, trying to find a way into his pants. Fielding kicked his foot out, causing the offending insect to fly across the room. His assistants jumped simultaneously and huddled together against the wall.

"We need to go deeper," he told them in their native tongue. He wasn't fluent, but he knew enough from previous digs to get by.

The two brown men nodded but made no further movement.

Looking down, he noted a slight groove in the sand where he'd kicked away the scorpion. "Hand me the water." He reached out his arm and one man, the braver of the two perhaps, stepped forward to give Fielding the canteen.

With his boot he moved additional sand away, revealing more of the groove. He knelt and poured a small amount of water into the crevice. The liquid bubbled with the sand, turning light brown, and then it thinned out, leaking somewhere below. Fielding scraped more of the sand aside and pressed his ear to the floor. Then he poured more water, this time a greater amount.

It disappeared into the crevice, and Fielding could hear the drips landing somewhere far below them.

"There is another chamber beneath this one," he told his assistants. "Look around for a way to open it." He pointed to the two men, who still stood pressed against the wall. "Shuffle your feet around; move the sand away from the stones."

When they still hadn't moved, he said to them, "And stop being so bloody afraid of a curse. This is a temple, meant to welcome people for worship." He didn't add that the closer they got to the legendary library, the more likely it was they'd run across some danger. People went to great lengths to protect items of value from treasure hunters like himself.

Another scorpion crawled across the sand-covered stone floor, making its path toward one of Fielding's diggers. The man jumped over the creature, landing hard on a stone to his right. Suddenly, the entire floor shifted, leaving huge gaps between the stones. The offending insect fell through the opened floor. Fielding grabbed onto the wall to his right.

"No one move," he warned.

For several seconds they all stayed motionless. Gingerly, Fielding took one step forward and then another. His third wobbled enough that he leaned into the wall, and when he did a loud click sounded behind it and the floor below him gave way.

He cursed loudly as he fell several feet into the chamber beneath them. He landed with a painful thud, the lantern he'd been holding shattering next to him, dousing the light. He could barely see the glow of his two assistants' lanterns above him.

"Throw me down a torch," he yelled.

They did as commanded, but the unlit torch landed somewhere to his left, swallowed by the shadows. Briefly he tried to feel for it, but remembering the scorpion was down here with him stilled his hand.

"Lower one of the lanterns on a rope so I can see."

The lowered lantern shed enough ambient light around the room for him to find the fallen torch. He quickly lit the thing, and warmth from the fire soon heated his face. A quick cursory glance around the room showed two more torches hung on the wall. He lit them both, and the room filled with a soft glow.

There was a tunnel going off to the right, which warranted exploration. Whether he found his client's ancient library or not, whatever he found down here would fetch a pretty price.

"Lower the rope back down so I can climb up when I'm finished." Neither of the men answered him, but the rope once again dropped to hang through the hole into which Fielding had fallen.

There were more hieroglyphics in this room, but instead of being painted on the walls, they were carved. Fielding inhaled deeply, the chalky chilled air filling his lungs. The tunnel proved smaller than he'd anticipated, and he found he would have to travel through it on his hands and knees. Not an easy task when one needed to carry a torch at the same time.

Carefully he set out down the tunnel, clumsily crawling on three limbs while he held the torch in his right hand. He was halfway into the narrow space when he realized the tunnel might not be complete. With his left hand, he tested the space directly in front of him, gauging the strength of the stone, but it held firm.

He inched forward, noting the darkness in front of him grew increasingly blacker. It was several rapid heartbeats before he could see the tunnel continued past a considerable gap in the stone.

He was getting close. Someone had gone to extreme measures to protect whatever was on the far end of this tunnel. He crawled to the edge and peered down into a rock-walled chamber that dropped off into darkness below.

Ordinarily his height was a hindrance to his job, as he was always having to squeeze himself into the tiniest of places. But in this regard, Fielding wagered he could make it across. He leaned over the edge, holding the torch low to see what fate he would meet if he were to fail. The sand at the bottom of the chamber was littered with bones and wooden spikes that shot up from the ground.

He took a steadying breath and, holding the torch in his teeth, made a leap to the other side. The distance was wider than he'd anticipated, and although he managed to get his upper body across the divide, his legs dangled down toward the yawning gap below. The bag around his waist shifted, changing his balance, and he began to slide. Using his hands and feet, he scrambled for a hold on the slick walls of the chamber and managed to stop his descent.

Hot ashes from the torch fell to his face, burning his eyes. He'd been in difficult situations before, he reminded himself. And he'd always survived.

With that thought he climbed back up to the ledge of the chamber, pushed himself up to his waist, and crawled back onto the stone floor of the tunnel. A moment later he found himself in an enormous room, this one with shelves built of stone. Scrolls and tablets covered every surface.

At long last, he'd found it. The lost Library of Alexandria.

He started with the shelf to his immediate right, careful to handle the fragile pieces with care. There was a fortune in this room. His client might have hired him to find a group of specific texts, but everything else he'd be able to sell to the highest bidder.

It took him the better part of an hour to sift through several shelves before he came across something with Socrates' name on it. He bundled the scrolls into his bag and turned to go. Tomorrow he'd come back with a team to retrieve the rest of the materials.

Getting back across the tunnel was much easier now that he knew to gauge the distance of the trap chamber, and soon he found himself standing below the rope his assistants had used to lower the torch.

"Tighten the rope," he called. "I'm coming up."

Fielding secured the bag to his waist, then began the climb up. He made it to the top and held out his hand.

Firm fingers grabbed his forearm and allowed him enough support to pull himself back into the antechamber.

He swiped at the dust on his pants, then stood straight. "Who the devil are you?" Fielding asked the man before him. He looked around the room but found no sight of the two men who'd climbed into the temple with him. "And what did you do with my men?"

"Your men were paid and sent home." The man held out his card. "I am a friend."

What kind of pompous idiot carried a card into an excavation site? Fielding grabbed the card and read it: *Jonathon Kessler, Solomon's.* Well, of course, a pompous member of Solomon's. And here he'd thought the scorpion was bad. Fielding flipped it back to the man. "Solomon's is no friend of mine." He did nothing to hide the coldness in his voice.

Kessler smiled and pocketed the card. "The men of our club wish to discuss a business proposition with you," he said. The man, several years Fielding's senior, had somehow managed to climb into the ancient tomb without getting even a speck of dust on his crisply pressed suit. Fielding fought the childish urge to kick sand onto the man's shiny black boots.

Instead he picked up the rope and wound it around his elbow and hand until it was in a manageable form, then he tossed it into his pack. "A business proposition. And they sent you all the way to Egypt to find me."

Kessler's mouth twitched with a slight grin. "Of course not," he said with disdain. "I was already in Alexandria. And now that you have found what you came for"—the man nodded to the bag tied at Fielding's waist—"you'll be returning to London. They wish to speak with you upon your arrival."

He had a lengthy list of things to do once he returned to London: a long, hot bath; a good glass of brandy, perhaps several; and about a week in the bed of a willing woman. A visit to Solomon's was nowhere on that list.

"I have no interest in Solomon's," Fielding said.

"Ordinarily the feeling would be mutual, I can assure you, Mr. Grey. But under the circumstances, I do believe a brief alliance would behoove both parties. Perhaps you will reconsider." The man withdrew a folded piece of parchment and handed it to Fielding. "This is an offer you simply *cannot* refuse."

Chapter One

———— ❧ ∼ ❧ ————

London, Mid-June 1887

One Friday night on a sleepy side of London, Esme Worthington yawned a most unladylike yawn, then sniffled her nose before looking back at the text on her lap. It was long past a reasonable time for bed, yet here she sat. Sometime after midnight she'd abandoned the hard chairs of her study for the more comfortable sofa in the parlor next door. But the plush floral cushions assisted only by lulling her to sleep rather than encouraging her to continue her research. She readjusted herself and blinked several times, trying to focus on the book before her.

She read the last sentence once again, trying to absorb the words. Some of these so-called scholars simply had no notion what they were suggesting. Precisely how was an artifact from ancient Greece supposed to have ended up in the jungles of South America? Preposterous. There was no possible way that Pandora's box had ended up on a Spanish explorer's ship.

Another yawn.

Her great black tom lifted his sleepy head from where he lay curled warmly over her thighs. His gold eyes were nothing more than slits as he yawned. "Horace, I do believe I shall retire for the evening. I don't seem to be getting any work done at all." She scratched him behind his ears, and he rewarded her with a rhythmic purr. Placing the heavy book on the table next to her, she stood. "You guard the books, and tomorrow morning I shall pour you some warm milk."

Esme doused the lamp, then stepped into the hallway. Horace followed her, and she scooped him into her arms. "Want to warm my feet tonight, do you?"

She stopped. Something had scraped against the wood floor in the very next room. It was far too late for Aunt Thea to be awake. Perhaps it was one of the servants, though they were normally early to bed as well. She padded over to the room and nudged the door open.

Two men, dressed head-to-toe in black, stopped what they were doing and faced her as the door swung open.

A scream caught in her throat when Horace leaped from her arms and strolled into the study where the villains stood, his tail high in the air. Evidently his feline sense of danger was sorely lacking.

Her heart thundered, but she couldn't very well leave them to continue their misdeeds now that they'd seen her. "I beg your pardon!" she said, straightening her back and trying to appear taller. "Precisely what do you think you're doing?" Her study was in tatters. Papers thrown about and books on the floor. What kind of barbarians . . . she picked up the book resting by her toe and clutched it to her chest.

They were of equal height, but one was clearly more athletic and stronger than the other. The larger one strode over to her and she realized, far too late, that she had nothing to use as a weapon against the brute. Even her slippers were worthless for that sort of deed. She supposed she could whack him on the head with the book she held, but it was her prized copy of *Gulliver's Travels*. She certainly couldn't risk damaging the book. Besides, she didn't want to wake her aunt or her elderly servants lest she put them in danger too, so Esme stood her ground.

"I can assure you I have nothing here worth stealing. You are in the wrong neighborhood for that," she said. "Although you are doing an admirable job of destroying my library." Then it occurred to her that her precious books might very well be what they were after. "I have no original texts," she lied. "These are all silly novels, not worth anything." Another lie.

The man took another step toward her. His eyes were wild and frightening, and when he ran them up and down her body, she became all too aware of the clothing she wore. Or rather the lack thereof. Granted, it was several hours after midnight, and a woman was generally given the right to sit in her own home wearing a night rail and robe. This man's intense gaze penetrated her and caused the hairs on the nape of her neck to stand erect. She forced herself not to shiver.

Surely they were not here to ravish her. Pulling her robe tighter around her, she eyed her opponent. She would certainly cause all sorts of noise if that was the case. No matter that the other three persons in the house were grayed and wrinkled, they could grab a fire poker or sturdy umbrella and fend off her attackers. And Aunt Thea had those ridiculously heavy candelabra in the dining room. Perhaps it would have been much smarter had Esme grabbed one of those before storming in here unarmed.

"Where's the key?" the man asked.

"Evidently you don't need keys." She pointed to the emptied drawers and shelves. "You simply force things open when you need to see within."

He closed in on her, his expression one of ravenous greed. He ripped the book from her grasp and whisked it across the room. It landed on its spine, the pages fanning out until they settled open. Esme winced. Panic fluttered in her chest as she considered the damage they'd already done to her desk and books. She didn't like to contemplate the damage such fiends could perpetrate on her person.

She narrowed her eyes at the man. "You should know that if you intend to ravish me, I will scream the house down," she said, forcing her voice to be as calm as possible. "And believe me when I say that the people who will come running to assist me will do you much bodily harm." An absurd notion.

He reached out and fingered the ruffled hem of her sleeve. His lip curled. "Tempting. But we only want the key." His voice was deep and raspy as he added, "And we've seen your staff." A smirk, then a vicious chuckle escaped his ugly mouth.

Bored with the exchange, her cat took that moment to flip his tail in the air and strut out of the room. Now she was utterly alone with these dangerous men.

She crossed her arms over her chest, mostly to hide her shaking hands. She hoped it made her look formidable. Not an easy task for one so small in stature, but she did her best. "I simply don't know which key you're referring to."

The man on the other side of the room twitched. "Thatcher, we don't have time," he said, his voice heavy with a Cockney accent.

"We take her, then," Thatcher said.

"You will do no such thing," Esme said, taking a step backward.

The man in front of her silently closed the door behind her, then shoved a cloth into her mouth. Furiously she tried to spit it out, then reached up for it, but before she could he grabbed her wrists and held them tight.

Esme tried scratching him while he manhandled her, but her blasted nails were so short, she caused little damage. She really must stop chewing them. With her feet she kicked and flailed, trying anything to deter them from taking her.

Nerves rippled through her stomach in sickening waves. She was in serious danger. With renewed effort, she kicked her legs about, desperately aiming to hit a target, but failing nonetheless.

This simply was not happening.

Her efforts to wrench herself from her captor's viselike grip only succeeded in exhausting her. She fought to keep her breathing under control lest she end up hyperventilating and suffocate herself on the gag. *Think, Esme.* She could find a way out of this situation.

Surely they had mistaken her for someone else. She didn't own anything valuable. Certainly not any keys. They didn't even have a cabinet to lock up the family silver. Of course, they no longer had any family silver. These foolish men were in the wrong house, kidnapping the wrong woman.

Thatcher yanked the tie to her robe and the loose folds fell open, leaving her exposed to the chill. "Waters, tie her hands together."

Waters did as he was told while Thatcher climbed out the library window. The thin satin sash became a harsh cord as he tightened it around her wrists. With the stronger of the two captors distracted, she doubled her efforts at trying to break free from Waters's clutches. But despite his slender body, his hands gripped her arms, sealing her in place.

"Hand me her feet," Thatcher said in a harsh whisper.

Waters complied, and in an instant she was being passed through the window as if she were nothing more than a sack of potatoes.

"Her bum is stuck on the window," Waters said.

"Well, lift her up." Thatcher's impatience was evident.

Waters gave her a lift. "She has quite the bottom for such a wee thing."

She glared at him, but he was not looking at her face. More than anything she wished to take the wretched cloth out of her mouth and give them both a tongue-lashing for speaking so cruelly about her bottom. Perhaps it was a bit on the large side for a woman of her size, but she had always been rather fond of it.

Once they were all out on the ground, Esme noticed the waiting coach. Four black steeds stomped impatiently. Clearly owned by someone quite wealthy, the large carriage was black with gilded filigree, and despite the dark night, Esme noted how it shone. A crest emblazoned the door, backed in red and in the center a great black bird, its wings spread as if it were about to fly away.

The street was barren except for the coach, but she was only a few steps from rounding the corner to a much busier lane. Now was her chance to try to get away. She bolted toward the front street, but the clouds shielding the almost full moon made seeing rather challenging. Nevertheless, she'd made it a far distance before one of the men crashed on top of her, knocking the air from her lungs and crushing her with his weight.

The damp grass chilled her immediately, reminding her all too well she was clad only in her aging night rail.

"You're not going anywhere, you little bitch." Thatcher pulled her to her feet and tossed her over his shoulder. In one swift movement he had dumped her on the dirty floor inside the carriage. Then he jumped in right behind her as they began jostling down the street.

"Get up on the seat," Thatcher snarled at her. When she didn't move, he lifted her and shoved her onto the seat. "You can't ride on the floor like that. We have a long trip ahead of us."

She kept her legs pulled to her chest, trying to warm her body. But the shivering would not still. Squeezing her eyes shut, she willed this scenario away. This couldn't possibly be happening. When she opened her eyes, though, it was all too real. Both villains were in the small confines with her. She pushed the curtain back as best she could with tied hands. If she couldn't escape, the least she could do was find out where they were taking her.

The dimly lit streets of London sped by, and she tried to keep a running catalog of all the roads they passed. But soon they turned down a road she didn't recognize and then another until she was thoroughly lost. She let the curtain fall back into place.

Esme was certain that the men could hear her heart pounding, so loudly did it beat in her chest. She willed her pulse to slow, taking steadying breaths. Esme closed her eyes. Perhaps if they thought her to be asleep, they would let their guard down just long enough for her to escape.

"What will we do with her?" Waters asked.

Thatcher cracked his knuckles. The sickening pops echoed against the small carriage walls. "We'll take her with us to the dungeon. Then we'll bring her to the Raven; he'll get her to talk."

Chapter Two

Fielding Grey stared blankly at the note in front of him. He'd read it at least ten times, and still the words remained the same.

Mr. Grey,

We have business to discuss. It is in your best interest to make yourself available. Contact us at your earliest convenience to schedule a meeting.

Sincerely,
The Members of Solomon's
28 King Street

Fielding pocketed the note and glanced once more at the clock ticking on the mantelpiece, wondering again why he'd bothered to come. Solomon's. Until the impromptu meeting in Egypt, he hadn't thought of this place, nor the men within, for a very long time.

These men with their pious attitudes and dreams of

artifacts fooled themselves into thinking they sought treasure for moral reasons. They'd fooled his father with that nonsense, convincing him to chase after one such treasure. Ultimately, the chase had led to the destruction of their family coffers, followed by his father's untimely death.

The room he sat in was typical of any gentlemen's club, with its large leather chairs that were heavily buttoned, ashtrays and pipe stands on every table, a sideboard with trays of brandy, port, and scotch, and a quiet atmosphere. These clubs were meant to be refuges where men could escape the noise and bustle of their nagging wives and crying children.

And this club, in particular, was where his own father had escaped his family.

Fielding stood and walked to the back of the room where framed photographs hung against a mahogany-paneled wall. He scanned the images. Some were faded; others looked new and sharp. These were the men of Solomon's. He recognized quite a few of them. Marquess Lindberg, who was rumored to be quite the rogue. Nick Callum, a second son, whom Fielding had known in school.

Each of these men represented a legend, or rather an obsession. Solomon's was the most secretive club in London and the most exclusive. It was rumored to have been started by King Henry VIII, a man who himself was seduced by the thought of hidden treasures. Each member of the club was invited to join only after proving themselves experts in the study of a particular legend or myth. Every man was held up to the light, and his obsession, as well as his intentions, was heavily scrutinized.

Only the pure at heart could darken the doorway of

the prestigious club. No one with practical motives such as earning funds to pay off debts was ever considered, making it all the more ironic that he himself stood in this very room.

Fielding knew all about Solomon's. These men would do anything for the opportunity to touch whatever treasure they sought. It mattered not if a member left a wife and son at home waiting and wondering if he would return.

Then a particular photograph caught his eye. Speaking of the devil. Fielding stepped closer to the wall for a better look. Second row from the top, fourth picture over—his father. Wearing his ridiculous hat and dusty clothes, he looked more like a servant than an aristocrat. Not much different, Fielding supposed, than he himself looked most of the time.

Damnation!

The similarities between him and his father ended there, he reminded himself. Fielding was not a dreamer.

Why had he come here? Mere curiosity, he'd told himself when he left the house this morning. Yet, standing here, facing his father's photo and the ghosts of his own past, Fielding realized it was far more than that. There were answers he needed within these walls. The men of Solomon's would pay for what they had done to his family.

The clock chimed the hour. Footsteps sounded down the hall. Perfect timing. From them, he expected nothing less.

A door to his right opened soundlessly, and a butler stepped forward. "Mr. Grey, they will see you now."

Fielding took one last look at his father's picture, then

allowed the butler to show him into the room. The door closed behind him.

As a boy, he'd longed for an invitation to enter this room. His father had told him many stories about the important decisions that were made here, such as who would or wouldn't be invited to become a member. "Only those who are worthy," his father had said. And now, worthy or not, Fielding finally stood within its four walls.

Fielding shoved the memories aside; he didn't have time for ghosts today.

Dark wood paneling covered the walls of the room, and a large table surrounded by straight-backed wooden chairs dominated the space. Swords hung on one wall along with a tapestry depicting a damsel in distress being rescued by a knight, his chest emblazoned with a red lion. As if the men of Solomon's believed they were the bloody Knights of the Round Table.

When he noted only three men gathered around the table, Fielding asked, "You didn't invite the others?" He did nothing to disguise the mockery in his voice.

"The others, as you put it," the eldest said, "are fully aware of our meeting."

"Do you require tea?" the butler asked.

Again the same man responded. He held his hand up, his long fingers withered with age. "That won't be necessary. The brandy"—he motioned to the crystal decanter at the center of the table—"will suffice." He was nearly Fielding's height, which was something considering that Fielding was tall for an Englishman. This man, however, was at least thirty years Fielding's senior, and while he certainly looked aristocratic with all his sharp facial features, Fielding doubted the man had ever been considered handsome.

Without an ounce of pretension or an invitation to do so, Fielding sat and stretched his legs out in front of him.

The men followed his lead. Again the tallest one spoke, gesturing to his left. "Mr. Grey, this is Maxwell Barrett, the Marquess of Lindberg."

Lindberg nodded. "We've met before, I believe," he said.

Fielding remained silent. He knew very little of Lindberg, only that he had a reputation as a lothario. Fielding suspected Max's golden hair and blue eyes made seduction rather easy.

"This is Mr. Nichols," the tall man said, pointing to the man on his right. "And I am Jensen."

"Merely Jensen?" Fielding asked.

"It is enough," Jensen said. The man's heavily lined face showed no emotion, but his shrewd black eyes—so black it was impossible to determine a difference in color between iris and pupil—spoke volumes. This was not a man one trifled with. He was used to getting his way, and he would do whatever it took to ensure that happened.

Well, Fielding wasn't so easily manipulated. He'd dealt with men far more powerful than these.

Max poured himself a drink, then stood. "We have a business proposition for you."

"So your associate informed me." He crossed his arms over his chest. "Impressive that you tracked me all the way to Egypt."

"We are aware of your existing profession as well as your previous . . . employment with the Raven," Mr. Nichols said, his voice wavering like a nervous hen's. The short, round man mopped at his brow with a handkerchief. "It is your experience with such matters that makes you uniquely qualified for our offer."

Fielding leaned forward, resting both arms on the table. "Are you offering me a position?" he asked. "I wasn't aware that Solomon's kept a staff."

"Aside from those in our employ who work at our club, no, we are not generally in the business of employing staff," Jensen said, his tone even and flat. "We try to keep our name and our existence as quiet as possible."

"But since I already knew about you . . . ," Fielding inferred.

"Precisely," Max said.

Fielding understood what they meant, what they weren't saying. They didn't want him to be here any more than he wanted to be. They'd invited him out of sheer desperation. Satisfaction spread through him. He would most certainly refuse their offer. No matter what the task.

He'd be a liar, though, if he said he wasn't the least bit curious. That was the one trait he shared with his father, and no matter how he tried, he hadn't been able to rid himself of it.

To hide his curiosity, he leaned forward and poured himself a drink. "What is it that you wish me to do?" Fielding asked.

"It has come to our attention that the Raven has potentially located a specific and rather valuable antiquity. We cannot allow him to keep or sell it," Jensen said. "Your uncle, after all, is not known for the most scrupulous of associations."

That was putting it mildly. "You want me to steal it from him?" Fielding sat back in his seat and pondered the idea.

"You cannot deny you have experience with this very thing," Jensen said.

"Stealing from my uncle?" Fielding laughed. "No, I

can't." Solomon's had had conflicts of interest with the
Raven in the past, but the men here had never resorted
to thievery. Whatever the artifact they were both after, it
must be worth a fortune. He waited only the briefest of
moments before asking, "What is the item?"

The three men exchanged glances as something went
unsaid between them. Finally Max leaned forward and
leveled his gaze on Fielding. "It's Pandora's box."

Fielding chuckled. The box from the children's bed-
time story? They must be joking. Then he realized none
of the other men were laughing. "You're quite serious."

Jensen nodded.

"The *real* Pandora's box," Fielding said. He really
shouldn't have been surprised. As members of Solomon's,
they were all legend hunters. Why would they not believe
in an ancient Greek myth?

"One and the same," Mr. Nichols said, his voice barely
registering above a whisper.

"As the story goes, Pandora allowed her curiosity to get
the better of her and opened a box, releasing plagues and
curses. It is this *cursed* box you seek?" Fielding asked,
unable to keep the derision from his voice.

Jensen set his glass down rather abruptly. "We do not
require mockery, Mr. Grey. We were under the impression
that you'd dealt with these sorts of antiquities before."

Fielding had never paid much attention to the antiquities he'd found; he couldn't afford to. To him they were
nothing more than the sum of money he collected. But
he knew from his own clients that many believed in the
magic of certain pieces. Despite his feelings about Solomon's, he felt obliged to be the voice of reason. "Could
it not simply be an artifact, a jewelry or trinket box from

ancient Greece and nothing more that my uncle has located?"

Mr. Nichols shook his head gravely. "If only it were that simple. This box is heavily cursed, sir."

Fielding shook his head. Curses were nonsense. "So why me? Why don't the men of Solomon's go after it? Your members are as skilled at the hunt as the Raven's men."

"We each have our own expertise," Lindberg said. "I myself am prepared for a different quest than that of Pandora's box. And some of us are content to merely be scholars of our subject. Mr. Nichols, for instance, has studied Pandora's legend for years, but his skill lies in research, not retrieval."

Mr. Nichols gave a weak smile and nodded.

Eyeing the man, Fielding could well imagine why Solomon's had not sent the meek Mr. Nichols to face the Raven. A headstrong woman would be a far better match against his uncle.

"You know the Raven's henchmen better than we do," Jensen interjected. "Know the sorts of behavior they exhibit, know where they'll take the box. You are the best prepared to handle such men. We are . . ." Jensen's voice trailed off with a wave of his hand.

"*Gentlemen*?" Fielding provided with a touch of bitterness in his voice. "Of course." Heat crept up the back of his neck. He should tell them to go straight to the devil. He too was a gentleman. At least he'd been raised one. He even had the title and coffers to prove it. But to the men of Solomon's, Fielding wasn't a viscount, he was merely a means to an end.

"Name your price," Mr. Nichols said. His stubby fingers twisted around his handkerchief, balling the damp cloth into a compact wad. "It is of utmost importance that we retrieve this artifact."

"Why is this particular piece so important? Other than Mr. Nichols's obvious affection," Fielding said.

Lindberg's easy smile disappeared. "Because it might be dangerous," he said.

"*Might* be?" Fielding asked.

"Most likely is," Lindberg corrected.

"We simply don't know," Mr. Nichols said, his voice nearing a fevered pitch. "There are many writings on the contents of Pandora's box, and we don't know which ones are accurate. But the potential . . ." His words trailed off. "The potential is catastrophic," he finally said.

"Tell him," Lindberg said.

Mr. Nichols eyed his fellow Solomon's members before nodding and turning back to Fielding.

"It is said there is evil within Pandora's box. That the gods put terrible things such as greed, hatred, disease, vanity, envy, and lust inside the box to punish Pandora for her curiosity. These curses, if you will, are believed to be embodied by actual artifacts within the box."

"Something you can hold or touch," Lindberg explained.

"Yes, yes," Mr. Nichols said. "Once the box is opened and these plagues are released, evil beyond imagining will fall upon our land."

"These evils, as you call them," Fielding said, "already exist in our world."

"They can't compare to the evils held within Pandora's box. And if that box got into the wrong hands . . ." Mr. Nichols wrung his hands again.

"And you believe my uncle has located the box?" Fielding asked. "I would not deny the man is good at what he does, but after all these centuries and hundreds of people searching for it, how was that it the Raven discovered its location?"

"He is not the first; others have found it before," Jensen said. "Perhaps you remember reading about the Black Death?" The man's smile was tight, his tone clipped.

"If memory serves me correctly, it was rats that caused the plague," Fielding said.

"Merely a vessel," Jensen argued.

"Your uncle is very good at what he does," Lindberg said. "No one can deny that. Regardless of whether you believe the warnings, were they proved true, the damage the Raven would surely cause with the box would be catastrophic. We need to stop him."

"Precisely," Jensen said. He steepled his long fingers beneath his chin. "We cannot risk his unleashing Pandora's curses. It is far too dangerous."

Fielding didn't believe a word of it. He'd heard of the myth, but that was all it was. Still, these men were quite serious in their concerns. But then the legend hunters of Solomon's were generally a serious sort.

If there was the slightest chance the box was dangerous, though, they were right: Allowing it to fall into the hands of the Raven would bring dire consequences.

"Where is it?" Fielding asked.

"We believe it to be in Portsmouth, in the ruins of a castle," Lindberg said.

"It was most recently a monastery," Mr. Nichols added.

"More importantly, that's where the Raven believes it to be," Jensen added. He slid a large stack of papers toward Fielding. "This is all the research we've gathered on the subject."

Fielding thumbed through the pages. They'd had the Raven followed, and the pages detailed his uncle's research as well as Mr. Nichols's. Fielding came upon a list with five unfamiliar names on it. "Who are these people?"

"Other scholars on the subject," Mr. Nichols said.

"Why is 'Mr. Spencer' marked through and replaced with the name Worthington?" Fielding asked.

"Spencer was a fictitious name used for protection," Mr. Nichols said.

"Worthington is the only one on that list who lives here in London," Jensen said. "Though we do not know precisely where."

"She guards her privacy well," Mr. Nichols said.

"Worthington is a she?" Fielding asked.

"Oh, yes, and a brilliant scholar in her own right. That much I know."

"You would, of course, have access to all our resources," Lindberg said. He pointed to the papers beneath Fielding's hand. "The location of the monastery is in those notes."

Fielding certainly didn't need their money, nor their resources. But having the opportunity, having them this desperate for his help, meant only one thing. They would be within his grasp, close enough for him to infiltrate their precious club and finally make someone pay for his father's death.

"I don't think you could afford me," he told them. "My fee is thirty thousand pounds." Fielding expected protests and sputtering, even laughter, but he never expected compliance.

"You'll have a banknote for half before you leave

today," Jensen said, not even blinking. "The other half when you bring us the box."

"Will you accept our proposition?" Mr. Nichols asked.

Fielding grinned. "I will."

Chapter Three

～✦～

Sometime the next evening, after an exhausting journey, the coach rattled to a stop. At some point during their long ride, the men had untied her hands and removed the cloth from her mouth, making it far easier to breathe. Esme was most eager to exit the vile enclosure so she might stretch her legs and relieve herself. Neither man offered her assistance, but she managed to climb out of the rig.

Of course her hope that they had stopped at an inn and she'd be able to seek help from a stranger was dashed when she saw no welcoming lamps. Instead she faced a barren landscape without a house or even a barn in sight. Her first few steps were unsteady, but she was able to maneuver herself behind the nearest bush.

"Stay with the girl and see that she doesn't try to run away," Thatcher yelled.

Desperate to avoid being seen by her abductors in such a state of dishabille, Esme hurriedly tugged her clothes into place. She stepped back onto the path. Waters grabbed her arm and led her through a clearing. She surveyed their surroundings as best she could in the dusky evening light. The moon hung heavy and low behind her, still rising but illuminating the stone walls in front of them. Off in the distance she could hear water lapping at rocks and gulls crying. She inhaled deeply and filled her lungs with crisp, salty air; they were on the coast.

It had taken them a while to traverse London, but once they were on the open road, they'd traveled all day and into the early evening. Not long enough to reach a western or northern coastline.

Waters grabbed her arm. "We won't hurt you if you just do as you're told." He led her forward toward a bank of crumbled rock walls.

"Considering I'm not certain of what you want, cooperation might be challenging." Esme waited for his response, but none came. Indignantly she jerked away from the man.

The ruins stretched on as far as her eye could see, in some spots nothing more than a pile of stone, whereas other sections still had full walls standing. He led her to a spot where the wall had crumbled down to nothing and stepped over the threshold into the ruins. Cold stone chilled her feet through her thin slippers, and the damp night breeze scattered goose bumps across her body. In a futile effort at gaining warmth, she pulled her thin robe tighter. The scent of damp earth and moss permeated the air as they moved farther into the decaying building, past more piles of rubble, through tumbled-down archways and heaps of rotting timbers.

"What is this place?" she asked.

"It was a monastery," Waters said.

They came to a steep staircase, which proved difficult to maneuver. The moss-covered stairs were slippery and lacked a railing, but with careful steps, she made it to the bottom unscathed. Water dripped into several puddles in an odd cadence, giving the large cavernous room a hollow feeling.

They said they were taking her to a dungeon, and they had made good on that promise. In the flickering light of the men's lanterns, she saw that a torture cage hung loosely from the ceiling across from her, though, thankfully, it looked to be in rather poor condition. Several sets of manacles were fastened to the wall, the ceiling above them partially collapsed. She suspected the thing off in the far corner was a pit. She shuddered to think of being crammed into the tiny box with nothing but the dark surrounding her.

"I believe you are mistaken," she said. "This couldn't possibly have been a monastery. Monks are not predisposed to torture—upon themselves, perhaps, but not upon others."

"This was an old castle before the monks inherited it," Waters said. "They've been gone a while now."

"If you two are finished with the history lesson, we have work to do," Thatcher growled. He set his lantern down and scanned the open room. His deep chuckle shot doom through Esme. "Put her there." He motioned to the far right wall.

Waters followed his gaze but made no movement. "In the manacles? Thatcher, a mite rough, don't you—"

But before he could finish his question, Thatcher silenced him with a steely glare. "Yes, you dolt, lock her up. She's a prisoner, not your betrothed."

Waters dragged her over to the far side of the room. The dungeon's air was damp and stale. The ground was so moist that mud clung to her slippers with each step. The dirt beneath her feet lent an earthy smell to the air that made her feel as if they were outside. Only she knew they weren't, and the likelihood of her escaping to the outside was slim. Even if she did, where would she go?

Panic rose in her throat, bitter and acidic as bile.

If only this were a scene from one of the adventure novels she read. In the books a handsome hero always came and saved the poor distressed woman. Esme knew that she had no such hero, handsome or otherwise, so it was likely she would rot hanging from those manacles. Or worse.

This time she didn't bother to suppress her shudder. If lurid fiction were to be believed, ruffians such as these were likely to use her poorly. Regardless of how they might feel about her large bum.

Waters untied her arms, then slid her right wrist into the manacle. As he closed the cold metal around her, she watched him slide the pin into place, locking it on her arm. She tried to kick him, but her feet caused no great damage, even when they collided with his shins.

He had more difficulty with her left arm, both because of her attempt to dissuade him from chaining her to a wall and because the pin on the left manacle was severely rusted. But he managed to force it into place. It certainly didn't look as if it would give way anytime soon.

Something scurried beneath her feet and she kicked out, sending the unsuspecting creature flying toward the men. *Rat.* She smiled at the irony.

Each man held a lantern that provided enough light for her to see them from her vantage point against the wall. Above her, there was a fair-sized hole in the partially collapsed ceiling, through which she caught a glimpse of cloud-strewn sky. She herself was shrouded in darkness except for the faintest shaft of moonlight.

"Start against that wall," Thatcher told Waters while pointing to his left. "You count forty paces. I'll start over here."

The men were several feet from their respective walls before Esme interrupted their counting. "At some point you'll realize you have the wrong woman. I have no key, nor any notion of what we're doing here."

Waters went back to his wall and started again.

"Whomever you were looking for, I'm not her," she said. "In fact, I'm certain you are unaware of this, but I am a very important person, and once my household discovers that I have disappeared, the whole of London will be looking for me. They've probably already notified the metropolitan police."

That sounded good, in theory. But none of it was true. Her aunt would certainly miss her, as would Mr. and Mrs. Craddock, their two servants, but no one would believe Esme to actually be missing. She had always had the bad habit of going off on her own whenever the desire hit, such as when she traveled to Oxford to buy the journal of the man who'd researched Pandora's box. She'd been gone three days and her aunt had barely noticed. So her household, as it were, was used to her disappearing every once in a while. Then again, they would know something was amiss by the state of her study. They would certainly know she would never treat her books in such a fashion. But they would not have noticed until long after the abductors had absconded with Esme.

Again Waters shook his head and went back to his starting point.

"Waters!" Thatcher yelled. "Get over here and hold my

place; I'll count out yours." He aimed his pistol at Esme. "And you, shut up!"

The man meant it. Even without clear lighting she could see the coldness behind his steely blue eyes.

Waters, while obviously still a menace, was clearly no match intellectually for a woman of her ilk. Facing him alone, she'd easily be able to outsmart him—if not over-power him. Thatcher, on the other hand, had the look of a man fueled by malicious intelligence and ambition. He was by far the more threatening of the two.

She said nothing more for a long while as the men counted and recounted their steps.

"This is the spot," Thatcher said. "Dig."

They set down their lanterns and picked up shovels.

This whole ordeal was growing stranger by the moment. Perhaps she really was having some sort of bizarre dream. She'd been reading at her desk, and she'd simply fallen asleep and was still sitting in her uncomfortable chair in her little study. She couldn't very well pinch her-self because of the current positioning of her arms. So she did the next best thing—she bit down on her bottom lip.

Damnation!

Not dreaming.

Of course she hadn't been dreaming. A dream couldn't be quite this painful. She'd never held her arms above her head for this length of time, and now she knew why. Her shoulders felt as if she were literally holding up the wall, and her muscles burned and cramped.

Another rat chirped and sniffed at her feet and she kicked out again, vaulting this one off to the right. "I still do not understand what I am doing here," she told her captors.

The men paid her no mind, so she instead turned her

energy to thinking of ways she could get herself out of this mess. Perhaps if she pretended to have a fit of the vapors, they would come to revive her and she could—

Could do what? Talk them to death?

"What are you digging for?" she asked.

"Pan—," Waters began, but before he got the word out, Thatcher clipped his shoulder with the shovel. Waters yelped in pain, jumping out of the way.

"Dig more. Talk less," Thatcher growled.

Esme's heart thundered. Could it be? What else started with "pan"?

Pantaloons. Pantomimes. Well, they couldn't possibly be digging for either of those.

Pandora's box. Here in England. Perhaps the story was true. She'd read about a sixth-century Saxon warlord who supposedly purchased the box for his new bride, and then they settled somewhere north of Cornwall. The bride had opened the box and brought destruction on the entire village until a priest stole the box and escaped with it.

It had always been a favorite theory of Esme's, but she'd never imagined she'd be present when it was found.

"Who told you Pandora's box was here?" she asked. "Is it that Raven person you mentioned earlier?"

"Our employer is none of your concern," Thatcher said, not bothering to look up from his digging. "Suffice it to say if he says the box is here, it's here."

The key! That's what they'd meant back at her house. They were looking for *her* key. Or rather, her pendant. Her father had given it to her only as a frivolity, a small token he'd picked up in a shop in Greece. He'd known she'd enjoy the fact that it had been advertised as the key to Pandora's box.

But how would anyone know of her pendant? She'd told

very few about the necklace or that lately her research had led her to believe that it might, in fact, be authentic. There were the two scholars she corresponded with, but they were mild-mannered, academic types. She knew they would never work with villains such as these. Aunt Thea knew, but she'd always believed it to be nothing more than a trinket.

Who else? Esme scoured her mind for some clue. Her sister knew, but they didn't even speak. Oh, and about three months ago there had been that man at the library. He'd been passing by, had somehow seen her pendant, and stopped to inquire about the origin. He'd seemed harmless, but perhaps she'd been fooled. She could feel the slender chain resting against her neck now, the gold pendant resting lightly against her chest.

Clearly, they fully expected that if they did find the box, she would use her key to open it. But that would never happen. She was no fool. All she needed to do was convince them the key was back at her house. They'd have to take her back to London; then, at least, she wouldn't die out here, a place no one would even begin to think to look for her. She could always demand they take her to this Raven person—anything to stay alive.

Perhaps if she deterred them now, they'd stop digging altogether. It was unlikely, but she could try.

"You'll never find it here," she said.

"Maybe she's right," Waters said.

"She is but a woman. What does she know?"

She gasped, momentarily forgetting the danger in her indignation. "I know a great deal more than you! That's for certain. Why, I—" But she swallowed her words. Her intellect was her greatest weapon against these men. No need to flaunt it before them.

Thatcher eyed her for a moment before continuing. "The Raven said we would find it here. So we will dig until we do."

It had been a silly plan, but she knew she had to keep her wits about her. If there was ever a time she needed her mind, it was now.

Esme scavenged her memory for any reading she might have done on an ancient monastery in connection with the box. She couldn't find any. Whomever these men worked for must have had resources completely different from her own.

The theory that Pandora's box was in Britain indicated it was much farther west than they were now. And they hadn't driven long enough to have hit a western coastline.

"I've found something," Waters yelled. He jammed his shovel back into the hole, and a great hollow thud sounded around them.

Esme's stomach lurched. Pandora's box, here in the same room. Well, same dungeon—or whatever this space was intended to be.

Thatcher moved over next to Waters, and they both began digging furiously. They must not have been far above the water table, because the ground quickly became saturated as they dug. Mud caked onto their hands and arms and flew against their clothing. Thatcher fell to his knees and put both arms in the hole up to his shoulders. For several minutes he sloshed mud and scooped it behind him, ever increasing the depth of the hole. Finally he pulled back what looked to be a square object dripping with mud.

"Bring that other lantern over here," Thatcher growled.

Waters ran to fetch the light, and together they bent over their discovery.

Esme strained her neck as best she could, trying to catch a glimpse of what they'd uncovered. Her heart thundered wildly, and she longed to run toward them and see what it was. Damn these manacles.

Whatever it was appeared to be wrapped in something, perhaps cloth of some sort, several layers of it too. Finally, when they had a pile of discarded fabric, Thatcher held it up to the lantern, inadvertently giving her a nearly perfect view. It was, most definitely, a box. About the size of a cigar box, yet not quite as ornamental, at least it appeared as such from what she could make out beneath all the dripping mud.

"Is that it?" Waters asked, his voice lined with disappointment.

"Let me see it closer," Esme pleaded, hoping they'd forget she was a prisoner and bring the box over to her. She itched to see what from her position looked to be engravings. How could she be this close and not be able to see it, touch it? She'd waited so long. It was far crueler to be denied a glance than it was to hang from this monastery wall.

"I don't think so," Thatcher said, turning toward her. "Now, about that key."

Chapter Four

———✦❧～❧✦———

Fielding had followed the sound of voices all the way to the innermost part of the ruins. The Raven's men had a woman with them, and she was quite the talker. He'd managed to find a ledge where he'd situated himself to see how many he was up against. Peering over, he wished they had a bit more lighting below.

"I will give you no such thing," a woman's voice said.

Where was the woman? He spied Waters standing in the middle of the room, and Thatcher looked to be walking directly toward Fielding. He crouched farther down to make certain he wasn't seen, then peered back over the edge. There, chained to the wall, was the woman, wearing nothing but a flimsy night rail. Since when were the Raven's men in the habit of abducting women? Evidently his uncle wanted this artifact badly.

Well, this certainly complicated matters. It would have been nice had Jensen and his Solomon's friends warned Fielding about the possibility of having to rescue a woman in addition to the box.

Of course he had no obligation to save her. She hadn't been part of his original agreement.

"Where is it?" Thatcher asked, his voice coming from between tightly clenched teeth.

"I don't know what you're referring to."

"The key to open this bloody thing." He held up the box in question.

"Let me see the box closely; it might jar my memory," the woman said.

"I know you have it. The Raven said the Worthington woman had the key. That's you, ain't it?"

There was a long pause before she answered, as if she'd been considering a lie. "Yes, that's me, but I don't have any keys with me. If you take me back to London, though, I'll be happy to retrieve all the keys I own for you to dig through."

Worthington. That was the name of the scholar on Mr. Nichols's list. Fielding again peered over the ledge. He'd imagined an old matronly figure with grayed hair and a shapeless body, her nose firmly implanted in a book. Not the slip of a woman below him. Even in the dim light, he could see her tantalizing breasts under the night rail.

Fielding wondered if the men of Solomon's knew about this supposed key. And if they did, why hadn't they warned him? There'd been nothing about a key in the notes they'd given him either. Bastards probably didn't share all their information with the hired help.

"Get your filthy hands off me, you beast," she said.

Thatcher was indeed putting his hands on her, searching her for some sort of key, from the looks of it. Although why he thought the woman could hide anything beneath her almost transparent nightgown, Fielding didn't know. He rolled his eyes. He'd never liked Thatcher, always felt the man took pride in being as vile and contemptuous as possible.

"What do we have here?" Thatcher asked. "That's an unusual pendant." He pulled his hand back, yanking the necklace free, and stepped away from the woman.

"That is nothing," she protested. "A frivolous gift from my father is all. It's not even real gold; I believe it's made of painted steel. It will probably rust in another month or so."

All Fielding could see was a slight glimmer against the lantern light. A bit of jewelry perhaps. So she *had* been hiding something.

"We'll see about that. Waters, get over here. And hold that light still."

"You have no idea what sort of trouble you could be in for," the woman warned. "That box is quite likely very dangerous. And I'd wager that your employer is paying you to retrieve it, not open it."

She was a smart one, Fielding would give her that. However, her common sense was sorely lacking. It was she who didn't realize the danger she was in.

While he'd never known Waters to harm a woman, Thatcher was the kind of man who took what he wanted regardless of what the implications might be.

"Look there," Waters said. "See that notch? It looks just like her trinket."

"Go ahead," she said loudly. "Open the box. All that lies within the walls of that box are evils. Death, destruction, pestilence. The plagues of Egypt. The ruination of humankind. Go ahead," she said again. "Unleash terrors upon yourself, it matters not to me. But I cannot watch."

She sounded remarkably like Mr. Nichols. Fielding

shook his head. He'd never understand adults who believed in such fairy tales.

"Perhaps she's right," Waters warned, his voice wavering with nerves. "The Raven did ask us to get the box, steal her key, and bring them back to him."

"You wouldn't want to disobey your employer's instructions," she said.

"We won't know if her key is the correct one," Thatcher ground out, "unless we try it."

"But she had all those books in her library. All of them were about this box. She knows something," Waters said.

"That's right," she agreed. "My library is extensive." The last word came out in a yawn. "I might be a woman, but I know of what I speak."

"Your incessant chatter is grating on my nerves." Thatcher hitched up his pistol and hit the woman hard on the head. "I said shut up!"

Fielding gritted his teeth as if he had been the one struck. The woman's head dropped and her body went slack, dangling from the manacles that affixed her to the wall.

Thatcher dropped the necklace into his pocket and walked away from the woman. "We'll wait in here for first light, then we'll take her to the Raven and he can decide what to do with her. Waters, build a fire over there."

From his perch, Fielding watched the two men build a makeshift camp, complete with a fire and ratty blankets to lie upon. Once the woman came to, her arms would ache fiercely from being shackled in that position, but the knot on her head would no doubt hurt worse. She was so small, her body frail and limp. He forced his eyes back toward the men. Fielding kept his post for another hour, waiting for the duo to settle in for the night.

Thatcher was unable leave the box alone, though. He went back and forth, picking it up to further examine it, then setting it back down and trying to fall asleep. Once more he picked up the box and held it close to his face. He nudged Waters with his foot.

"Waters," he whispered.

The other man sat bolt upright. "What?"

"Listen. Do you hear that? Do you hear the voices?"

"Only your voice," he said groggily.

"Here, listen." Thatcher held the box out to the other man, who, in turn, took it and held it up to his ear.

A moment later Waters threw the box away from him as he sat up abruptly. Thatcher caught the box before it fell to the ground.

"You heard it, didn't you?" Thatcher said.

"Bloody 'ell," Waters said. "I heard my name."

Thatcher dug into his pocket and pulled out the woman's necklace. The pendant caught the fire's glow and cast flecks of light around them.

"What are you doing?" Waters asked.

"Opening it."

Thatcher pressed the metal pendant against the box, and a latch audibly released. Even from a distance, Fielding could hear it. He shook his head, certain he must have been mistaken. His own mind must be playing tricks on him from lying still so long.

In one swift movement Thatcher popped open the lid. Both men sat for a moment looking around them, presumably waiting for the terrors to be unleashed upon them, but nothing happened.

Fielding rolled his eyes. Damned superstitions.

"There's nothing in here," Thatcher said.

"Let me see," Waters said. "What's that on the bottom?"

Thatcher dug his hand in, perhaps searching for hidden compartments, then pulled his hand back. "Nothing."

"What's that on your wrist?" Waters asked.

Thatcher held his arm up to the firelight, and a thin band of gold shimmered against his dirty flesh.

"A treasure," Waters said. "Give me the box." He too put his hand in the box and pulled back with a band of gold on his wrist as well.

They eyed their matching bands for several moments. Thatcher laughed. "Why, that's a pretty find. But we'd better take them off. Don't want to damage them before we can get the box back to the Raven." Then Thatcher tried to remove his bracelet. "It won't come off," he growled.

Waters attempted to remove his own, and his bracelet would not budge either.

"What do we do?" Waters asked, his voice rising a notch.

"We'll get them off tomorrow," Thatcher said. "The Raven will help."

"We can't tell the Raven. He'll kill us for trying to steal from him."

"I can make him understand," Thatcher assured him. "Now go back to sleep."

Fools.

The Raven would never understand. And he didn't deal lightly with those who betrayed him.

Fielding wouldn't have to wait much longer. He needed them to doze off for only a little while before they'd be too bleary-headed to fight him. He checked his waistband for the pistol and found it snugly in place. Ten minutes later Thatcher's loud snores echoed through the dungeon.

Fielding waited a little longer before he crept down from his ledge and into their makeshift camp. Snagging Thatcher's bag with the box hidden inside proved easy enough, as was snuffing out their lanterns, leaving only the remnants of their fire as light. But as Fielding turned to go, he saw her.

Her frail body hung limply from the manacles, and her brown hair was matted with dirt and a small patch of blood. Her nightdress was covered in Thatcher's muddy handprints.

Blast it all.

There was no way Fielding could leave her here. He glanced over his shoulder. The two men were still sleeping, so he slowly moved to stand in front of the woman. He tightened the cinch on the bag to ensure it was secure over his shoulder before placing one hand firmly against her mouth. Her eyes flew open, but his hand muffled the sound she made.

He shook his head. "Be quiet," he whispered. "I'm not going to hurt you. I'm going to get you out of here. Nod if you understand."

Her wide eyes rounded, but she nodded nonetheless.

"If I move my hand away from your mouth, do you promise not to scream?"

She nodded fervently.

He waited a few heartbeats, then he slowly took his hand away.

"Please hurry," she urged.

Reaching up, he worked on the right brace, nudging the pin out of its confines. The rusted metal scraped and groaned as it moved, but it eventually gave way and he was able to remove her hand. Being hung from the wall as long as she'd been, her movements would be unsteady and sluggish. He couldn't afford to be slowed by her. As she lowered her arm, she winced, confirming his suspicions.

The men stirred. Fielding and the woman froze, waiting to see if either man awoke, but the snoring continued.

He moved to remove the other pin, but unlike its counterpart, this one would not budge.

"He had trouble with that one," she whispered.

Fielding nodded and continued trying to work the pin out, but it remained lodged firmly in place. If he'd had a sword he could have snapped the chain in half, but seeing as he wasn't in the habit of carrying swords around with him, that wasn't an option. There was something he could do, although it would most certainly wake Waters and Thatcher. He didn't even know this woman, and already she was more trouble than he'd wager she was worth.

But damn it all, he couldn't leave her.

With brusque motions, he began to run his hands along the skin of her arms, massaging the tender flesh there.

She gasped. "What are you doing?" she asked in a whispered hiss.

"Kneading your muscles."

"Well, I insist you stop at once. It's most improper! Furthermore, I can do it myself once you release me."

"Once I release you," he explained with forced patience, "we are going to have to move quickly. A cramped muscle could mean the difference between life and death." He paused to meet her gaze. "Understand?"

Her eyes were wide in the darkness, her breath coming in nervous pants, but she nodded.

He returned to the task at hand, working on her arms first and then turning his attention to her legs, which were longer than he expected for a woman of her diminutive height and surprisingly sturdy. Supporting her feet, he bent first one knee and then the other, massaging the muscles of her calves and thighs as he did so. Her sinewy flesh convulsed beneath his touch.

He worked quickly since there was no time to waste. But even so, he couldn't help noticing her generous curves and the enticing flesh beneath his hands. His body leaped in response, though he tried to stifle his reaction. Much more of this, and she wouldn't be the only one moving slowly.

"I believe, sir, that my muscles are quite relaxed now." Her tone was both husky and tense, whether from the situation or his ministrations, he couldn't tell.

Fielding reached into his boot and withdrew a dagger. He handed it to the woman. "If they come after you, do not hesitate to use this, do you understand?"

She looked down at the knife in her free hand and nodded, but he was uncertain as to whether or not she could actually follow through with such a task. There was no room for error at the moment, else he and the woman would both find themselves prisoners of the Raven.

"Do not bother slashing at their arms. Go straight for their bellies, where you'll do the most damage," he instructed.

She shuddered but nodded.

He stepped away from her and aimed his pistol at the top of the chain.

"Are you mad?" she hissed.

He ignored her and took the shot. It did the trick and the chain broke free, but the ricochet rang throughout the room and Thatcher was on his feet in a matter of seconds. Fielding had already grabbed the girl, though, and they were making their way up the stairs.

"Where do you think you're going, Grey?" Thatcher snarled. The man searched for his gun, but Fielding had already removed it. Just as he'd also disabled their carriage outside and sent their horses running.

"Thatcher, it's not your style to abduct unsuspecting women." He slid another bullet into his pistol and leveled it at the men.

Thatcher took a step toward them but stumbled in the darkness. "Grey, you and I both know you're no different than us, despite that title of yours."

Waters felt around the camp, crawling on his knees, searching under their bedding, no doubt also looking for a weapon.

"Ah," Fielding said, "but there is one difference. I have the box and the girl."

Thatcher snarled. "Give us the box." He took another step forward. "We'll split our share of the money with you."

"Don't make another move, or I will shoot you," Fielding said as they backed their way up the stairs. "We'll be leaving now." And with that, they turned and ran.

Fielding dragged the woman behind him, knowing that her slippered feet were taking a beating against the cracked stone, but that wasn't his concern. Carrying her would only slow them down, and he could already hear the men scrambling after them.

He and the woman reached the outside, and the chilled night air slapped at them. With one arm, he jumped onto his horse, then pulled the woman up in front of him. Facing him, actually, which proved a bit awkward, but there was no time to rectify it. He kicked his horse into action, and they rode off just as Thatcher and Waters appeared outside the ruins.

"Thank you for rescuing me," she said breathlessly.

It was hard not to look at her face when she spoke to him, as she was sitting directly in front of him. And the moon hanging above illuminated her perfectly. She was close enough for him to see the freckles that splattered across her nose and her large, thickly lashed, river-green eyes. Her hair smelled of lilac, despite the mud covering her.

He merely nodded and returned his attention to the landscape before them.

"Won't they come after us?" she asked.

"Probably." Her legs brushed against his, and he looked down—milky white thighs straddled his own. He couldn't help remembering how those thighs had felt beneath his hands. Firm yet pliant. His senses stirred as his body once again responded to hers. Damn it all.

He could only imagine her indignation if she happened to notice his growing erection. He'd heard more than enough of her prattling earlier to know she was a well-bred lady. A prim one at that, despite the fact that her body was obviously made for sin.

They couldn't very well ride back to London this way. It was more than twelve hours away, and if she noticed his reaction, chatterer that she was, she'd no doubt preach to him the whole way about sins of the flesh or some such nonsense. The ride would be interminable even if his body didn't have a mind of its own.

They needed to either take the train or find a coach. He eyed her mud-splattered nightgown. Clearly they couldn't take the train and avoid being seen, even with a private car. He didn't even know who this woman was. The last thing he needed was some angry papa coming after him demanding Fielding marry the girl. That left finding a carriage. He'd seen a sign for a carriage house on his way to the ruins.

As he turned his horse down the appropriate road, he detected the sound of pounding hooves behind them. He did his best to isolate the noise, to be certain of what he heard. Definitely horses coming their way.

"Hold on tight," he told the woman.

"Why?"

"Because we're being followed."

Chapter Five

———❧〰❧———

Esme wrapped her arms around the man's torso and did as he bade. He turned the horse so abruptly she was certain they'd all fall to the ground, but the steed kept his footing. They cut into a dense patch of trees. Branches and leaves swatted at her bare legs as they made their way deeper into the forest.

He slowed the horse to a trot, then stopped him altogether. "Shhh," he told her.

She could see only his face as they waited in the trees for their pursuers to catch up, and his expression told her nothing. The moments stretched by, and Esme's own labored breathing and pounding heart roared in her ears so loudly she was almost certain their hiding place would be discovered. The man's hands tightened on the reins. Those same hands that had caressed her body only moments before. Her cheeks flamed as an unfamiliar rush of heat spread through her.

The hooves got closer and closer, slamming against the dirt road. The two horsemen slowed to a trot.

"I don't see 'em," Waters said.

Esme couldn't see the road, but she could gauge how close the men were by the dark expression on her rescuer's face. A muscle in his jaw ticked, but he made no movement. She wasn't even certain he blinked.

"We've lost 'em," Waters cried.

Thatcher let out a string of curses that had Esme's ears burning. "We'll catch him. We know all his hiding places."

Then the men turned and rode back in the direction from which they'd come.

Esme released a breath and sagged against her rescuer. "That was close."

They waited a handful of minutes longer before continuing on their way to the carriage house.

Nearly an hour later, Esme pulled the overcoat tighter around her. She didn't think she'd ever been so cold or filthy. But the warmth of her savior's coat was certainly helping. Not to mention the enclosed carriage as opposed to the frigid air she'd been exposed to on the horse ride. He'd hired a driver and currently sat opposite her inside the rig.

So much had happened in the last day. The kidnapping and subsequent rescue by this handsome stranger. And Pandora's box had been found. She wished it had been under different circumstances so she could have fully enjoyed it. And she wished her father were still alive to share the discovery with; he would have enjoyed the adventure of it. Well, with the exception of his daughter being abducted.

"Where are you taking me?" she asked.

"London."

She sighed heavily. He wasn't a man of many words.

And he seemed a bit of a contradiction. While he dressed and moved as a gentleman would, he did not keep gentlemanly company, as he'd known her captors. Granted, it seemed as if they had an antagonistic relationship.

With no thought to the propriety of the matter, she openly examined him. He was a handsome man, that she could not deny. With his dark eyes and equally dark eyebrows slashing shrewdly above, he looked rather intelligent. His full lips, though, gave him a sensual look. Yes, this stranger who had saved her was particularly dashing.

Perhaps this was how he earned his living. Tracking down thieves and stealing from them whatever artifact they'd managed to find. No doubt he then donated it to a museum or someplace else secure. She'd heard of such men, employed by museums. She smiled. He was an honorable man, and she was safe.

"Who were those men?" she asked.

"First tell me your name," he said flatly.

Honorable, albeit rude. "Esme Worthington," she said.

"And to whom do you belong?"

"I beg your pardon; I don't *belong* to anyone."

He took a silent breath and closed his eyes. "Who are your parents?"

"My parents are deceased." Crossing her arms across her chest, she nodded once. "I am my own woman."

His eyes narrowed. "You live in London?" He stretched his long legs out in front of him, coming close to brushing her own in the process. "Alone?"

She waved a hand in front of her. "Not completely alone. I live with my aunt, and we keep a small household staff."

He nodded thoughtfully. "How is it that you know so much about Pandora's box?"

"I am a scholar. What I know I've learned from much study and research." She thought she detected a slight smile before he turned to look out the darkened window. Many people—many men—held women such as herself in disdain. However, she did not care if he thought her refusal to suppress her intelligence made her unwomanly.

"Did you lie to our friends back at the ruins? All your warnings about the dangers of the box?" he asked.

Her shoulders rose in a light shrug. "There are many stories about Pandora's box and what it might contain. Personally, I've never subscribed to any of the theories that it holds plagues and all other sorts of nastiness. I was simply attempting to save my neck and warn those two oafs in the process."

"It's unlikely they would have heeded any of your warnings no matter how grave." He paused, then continued, "I wouldn't have."

The stranger smiled at her and her breath caught. He looked much younger when he wasn't scowling. She glanced at the ratty bag sitting next to him on the seat. Her heart stopped and she held her breath. "Might I see it?" She had waited long enough.

He eyed her for a moment, then reached into the bag and withdrew the box. "Don't break it."

"That is a priceless relic. I'd no sooner break it than I'd smash the Rosetta stone."

"I need it unscathed when I deliver it," he said.

"To whom?" she asked, smoothing her hands across the wooden sides.

"None of your concern."

She narrowed her eyes at him. "At least tell me your name and who those men were."

"Fielding Grey. And those men work for a man known as the Raven."

Ordinarily she would have pressed him for more information, but right now she couldn't seem to take her eyes off the box. She couldn't see much of it in detail since the interior of the carriage wasn't well lit. But she could see the recessed shadows of carvings and felt the smooth etched metal beneath her fingertips. Now that she held it close, she could see that it was made of solid gold.

Anticipation skittered her nerve endings. Here it was, in her hands, her life's ambition.

And she wasn't supposed to open it.

She'd read many of the legends; she knew almost all of them told of the inquisitiveness that led to Pandora's demise. She knew of the warnings and dangers that went along with lifting the lid of a seemingly simple box. Even knowing all the potential hazards the box represented, her desire was strong for one . . . tiny . . . peek.

The carriage jolted and Esme sat upright. She pulled back the tightly gathered curtain and saw that daylight had arrived, although it proved to be a dreary, rain-filled day. The flat coastland had given way to gentle hills. Pushing the curtain back in place, she examined the man across from her.

He still slept, and his features had softened in his slumber. His brown hair was cropped short, leaving his face open for her perusal. At least two days' worth of beard lined his jaw and would have given him a hardened look, were it not for the seductive curl of his lips. She caught herself before she sighed, then rolled her eyes.

Honestly, he was merely a man. A handsome one, she'd grant him that, but a man nonetheless. She was eyeing him this way only because he'd saved her life. It had absolutely nothing to do with the fact that she longed for male companionship, a relationship like all her friends and her sister had found. This happened in every adventure novel—the damsel always harbored romantic notions about her hero. It was a purely natural reaction. But it needn't mean anything.

Without his intense brown gaze upon her, she reached for the tattered bag sitting on the carriage seat next to him. The carriage jostled again, and she paused to see if Mr. Grey would awaken. But he did not. Evidently he was a sound sleeper, which boded well for her, at least in the current moment.

She reached into the bag and felt a thin chain loop around her finger, her pendant. She'd feared Thatcher still had it, but apparently he'd stashed it in the same bag in which he'd stowed the box. She pocketed the trinket, then pulled out the box. It didn't look as dingy as it had the night before. The gold shimmered in the morning light. She could see the etchings more closely and admired the handiwork.

On each side was a miniature carved mural of gods and goddesses. Zeus was, of course, prominently displayed on the top, with other deities carved into the sides. She quickly looked at each in turn until she found what she was looking for. There! Eros and Aphrodite, each a symbol of love and passion. Satisfaction surged through her. Her theory was right. It had to be. Within this box lay Pandora's charms, the very key to being irresistible to men.

Some women, like her sister, were simply born with

such charms. Esme knew she and Elena were different, not simply in age and appearance but in demeanor as well. Elena always had suitors lined up waiting for a chance to spin her around the dance floor, while Esme had been resigned to the seats lining the ballroom—the chairs reserved for elderly women and the girls no one would dance with.

It wasn't only her sister, though. It seemed most women had at least a modest ability to seduce men, to walk into a room and command attention, as all the girls she knew had managed to snag a husband. But Esme, well, she'd never so much as caught a rogue glance in her direction. Then again, she'd been the only one to correct the Duke of Devonshire in a roomful of people. She shouldn't have, probably wouldn't have, if he hadn't have been spouting off incorrect history.

Thus had ended her short-lived time in the marriage market and any hope of landing a good match. So here she was, seven and twenty and as undesirable as ever.

What other woman in all of England could manage to get herself abducted by a pair of nasty villains and come out of the experience with her virtue completely unscathed?

Of course she didn't *want* to be ravished. Well, not by the first two men, at least. But Mr. Grey . . . She mentally chided herself for the thought. A thought made all the worse by her realization that she was staring at the man, studying the fullness of his lips, the growth of beard shadowing his cheeks.

She shook her head to rid herself of such useless thoughts. There would be no ravishing from anyone. And there was little point in feeling disappointed by that.

But she could lay claim to those female charms now. All she needed to do was open the box.

Which, of course, she couldn't do. She placed her hand on the lid of the box to make certain she didn't open it. At least not intentionally. But if by sheer will she could force the lid open and not have to take responsibility for her actions should any evils come pouring out, that would be another matter. She stared intently. Nothing happened.

Then she saw it, what looked to be an ornately swirled infinity sign. A carving that perfectly matched her necklace's uniquely shaped pendant. Undoubtedly this was how she could open the box, which she wouldn't do.

But what if she merely took a tiny peek? What if this was her destiny? Why else would she be the one to have this pendant? The key that opened the mystical box. Perhaps she was meant to open the box. Surely that meant no harm would come to her.

She'd barely had time to put her hand in her pocket to reach for the necklace when the carriage pulled to a stop.

"What exactly do you think you're doing?" Fielding grumbled.

Her thundering heart seemed to stop beating. She met his gaze before it focused on the box in her lap. "I was merely admiring the box. It's quite the treasure, as you can imagine."

"Indeed." He took it back from her and tucked it into the bag. "We're here."

The carriage door opened and a footman extended his hand. "Miss," he said.

She poked her head out. "We're where?"

"My family's home. It's about halfway between Portsmouth and London. I thought we could rest and wash up."

When she still didn't move he nudged her. "Get out of the carriage, Miss Worthington."

The estate sat beyond the circular drive, classic in architecture. Several stories high, it peaked with at least six chimneys and two picturesque wings flanking each side of the home. They were nearly cathedral-like in structure.

"Come along," he said, but he did not bother waiting for her to follow.

Esme had always wondered what it would be like to have a bevy of servants bathe and dress her, and today she'd found out. One washed her hair, one kept the water temperature just so, and one scrubbed her back. Then two more had helped her dress and attended her toilet.

The dress they'd put her in was a couple of decades out of style with its butter-yellow full skirt, velvet sash, and squared bodice, but it was clean and warm. Miraculously, they'd found a pair of boots that came close to fitting her. The leather had hardened with age, clearly conforming to the previous owner's feet. On Esme they were tight across the arch, but loose in the heel and longer than necessary. She tugged at the ill-fitting dress, which clung too tightly to her hips.

She would have liked nothing more than to toss herself upon the luxurious-looking bed taking up the center of the room, but Mr. Grey had not said how long they'd be here and she had some exploring to do. Namely, she wanted to find Pandora's box and have another look.

Walnut paneling covered the lower three-quarters of the hallway walls and positively gleamed with lemon oil. The fresh scent invigorated her as she proceeded down the large marble staircase. Mr. Grey had said this was his family estate, yet the servants had been most surprised to see him when he'd stepped out of the carriage. Or perhaps it had been the mud-covered, scantily clad woman he'd brought with him. But somehow their dismay had seemed clearly aimed at him.

As if they hadn't seen him in years and had never expected his visit.

Fielding Grey was a most curious man, Esme decided. She would rather enjoy learning more about him, but for the time being, she'd have to settle for investigating his home. Where would he put the box while he rested and bathed? Starting at the door closest to the back of the house, she worked her way through the myriad halls. The home was spotless and the rooms fairly standard: a couple of parlors and a library, a room she'd longed to further explore as the books beckoned her like new friends, but she forced herself to keep moving. She then came upon a conservatory, a billiards room, and a study.

She had nearly closed the door on the study when she spied Thatcher's tattered bag sitting on the massive mahogany desk. Slipping inside the room, she assured herself that no one was watching, then closed the door behind her. After a cursory glance to make certain she was alone, she quietly made her way to the desk. And before she knew it, she was seated in the large leather chair.

The stiff chair was exceedingly uncomfortable and so large that her feet dangled several inches above the floor. She ignored the fact that she felt more like a girl than a woman. Gently, she retrieved the box and set it in her lap.

Pandora's box!

Esme stifled a giggle, again feeling very much the young girl with a new toy. Every time she looked upon it, the carvings became more and more beautiful. She ran her fingers across the gold, reveling in the feel of it. Then she heard it—a whispering. Just the faintest of sounds, like a voice being carried on a wind. She whipped around to look behind her but found no one there. Straining to listen to the voice, she was unable to decipher any of the words.

"Hello? Anyone there?" she asked. Yet there was nowhere in the room for someone to hide and only the door through which she'd entered.

She shook her head and looked at the box. Again she heard an unmistakable whisper. It was a sound filled with the promise of fulfilled longing. Suddenly she was overtaken by the sweetest yearning. With a sense of hope and the possibility of joy. Although the words were still undecipherable, she could have sworn she'd heard her name. But that was impossible.

She continued stroking the box, tracing each engraving, noting each detail. Something pricked her finger and she drew it back; a fleck of blood bubbled from a tiny cut. Strange, considering the gold was perfectly smooth. She lifted the box for a closer inspection and noticed a slight abrasion in the metal near the etching that matched her pendant.

Her heart quickened. It was as if the box were asking her to open it—no, begging. One little peek wouldn't hurt. For so many years she'd longed to open it, how could she now deny herself this moment?

She had the opportunity; she had the key.

She scanned the room once more before removing her necklace. Carefully she lined her pendant piece up with the carving, then took a deep breath before pushing it into place. She heard something give way within. Slowly she exhaled.

In one swift movement she opened the lid and squeezed her eyes shut. She waited for a swarm of locusts or screaming—something. Nothing happened.

One eye popped open to inspect the inside of the box, then she opened the other.

Empty.

There was nothing inside the box. She waited a moment to see if she felt any different, to see if some invisible power had settled over her. But she felt nothing.

Disappointment poured through her, and she was about to close the lid when she noticed something at the bottom. It looked as if it too might open, so she slipped her hand inside. Something touched her. She pulled back. A shimmering gold bracelet dangled from her wrist. It was beautiful. Thin and unadorned, the band was simple and elegant.

Excitement fluttered in her belly. Perhaps this was it— Pandora's charm. Was it possible that by simply wearing the band men would want her? That she could finally know what it was like to walk into a room and have all men's eyes turn to her?

A giggle erupted from within her. It was a mythical box, not a miracle box. She ought not get too encouraged. Perhaps it would assist her in the ways of womanly charms, but the chances of her becoming an irresistible siren were slim.

She held her arm up in the air, moving her wrist about. The light played against the sliver of gold. Something caught her attention, and she held the bracelet up to the light to admire it and noticed an engraving. A closer look proved the impression to be ancient Greek; a language she could read, but not one she was proficient in. Luckily for her, the text to decipher was short, only one word. She read the word and thought on it a moment, unsure if she'd translated correctly. Another glance and she was certain. *Lust.*

With her other hand she attempted to remove the gold band, to put it back in the box, but it would not budge. No matter how much she tugged, the bracelet would not move past her thumb.

Splendid.

Her heart raced to a wild beating and her breaths came in short surges. This changed everything.

This wasn't a charm.

This was a *curse*.

Chapter Six

———— ❦ ————

M̲r. Grey! Mr. Grey." Esme came barreling down the looming staircase and stopped just short of running headlong into him. "Oh, there you are."

Fielding nodded to the butler, and the servant turned and left. Here in his well-lit hallway, he could see now that her hair was clean it was more of a reddish-brown, with hints of gold peeking through the soft curls. "What is it, Miss Worthington, that is so pressing you must tear through the house bellowing my name?"

She frowned, and two small lines furrowed her otherwise smooth forehead. It transformed her face, and something about her ridiculous expression tugged at his lips, urging him to smile.

"I was not bellowing," she said, attempting to compose herself. "I merely needed to find you in a hurry, and this place"—she made a sweeping gesture with her hand—"is rather large. I almost got lost on the third floor when you were nowhere to be found on the second."

"Yes, well, you've found me now. I've made arrangements for our travel, and I see you've cleaned your-self up and found something suitable to wear. Although that dress is too long for you." Not to mention a little snug around her generous hips. Esme Worthington had a lus-cious bottom. He'd noticed that straightaway through her thin nightdress, and still she was unable to hide it beneath this dress and all the underthings he knew women lay-ered on. He cleared his throat, annoyed with his train of thought. "We may leave."

"Yes," she said excitedly. "Yes, let us leave; you must take me home at once. And I'm afraid I must speak with you." The frown again touched between her eyes. "It is of grave importance."

She fell into step beside him as he made his way to the study. He gathered the box and a stack of unopened mail. "How is your head feeling? Thatcher struck you fairly hard."

"Your maids were able to remove all the blood, and one of them rubbed on an herbal poultice, which has all but removed the dull ache. I believe I shall recover quite nicely."

"Glad to hear it," he said.

"Now, then. There are many legends of Pandora's box, and I've read quite a lot of them because, well, because as I said earlier, I've been studying the legend of Pandora's box. I have many volumes that cover nothing but that par-ticular subject." She scarcely took breaths in between her sentences, and Fielding found himself growing anxious listening to her as they left the house.

He helped Miss Worthington into the carriage, and she never missed a beat.

"As you can imagine, with all the varied approaches

and theories there are, a student of the subject would begin to lean toward some of them and away from others."

He shook his head, unsure if he was following her logic. "Precisely what are you trying to say, Miss Worthington?"

"I had come to favor one particular theory about the box." She leaned forward, and for the briefest of moments her enthusiasm was nearly contagious.

"You see, according to the legend, Pandora was known as a consummate beauty, and she was presented, as a gift, by the gods to the brothers Epimetheus and Prometheus. Epimetheus walked away from her because he felt she was too much of a temptation and would lead him astray, but Prometheus accepted her as his wife."

Fielding didn't bother trying to ask questions. He'd heard enough from the men of Solomon's. Curses, Greek gods—it was all rubbish as far as he was concerned.

"Some scholars theorize that within the box are all the aspects that made Pandora the temptress she was," she continued. "Her charms, if you will."

Esme was talking so fast Fielding had a hard time following her words. He didn't, however, neglect watching her mouth as she spoke. Her lips were full and lush and ever so tempting.

"I had subscribed to this theory as well." She took a deep breath. "But it seems as if they, and I, were wrong. Terribly so."

"You can't honestly believe Pandora's box was created by the Greek gods," he said, not even bothering to hide the bite in his tone.

Esme stiffened. "Of course not. That would be blasphemy." Light sparked in her eyes as she leaned forward, the insult apparently forgotten. "However, I do believe that

Pandora's box exists and that it has powers, as unexplained as they may be. There is simply too much evidence to be ignored."

"So where do these powers come from?"

"No one knows, of course. But there are many references to Pandora's box, dating back to 500 BC. Cleopatra herself was said to possess a box that gave her the power to rule all of Egypt. By all accounts, she was a physically unremarkable woman, yet the most powerful men in the world were devoted to her. What if she used Pandora's box to control first Julius Caesar and then Marc Antony?"

"Or perhaps she was simply beautiful," he said. Beautiful in an interesting way as the woman before him was. Esme wasn't a conventional beauty; her features had too many angles, and with her narrow nose and straight eyebrows, her face was not one of delicate curves. Still, there was beauty before him. Thick lashes framed her wide green eyes, while sweet freckles smattered across her nose, and her pouty mouth had a heavier bottom lip that begged to be nibbled.

Annoyance flickered across her face, but she ignored his comment. "And then there is the theory that Pandora's box holds not charms but curses. There was the plague that traveled from Egypt to Byzantium along with a group of Egyptian traders who brought with them a box that spread death."

"Yes, yes," he said impatiently, "and we mustn't forget about the Black Death."

Her eyebrows rose. "Why, Mr. Grey, I see you've done a bit of research yourself. Yes, some believe the box caused the great plague. For example, Pliny the Elder described a box of mystical properties that spread greed and disease throughout the empire. He believed the box was responsible for the sacking of Troy. Don't you see," she said, "there is one thing all these stories have in common. A box. That can't be a coincidence."

His interest piqued, Fielding leaned forward. "Do any of these writings explain how Pandora's box made it to jolly ol' England?"

She frowned. "There is one. A modern scholar, George Winthrop, has found reference to a sixth-century Saxon warlord who gave his wife a spectacular box he'd purchased from an Egyptian peasant. He described the box as a gift from the gods, but later said it brought horrible death. I believe all these boxes have been the same box. Pandora's box."

"You have certainly done your research. But did you intend to merely dazzle me with your extensive knowledge or does this conversation have a purpose?" he asked.

She glared at him. "There is another theory that, frankly, I've never spent very much time on because, well, because it seemed ludicrous to me. But now I believe otherwise."

He didn't point out how ludicrous all of this sounded to him. Instead, he waited for her to finish.

She held her arm up to his face, and he pushed it back to see what she was trying to show him. With her other hand she shoved back the sleeve of her dress, only to have it fall back into place. "This is why we must make haste to my home."

"Because of an ill-fitting sleeve?"

She looked down and made a growling sort of noise before switching arms. "No, this," she said, pointing at the gold band encircling her right wrist.

The same sort of band that Thatcher and Waters had pulled out of the box. So, she had opened the box herself.

Sneaky little thing.

"I really wish I'd paid closer attention to those writings, that I hadn't judged them so hastily." She swallowed visibly. "I need to put the pieces together and discover what we must do to get this infernal thing off my wrist."

"It won't come off?" he asked.

"No, I tried." Once again she held her arm out to him.

He tried to remove the band by slipping it off her hand, but that did not work. Then he tried to open the bracelet somehow, but there were no grooves or clasps to be found anywhere.

"It does seem to be affixed quite securely," he said.

She looked up at him, her green eyes full of emotion. Apprehension, annoyance, anger. He wasn't certain which, perhaps all. "Yes, I see that," she said tartly. "There is more."

"More what?"

"More to my story. The bracelets, as I'm assuming there are more inside the box, have engravings that identify them. At least this one does, so it stands to reason the others do as well."

"And?"

"I have lust," she said in a tight whisper.

"I beg your pardon."

"*Lust!* On my wrist."

He fought the urge to laugh at her. That would settle nothing. He'd been in mummies' tombs and pirates' caves, all of which came with warnings of curses, and he'd come out unscathed. No, he did not believe in curses. But clearly Miss Worthington did. As did the men of Solomon's. They were all a bunch of superstitious fools.

"And what does all of this have to do with your house?"

"I have books on the matter, and journal articles. Ones I haven't even read because, as I mentioned, I thought this particular hypothesis imprudent." Esme took a cleansing breath. "Perhaps I should contact my scholar friends, see what they make of the situation." Then she shook her head as if arguing with herself. "No, that will never do; no reason to alert them to my foolishness."

His head was beginning to fog from trying to follow her circuitous logic. "Can we start at the beginning? Tell me about the theory of the bracelets," he said.

"Well, I can tell you all I know, but I admit it isn't much."

"Tell me what you can."

She nodded. "There are those who believe that when the gods made the box and sent it with Pandora they cursed it, thus cursing her and any who opened it. Inside the box, they put disease, greed, hope and lust. Legend says that when Pandora opened the box she released all of the curses. Then she panicked and slammed the lid down, sealing hope inside. It was a cruel jest at the hands of the gods."

Mr. Nichols had mentioned believing the curses were contained in material items. "You mentioned something about an inscription," he said.

She held her hand out to him. "Here," she said, pointing to the tiny engraved text.

"What language is this?"

"Some derivation of ancient Greek. I admit, it's not my best language; I am much better with Latin. But I know enough to know that's 'lust.' " She tilted her head. "I don't suppose you know Greek?"

"I can speak a few words, but that is all." He looked

back down at the band. "So each bracelet represents one of those elements? Theoretically speaking," he said.

"Yes, I believe so."

He nodded. "Which means there's at least one remaining in the box."

Esme opened her mouth, then frowned. "One more band?"

"The men who kidnapped you opened the box, and they both received similar bracelets for their trouble."

She buried her face in her hands. "Oh, this is positively dreadful." Her voice was muffled. "I'm quite certain the bracelets that have been unleashed will wreak havoc on the wearers."

He looked from the bracelet to the woman wearing it. Wreak havoc on the wearers, indeed. Esme seemed to have a knack for wreaking havoc, with or without a bracelet.

Fielding swore, which garnered a look from his carriage companion. He'd wanted to deliver Esme Worthington back to her aunt, hand this bloody box over to Solomon's, then collect his fee and be done with it. Now he could do none of those things. The men who hired him had warned him about the evils within the box, and while Fielding certainly didn't believe any of that nonsense, chances were they meant those bracelets. Which meant they belonged inside the box, and until they were all returned, his job wasn't complete.

He might not be the most honest man in London, but he'd never cheated anyone who'd paid him.

"Then I suppose there's only one thing for us to do," he said.

"What's that?"

"We have to go after the bracelets."

* * *

"What do you mean, we have to go after the bracelets?" Esme asked, certain she'd misunderstood him. "Aren't we currently running *from* the men who wear two of them?"

He inclined his head. "We are. But without all the bands in the box, I cannot complete the job I've been hired to do. Which means until we remove that bracelet from your wrist, you're my responsibility."

"So honorable," she said, her eyes skimming his strong form. His broad shoulders and strong, shapely thighs were evident in his new clothes, and she wondered why he didn't dress in such tailored finery more often. Oh, no, it was happening. The curse was taking effect. She brought her hand to her throat. "I must be truthful, Mr. Grey." His eyes were a warm brown when she settled on them. "I find myself utterly drawn to you. The fine chisel of your jawline and the intensity in your gaze. You are quite the specimen." Esme sat taller in her seat. "So I do ask that you be a gentleman lest we end up in an unfortunate position."

His brows arched. "I am a gentleman by title and birth, Miss Worthington, but I've never been that good at behaving as one. You'd best not trust your virtue with me."

She was unable to turn away from his molten gaze. Had that been a promise or a threat?

"Instead of tallying my merits," he said, "perhaps you should focus on something more pressing." A seductive smile slid into place. "Unless you have a better use of our time. We still have more than four hours to go before we arrive in London."

The hot flush that crept up her neck settled in her cheeks until they burned. So it had been a promise. Suddenly she found it quite difficult to breathe. She remembered his hands rubbing her sore muscles in the dungeon. Her internal temperature climbed several degrees.

Perhaps Mr. Grey was right: If she focused on the task at hand, she wouldn't think about his long legs and the way his thigh muscles pressed nicely against his trousers. And she wouldn't notice the crisp crinkle of brown hair on his forearms that his rolled-up sleeves revealed.

"Oh, for mercy's sake!" She mentally shook herself. *Talk, Esme; put your mind off of him.*

"I suspect most people believe Pandora's box to be nothing more than a fable, but most of us who study the legend know the truth of its existence. Which clearly we were quite right about."

"Clearly," he said dryly.

"I'd always subscribed to the theory that the box was not actually a box at all, but rather a bottle or an amphora. Many agree with that assessment, I can assure you. But it does appear that we were wrong in that regard. It is, after all, an actual box."

"So it appears," he said.

"In all these years of studying, how did I miss the legitimacy of this theory?" She shook her head in confusion. "What we'll be looking for in the books is information on the bracelets and precisely how we're supposed to get them off."

"Ah, yes, the books."

"Mr. Grey, do you find humor in my being a scholar?" she asked. Her delicate chin rose, and she eyed him square in the face as if she weren't head and shoulders shorter than he.

He shrugged. "It's not you, but the practice. I find it a waste of time. Tell me you're not the least bit interested in this antiquity because of its value."

"Its value? Why, of course I am. Think of what we could learn by studying such an artifact. Think of the insight we could gain into ancient cultures. Not to mention—"

"Not academic value. Monetary value."

"Monetary?" she scoffed. "That's insulting."

"It's made of solid gold," he said.

"That's completely irrelevant," she insisted.

"Miss Worthington, you are vastly entertaining."

"Splendid. Precisely what every woman longs to hear. I'll have you know I was not attempting to be entertaining. I am quite serious about my studies."

He almost believed her. *Almost*. But Fielding knew better. He'd seen his father's fruitless research dry up the family's fortune. Books and studies were a complete waste of time unless they brought a profit in the end. Anyone who thought otherwise was fooling themselves.

"There is a difference between a dreamer and a scholar, Miss Worthington."

"And you are suggesting that I am the former rather than the latter." She shook her head in annoyance. "You men are all the same."

He ignored her comment, though it intrigued him. Instead he settled on giving her instructions about what would happen once they arrived in London. "We'll need to make haste at gathering these books you need," he said.

"Yes." She nodded fervently. "I am most eager to remove this curse."

"No, I meant we can't stay at your home long. Waters and Thatcher know where you live, and they will likely return."

She frowned. "But you said we needed to find them."

"We do, but it would be better if we knew how to

remove the bracelets first. I'll take you somewhere to stay where you can be safe in the meantime."

"Oh," she said. Although no sound came out, everything on her face went round. Her eyes were like big green emeralds, and that mouth of hers parted in a silent "O."

"And what of my aunt? My household?"

"We'll bring your aunt with us."

"And my cat?" she asked.

Her cat?

Her books, her aunt, *and* her cat? Was he to cart her entire household across London? Perhaps she had a neighbor or a shopgirl down the lane he could accommodate too.

He gritted his teeth. "And your cat. Send your staff to their own homes for a while or to visit family."

She nodded and gripped the folds of her skirts. "Where shall we go?"

"The last place the Raven will look for me. To the home of a member of Solomon's." Were it not useful in that regard, he'd never seek out this man for assistance. It could work to his benefit, though. The closer he got to the club's members, the easier it would be to uncover the identities of the men he sought. The men who'd been with his father when the accident had occurred; the men who were responsible for his death.

Chapter Seven

~~~~~

Did you say Solomon's?" she breathed. "*The* Solomon's?"

"Unless there is another group of treasure hunters pretending to be scholars, then I suspect yes, *the* Solomon's. You've heard of them?"

"Of course I've heard of them. They are a legendary club whispered about in the shadows as if they were armored knights." She tried to slow her breathing or at the very least the rate of her speech. "And you are one of them?"

He scoffed. "No. They hired me to find the box."

"Ah." She sank back against the seat. "They hired you." It mattered little that he was not himself a member. Solomon's reputation was impeccable. They would work with only the most honorable of men.

"Yes. One of their members has devoted his life to Pandora's box and is extremely concerned with the antiquity falling into the wrong hands. So he and his friends"—he stumbled over the last word—"hired me to retrieve it from the Raven and return it safely to them."

"They must certainly trust you."

He shook his head. "No, I was merely the lesser of two evils. I can do things they are unwilling to do."

"Solomon's," she whispered. His self-deprecation did little to dampen her interest in the matter. Quite the opposite, in fact. His modesty was charming.

"They are only men. Nothing exciting about that," he grumbled.

She smiled, feeling content and greatly relieved. "I trust the men of Solomon's implicitly to care for Pandora's box. Therefore, I must deduce that you are trustworthy, or they would never have employed you."

Her confidence seemed to further annoy him. His jaw twitched.

As challenging as it was, she said nothing else for the duration of their trip. She wanted neither to annoy Mr. Grey nor to waste the opportunity to think of a possible solution. Two hours later they had arrived at her home, and Esme still had no idea how to remove the bracelet. She shuttled Fielding into her study.

"Mr. Grey, please wait in here." Horace jumped off a wingback chair and twined himself between her legs. She bent to scratch him behind the ears. It was nice to be missed. "I need to notify my aunt that we'll be going away for a while and she'll need to pack a few things. I'll be down directly to help gather the requisite books." She scooped up her cat, then left Fielding standing in the midst of her study.

Esme inhaled deeply. There had been moments when she'd feared she would never again see her aunt or her books or her home. Her home that smelled of freshly baked bread and was usually full of the sounds of her aging servants speaking too loudly to each other to make up for their diminished hearing. She made her way through the house and found her aunt coming down the stairs.

"Oh, me, you're home, child. I heard the door; I hoped it was you." She took several deep breaths. "We were so worried." Her aunt was a round woman with rosy cheeks and bright blue eyes. Esme had always thought she resembled an aging cherub.

"Yes, I'm home. You will never believe what has happened to me, Thea." She gave her aunt a squeeze. There weren't many adults shorter than Esme, but Thea was one of them. "There is no time to explain it now, though. Rest assured that very soon I shall have a story to tell you that will make that curling rod of yours unnecessary." She leaned in and kissed her aunt's cheek. They might not be blood-related, but Thea was the only family Esme had. Their relationship had begun simply enough, a mutual love of books, but they were so much more now.

"I shall look forward to that." Thea paused. "We tried to clean up your study as best we could."

"Thank you." Esme gave Thea an encouraging smile. "I know it won't make any sense, and I don't have time to explain right now, but we must leave. All of us. Within the hour."

Thea's hand flew to her ample bosom. "You are giving me such a fright, child."

"All will be well." Esme gave Thea another squeeze. "You go and pack some of our belongings. And let Mr. and Mrs. Craddock know they should go and visit their family until further notice."

At Thea's worried expression, Esme gently patted her shoulder. "I promise, all will be well. I shall be in my office with a visitor."

Thea nodded cautiously, then disappeared through a doorway.

The woman was featherbrained, to be certain, but she was kind, and Esme was grateful for her financial contribution that had allowed the two of them to purchase a suitable house on the edge of Clareville Grove with a lovely garden that Thea faithfully tended.

Esme felt a pang of guilt. Poor Thea and Mr. and Mrs. Craddock. It was not their fault that suddenly Esme found herself embroiled in some strange circumstances involving a secretive man named the Raven and cursed bracelets. It at least gave Esme some peace knowing that she'd be able to bring her aunt with her to wherever it was Mr. Grey was taking them.

Esme slipped back into her office and found Mr. Grey perusing the shelves full of books.

"You have an impressive collection," he said.

Pride swelled within her as she followed his gaze to her vast array of bound volumes. No doubt a man like Fielding—one trusted by Solomon's—would appreciate such an extensive library. Even if he didn't appreciate the woman in possession of it. "I don't suppose we can take all of them," she said, more to herself than him.

"We have neither the room nor the time."

"I can't imagine what's made you so prickly," she said. "Now, let's see what we can discover about removing this infernal band." Knowing it was utterly futile, but unable to stop herself, she tugged on the gold encircling her wrist. It did not budge. "I seem to remember," she said as she climbed onto the ladder, "there was mention of the bands in one of these." She traced her finger along the row of green leather books. "Professor MacAdo is rather eccentric in his views."

"Do you want me to help you with that?" Fielding asked.

"I believe I can manage." She stretched, and with the tip of her finger managed to work the last book on the row out of its place. She held it out behind her, and when he didn't immediately take it from her, she shook it impatiently.

He pulled the book from her hand, their fingers brushing during the exchange. Heat coursed up her arm, and for a moment she closed her eyes to revel in the sensation. He cleared his throat. She jerked her hand back, yet the heated sensation remained.

"There are others, though," she continued. "One more recent, perhaps one of those journals on the desk." She continued pulling books and handing them to him, careful not to touch his hand again. One after another she collected books until he finally spoke.

"Enough. You have selected a quarter of the books in this entire library." His tone was fierce, but Esme felt no fear.

After retrieving three more books, she began descending the ladder. "Oh, and this one might have some tidbits." She pulled a small brown book from its shelf.

He eyed the stack in her arms. "You can't bring all of them with us. Go through them and select only the essentials." With his arms crossed over his chest, he seemed forbidding, but all Esme could think about was the sensual line of his jaw.

Unable to withstand the temptation any longer, she reached over and, with one hand, ran her fingers across the stubble that covered his chin. Bristly, yet not all together an unpleasant feeling. His jaw seemed to clench under her fingers, but when he had no other response, she forced herself to step away from him.

She smothered her disappointment. After all, it was she who was affected by the curse of the bracelet. She couldn't expect him to feel the same rising passions for her that she felt growing within for him.

"We can examine the books over here," she said, pointing to the large table by the windows.

Men didn't choose women with brains; he'd said so himself earlier—books were a waste of time. And he thought her to be a dreamer. She had no business tempting herself like this. Not unless she was content to live as someone she was not for the rest of her days, to stifle her intelligence and play the part of an addle-brained female.

"It is most bothersome to be wearing this cursed band. Under any other circumstances, I would find you unpleasant and rude," she said.

He cocked one eyebrow. "And instead?"

She released a short puff of a breath and dropped the books onto the table. They scattered in an uneven rainbow. "Instead I should like nothing better than to kiss you, Mr. Grey."

"I can assure you, Miss Worthington, that whatever romantic notions you are having are completely misguided." He leaned forward. "Kissing me will not"—he paused for a moment, letting his eyes roam the length of her—"cure what is ailing you."

Warmth spread through her like the richest of chocolate. She didn't believe him. Surely, kissing him would prove to be the most perfect of cures.

As if he'd read her mind, he said, "If you wish to flirt with temptation, I will not stop you." He held his hands up as if he were defenseless.

Taking a cleansing breath, she turned away from Mr. Grey and focused her attention on the books in front of them. "Yes, thank you for that reminder. I assure you, I am trying to keep my attention on our current predicament and not my"—her voice dropped to a whisper—"*lustful* feelings for you."

Merely saying the word *lust* seemed to stir the feeling within her. It seemed such a forbidden word. She doubted she'd ever even said it aloud before now.

Since such thoughts were hardly helpful, she pushed them aside and said, "Let us start digging. I don't suppose we have much time to select which books to bring with us."

Once they were both seated, she tried to focus on the words on the page, but from the corner of her eye she could see his long fingers make delicate work of turning the pages in the book he perused. The masculine scent of sandalwood soap seemed to waft toward her like candle smoke. *Oh, for mercy's sake.*

Several moments passed, and she finally forced herself to stare at the words until she'd managed to read, and comprehend, the paragraph before her. But her mind would not still. He was sitting so close to her she could feel the warmth pour off his body. She closed her eyes and instantly became aware of his steady breathing, the sound of his hands stroking through the pages of the book before him.

In her mind she saw him turn to her, his eyes darkened with passion as he lifted her to the table. He said nothing, but bent forward to kiss her throat. Shivers of desire scattered across her arms and down her chest. Then his mouth made quick work of the skin at her shoulders before he finally kissed her full on the mouth.

A chair scuffed against the wood floor, jarring her out of her fantasy and back to the book in front of her.

She slammed the book closed and reached for another one, flipping it open. After scanning a few pages and reading only more of the same, her eyes lit on an illustration.

"Mr. Grey, look at this."

He leaned over and glanced at the image.

Her cheeks flamed as she realized what she had just shown him. A drawing of a nude woman reclining with nothing but a scrap of fabric draped over the apex between her thighs. Her breasts, however, were quite bare, the nipples pronounced. One hand was placed on a vase, and dangling from her wrist were four small bracelets.

"It says here"—she cleared her throat—"the gods wanted to curse her for her beauty . . ."

Heat from his body engulfed her as he rose to stand behind her chair. He'd bent forward, placing his head a mere breath away from her own. She stopped reading and swallowed.

"Continue," he said, his deep voice caressing the wisps of hair that dangled around her face.

"Can you not see the text yourself?" she asked, her voice airy.

His breath whispered against her ear. She met his gaze and nearly forgot her name or where she was. This close, she could see gold flecks swimming in the brown depths of his eyes. Her mouth went dry. A sensual smile curved his lips, and he looked as if he was prepared to devour her. Not in a lecherous fashion, but rather in a way she instinctively knew would be incredibly pleasurable. She wiped her palms against her skirt.

Without a second thought she leaned in and pressed her lips against his. With a gasp she pulled away, appalled at her behavior. After sitting back she eyed his reaction. He said nothing, merely gazed at her with silent amusement. Which, frankly, was rather annoying.

"Miss Worthington, if you're going to kiss me, you must do so with more passion than that. It is lust you have on your wrist, is it not?"

She looked down at the gold band, then back at him.

He smiled.

She frowned.

Then he placed one hand beneath her chin and nudged her forward. She kept her eyes open and watched as he leaned toward her; she didn't want to miss anything. But once his soft lips feathered across hers, she lost herself in the sensation, and her eyes fluttered closed.

Absently, she realized that his other hand had found its way to the back of her neck and was kneading the flesh there. But his mouth demanded most of her attention as it moved elegantly, seductively across her own.

This was kissing.

There was no time to consider how much of a fool he must have thought her with her schoolyard kiss. There was only pleasure. Radiating from her lips and sliding over every inch of her flesh like the lushest of silks.

His tongue ran across her bottom lip, and she gripped the arms of the chair to keep from sinking to the floor. Infinitely better than her imaginings, his lips teased and coaxed her own. Gracious, but this man knew how to kiss. Then, as quickly as it had started, the kiss ended.

She opened her eyes and undoubtedly gave him a wistful smile. "Well, you certainly are much better at that than I am," she said.

He cleared his throat. "I suspect you could catch on rather quickly," he said, his voice tense.

For a moment neither said anything, then without warning, Fielding fell back into his chair and pointed at the book she'd been studying. "Does it say anything about the bracelets or a curse?"

Esme glanced back at the book and skimmed the pages surrounding the drawing of the woman. She shook her head. "It doesn't even mention the bracelets, other than to say they are part of yet another theory surrounding Pandora's box." With one fluid motion, she rose to her feet. "I'm going to check and see how my aunt is faring with the packing."

The truth of the matter was, she needed some space. Some distance from the increasingly attractive Mr. Grey. Resisting him had been hard enough before she'd known his skill at kissing.

The hall outside her study was quiet as she made her way up the stairs. Why had he kissed her? Well, why wouldn't he when she'd practically crawled into his lap? Perhaps willing women were more difficult to come by than one might think.

But oh, that kiss. The memory of his warm lips on hers sent gooseflesh popping up all over her body. Fielding Grey was a man of the world. He was an experienced lover. She could tell by his expert kissing. True, she had no means of comparison, but still, a woman could tell when a kiss would have curled the toes of a seasoned mistress.

She knew one thing for certain: she would kiss Fielding again. And for a bit longer. There was something in the way he'd moved his tongue against her bottom lip that promised more. She desperately wanted to know what that more was. And she couldn't help it. Not really. The curse was far too strong and Mr. Grey far too tempting.

Besides, kissing was harmless. And in any case, she

was a woman without a name, without any prospects for marriage. She'd given up that opportunity years ago.

So there was no need for great concern regarding her reputation. She only hoped this blessed curse would stop before she ruined herself altogether.

Chapter Eight

~~~

Fielding watched Esme slip out of the office. He leaned back in the straight-backed wooden chair and rubbed his hand down his face.

He'd never believed in foolish curses. Esme fancied him only because he'd rescued her. The kidnapping and subsequent hanging from manacles would have been an ordeal for anyone, but for a genteel lady such as Esme, it was too much. It was no wonder he had become the object of her affection.

Oh, perhaps she was attracted to him to some degree. He supposed there was no way she could act so beguiling were she not. But Esme didn't want him, specifically; he was merely convenient.

She was a grown woman, though, and who was he to deny her something she wanted? He'd certainly played into her charms and kissed her when he ought to have kept his hands to himself.

But when she'd pressed her lips against his in that innocent way, he'd been unable to think of anything else but kissing her properly. Although propriety had been the furthest thing from his mind when he'd pulled her into his arms. He'd done it to teach her a lesson, show her that toying with him would not benefit her in the end. Yet it seemed that he was the one who had learned a lesson—that touching and kissing Esme would only whet a desire he knew he'd never be able to quench.

He'd told her from the beginning he was no gentleman, and he'd meant it. If she wanted to play with fire, he'd hand her matches. Yet, as sweet as seducing Esme sounded, he had more pressing matters to handle. Namely, protecting her until he could get the blasted bracelets back into the box.

Stepping out onto her front step, Fielding examined both sides of the street. He knew the Raven's men wouldn't be far behind them. And just then, as if not to disappoint, Fielding caught sight of his uncle's red crest on the shiny black carriage parked on a cross street a quarter mile up the lane.

"Esme," he yelled as he entered the house again. This was no time for formalities. "We must leave. Now."

She appeared in the hallway, breathy from her exertion. She'd changed into one of her own dresses, and the soft pink matched the stain on her cheeks. "What's the matter?"

"They've found us."

"Who's found us?" Thea asked in a panic.

Esme eyed Fielding before she turned to her aunt. "The men who abducted me," she said plainly.

If that was how she intended to soothe her aunt, she failed miserably. As it was, the older woman swayed on her feet and reached her hand out to the wall to steady herself.

"Gracious," she muttered.

He wasn't used to handling women. He knew how to give instruction to men, tell them where to dig or where to shine the light, but this hero business was damned challenging.

"I will ensure we leave safely," Fielding muttered, hoping it eased their worries.

"Are they coming back in the house?" Thea asked. Her voice wavered, and it sounded as if at any moment she would be reduced to sobs.

He released a string of curses that had both women turning clashing shades of red. "No, I'm sure they only mean to watch us and follow us should we leave. But we can get around them. Trust me."

With that, he went to the driver still waiting in the hired rig in front of Esme's home. He paid the man, then instructed him to leave, telling the driver that they'd changed their plans and were no longer in need of a coach. On the chance that the Raven's men stopped the driver and paid for information, Fielding wanted to ensure they got nothing for their money. Proceeding to the alleyway behind Esme's house, Fielding checked to make sure the Raven hadn't stationed men there as well. Hiring a new rig was as simple as whistling through his two fingers. It was a considerably smaller carriage, but it would have to do.

"Hurry," he told the women as he stepped back into the house. "We need to leave now." When Esme started for the front door, he grabbed her arm. "This way. We're going out the back." He held the door open for them as they shuffled out to the waiting carriage.

Several minutes later, after their luggage had been quickly loaded, they were packed tightly in the hired coach—Fielding, Esme, Thea, and a surly-looking tomcat nestled in Esme's lap.

Her aunt fluttered her hands. "First you disappear for two days, then you return and demand we abandon our home. I could have accepted any of that, but sneaking out the back door? And this mention of someone called the Raven?" Thea's eyes grew large, and her voice pitched higher and higher.

"Thea, there is no reason for a fit of the vapors." Esme reached over and patted her aunt's knee. "But if you find you simply cannot abide it, I did bring some of your salts. Mr. Grey shall take excellent care of us." She smiled sweetly. "He's taking us somewhere safe. Somewhere I can read the journals and plan our next step."

Her complete faith in him was unsettling. Not to mention unwarranted. The only thing that would come out of their time together would be disappointment for Esme. He looked out the window and saw the Raven's carriage still stationed at the front of the house.

"I believe we'll all be safe at the marquess's house," Fielding said.

"A marquess?" Thea asked, obviously impressed.

"Mr. Grey is a viscount," Esme said.

"Indeed?" Thea's thinned eyebrows rose. "Well, you shouldn't be calling him mister; he has a more appropriate title, I should think."

Fielding shook his head. "I prefer Mr. Grey. It is how I am known in my profession. But your aunt is right; we're beyond formalities. Call me Fielding." He scanned the street but found no sign of his uncle's carriage.

"Fielding," Esme repeated, then caught herself. "Thea

loves her gossip rags; I'm afraid she can't read enough about the scandals and goings-on in proper society," Esme explained.

"What's your title, dear?" Thea asked him.

"The Viscount Eldon."

"Eldon. Can't say that I recall reading anything about you," Thea said.

"Too scandalous," he said and winked at her. "They wouldn't know where to begin." For the most part, they simply didn't pay any attention to him. He was a man who worked for his money, and to most of society that meant he'd walked away from all things proper.

Her aunt was fanning herself with a handkerchief so Esme directed her attention there. "Oh, Thea, think of this as a grand adventure."

"I do believe I'm too old for adventures," Thea said with a weak smile.

"Nonsense. You don't look a day over forty."

They wound up one street, across two, and down another, all in the name of confusion should anyone be following. It wasn't much longer before the carriage stopped.

Esme pulled the curtain back to survey their surroundings. "Is this the marquess's house?"

"If you would wait here," he replied, "I shouldn't be long." He stepped down and closed the small door behind him. He spoke briefly to his driver to guarantee the ladies would be safe during his absence; then he climbed the stairs to Lindberg's large columned home.

The butler answered the door practically before Fielding had a chance to knock, as if he'd been poised, waiting for the first sign of a visitor. Fielding was shown directly into Max's study, where the marquess stood behind his desk, poring over a large map.

At the butler's announcement, Max looked up. "Grey. This is a surprise." He stepped around his desk. "Have you already found the box?" He did nothing to hide the enthusiasm in his voice.

Fielding ignored the question. "Actually, I need your assistance." He paused, trying to think of the right words to say. "We might need a drink for this." He took a seat in a reddish-brown leather chair that groaned under his weight.

Max complied and poured them each a glass of sherry, then sat opposite Fielding.

After taking a bracing sip, Fielding informed Max of Miss Worthington's kidnapping and the lady and her aunt's current need for sanctuary. For the time being, he left out the business with the cursed bracelets and made no further mention of the box. He didn't trust Solomon's and saw no reason to disclose such information to them. Besides, he didn't normally present a step-by-step process of his excavation for his clients. "I know the Raven well enough to know he won't look for me anywhere near a member of Solomon's."

More to the point, the Raven knew him well enough to know Fielding would never ordinarily ask for assistance. Which, under the circumstances, meant refuge here would bring them safety.

"Obviously, your house is out of the question," Max provided.

"Precisely. So now I find myself with two ladies and nowhere to put them."

Fielding hadn't known what sort of reaction to expect

from Max, but laughter hadn't been at the top of his list. Yet that was exactly his response.

"We certainly didn't intend to send you on a mission that entailed rescuing a damsel in distress," Max said with a chuckle.

"You learn to expect the unexpected when it comes to dealing with the Raven," Fielding said. "Although I admit, when I worked for him we were never in the practice of abducting innocent ladies."

"The Raven obviously believed she had valuable information." Two creases pinched Max's forehead. "And you say you have her with you?"

Fielding nodded. "In the carriage outside. With her aunt."

Max smiled as he walked to the door. "Let us invite the ladies in and make them comfortable. All three of you may stay as long as you need. I have an entire wing of the house that I scarcely use." He motioned to the other end of the hall as they made their way to the front door.

"I should warn you, Miss Worthington is not your typical woman. She's unique and can talk your ear off."

Max's eyebrows rose. "I'll heed your warning and guard my ears accordingly."

Within moments they had gathered the women, and the four of them were seated in a heavily windowed parlor with a tray of tea and frosted biscuits at their disposal. Esme and her aunt sat together on a blue-and-gold settee, simultaneously soaking in every detail. From the plush gold-colored carpet to the blue draperies, they seemed awed by the opulence that surrounded them.

Fielding sat on the edge of a small wingback chair, clearly built for one of the fairer sex. Besides the delicate size, the pale-blue-flowered print made him feel utterly foolish. He balanced an equally small and dainty teacup on his knee.

"Oh, my dear boy, I do believe my frazzled nerves are finally beginning to calm," Thea said, sipping her tea.

"Glad to hear it," Max said.

"Your home is beautiful," Esme said. "Thank you so much for welcoming us."

"I hope your ordeal wasn't too overwhelming, Miss Worthington," Max said.

Esme smiled at Fielding, and it was so genuine, he found it difficult to look away from her.

"Thankfully, Mr. Grey was there to rescue me," she said. "Otherwise, I'm not certain what I would have done. I suppose eventually the rats would have eaten me."

"Mercy, child, don't say such a thing," Thea exclaimed. "You're safe now," she said, patting Esme's hand. "That's all that matters."

"Well, it was a distinct possibility," Esme said. She bit into a biscuit. Her eyes closed as she savored the bite. She washed it down with a decidedly feminine sip of tea.

One minute Thea had been engaged in the conversation and the next she'd fallen quite asleep, though her teacup and saucer remained on her lap without a drop spilling.

Fielding could not have felt more out of place had he been sitting with the queen herself. He could sometimes go several days without speaking to anyone, save the few he kept on staff at his home. And when he was in the field hunting for an antiquity, he hired the bare number of men necessary to complete the task. Yet it appeared he now would be surrounded by people, at least for the time being.

"Worthington," Max said casually. "Tell me, why do I know that name?"

Esme shifted in her seat, and her cheeks pinkened ever so slightly. She set down her plate and straightened her skirt, paying particular attention to one of the pleats.

While he'd known her only two days, Fielding noted he'd never before seen Esme look nervous, despite the ordeal she'd been through.

She bumped up her chin, then licked her lips. "You might know my sister." She uncrossed and crossed her legs at the ankles.

Max was silent for a brief moment. "Elena," he supplied in almost a whisper.

Esme shifted again, moving forward ever so slightly. "Yes," she said, her voice tight.

Max was going to think him a liar for making Esme out to be a talker when she seemed intent on providing the marquess with tight-lipped answers.

After a thoughtful sip, the marquess spoke again. "Pretty girl. I believe we danced a few times." He gave Esme a sly grin. "Before she saddled herself with Griffin."

"Yes, she's quite lovely," Esme agreed, her voice seeming to thin.

Fielding tried to determine the emotion that darkened Esme's eyes.

Jealousy, perhaps. Resentment, maybe. Sorrow, a touch.

Max had inadvertently hit on a sensitive subject. So there was more to Esme Worthington than first met the eye. More than her incessant chatter and innocently brazen behavior. For some reason that pleased Fielding.

"How is your sister?" Max asked.

Esme stiffened and took several breaths before answering. "I presume she's doing quite perfectly."

Fielding knew there was something more. Something Esme left unsaid.

"Thank you, my lord, for your kindness in offering us sanctuary. I do hate to be rude, but I believe my aunt needs to rest." Esme stood and placed her hand on Thea's shoulder, which instantly roused the woman. "Could you point us in the direction of our room?"

"Of course. I've put you in adjoining rooms in the north wing." Max rang a bell, and a moment later his butler appeared. "Please take the ladies to their rooms."

Fielding grabbed Esme's elbow. "When you get settled, come back down and we'll get back to those books."

After the ladies left the room, Fielding nodded to Max. "You know her sister?"

"Not in the biblical sense, Grey, if that's what you're asking. But I do recall meeting her on occasion. And that husband of hers."

Esme had told Fielding she had no family, that she lived only with her aunt. He did not appreciate being lied to, no matter what the reason. Still, he felt compelled to ask, "What do you know of them?"

"Raymond Griffin, the Earl of Weatherby," Max said. "I can't say that we've ever exchanged more than salutations. My impression, though, is that the man is a bastard."

Fielding rose from the ridiculously small chair. " 'Bastard' covers a multitude of sins," he said. Undoubtedly there were a great many people in London who would use exactly that word to describe him. He gripped the back of the dainty parlor chair.

"Rumors," Max said, his usual cool facade disappearing. "I don't remember much, as I rarely pay any attention to societal scandals, but I do remember word of Elena's younger sister causing quite a stir. And then she was gone, sent to a country estate after a reported illness."

"Convenient for them," Fielding said. "Perhaps I need to pay the Weatherbys a visit, inform them of Esme's safety." And assure them that he would not be party to any rumored scandal that required he make an honest woman out of Esme.

Chapter Nine

Esme hadn't wanted to talk about her sister. Nothing good ever came from that. She flung open her trunk, fully intent on unpacking her belongings, but found the task had already been completed for her. The armoire was filled with the dresses Thea had crammed into the case and her personal belongings—her hairbrush, combs, and the few pieces of jewelry she owned—lay sorted on top of the dressing table.

With a resigned sigh, she walked to the door. Esme had tried to continue her relationship with her sister, had tried to see her a few times, but Elena had not been interested. All Esme knew was that she'd stood on Elena's doorstep and been asked to leave by a servant. Despite her best efforts, Esme's relationship with her sister had dissolved to the occasional letter at Christmastime.

But she hadn't wanted to say any of that either. Living an anonymous life was rather easy when one stayed home and ventured out only to libraries or obscure bookstores. Besides, no one knew she was still in London. As far as

Esme knew, Elena was still telling everyone that Esme preferred the solitude of country living.

Quietly, she made her way down the massive staircase to the main hall. Here, in the house of a marquess, though, she was bound to have her identity discovered.

Did that mean Elena and Raymond would discover all the trouble she'd gotten herself into as of late? The empty marble expanse seemed to echo with her thoughts as she made her way through it. She turned a corner to find Fielding standing with Lord Lindberg, and they were quietly having a discussion.

Having Elena and Raymond find out about the kidnapping would only further prove to them that they'd made the right decision in leaving her to her own devices. Wouldn't they relish all the details about her being abducted and the ancient curse she was under, a curse that was turning her into a wanton? Right now, at this very moment, looking at Mr. Grey standing at the opposite end of the hall, Esme wanted to press herself against him and experience another of his knee-weakening kisses.

Fielding saw her standing there, and his brown eyes flashed with acknowledgment, but he continued his conversation. She decided he was undoubtedly the most handsome man she'd ever set eyes on. Esme took in Fielding's height, the sheer length of his legs, and her heart rate accelerated.

The marquess was also an attractive man, especially if one was the sort to prefer dark blond hair and an easy smile over Fielding's darker features. Fielding, though, had a smile that, while slower to appear, came with tight dimples that pierced his scruffy cheeks. And eyes that seemed to bore into her and make her want to admit every secret she'd ever hidden.

She didn't have many of those, but for him, no matter the cost, she would share the secrets she did have.

The two men both had the physique of an athlete, although Fielding's shoulders were broader, and his added height put him at least a head taller than the marquess. While the marquess's clothes were impeccably pristine and wrinkle-free and his face freshly shaven, Fielding's shirt was open at the neck, revealing a swath of dark hair, and his own face had not seen a razor in days. Unkempt and unmade like a just-slept-in bed. Esme sighed. Fielding Grey did not look like a true gentleman with his rough edges and lack of polish, but to her, he was all the more attractive for it.

She tried looking at the marquess, searched for something in his clean good looks that would draw her in, make her heart skip a beat. But she felt nothing. It appeared her lustful curse had chosen its mark.

Suddenly the marquess slapped Fielding on the back and strode away. Fielding turned toward her, and her heart not only skipped a beat, it seemed to stop beating altogether.

"Come along, Miss Worthington."

She wondered for a moment if her feet would move, but they seemed to respond to him on their own as a dog to its master. If he beckoned, she would follow. Perhaps she should be humiliated by such a realization, but she was only eager for more time spent in his presence. Infernal curse. She supposed she should be thankful her lustful thoughts were for him and not some wretched man with rotting teeth and crossed eyes.

"The marquess has prepared a room where we can study those books and journals of yours and hopefully find out what needs to be done to remove that bracelet from your wrist."

"Very good," she managed. She followed him down a hall toward the back of the house. They turned left and then entered a room through a large open doorway.

The room was perfect for such a task. Normally, it must serve as a smaller dining room, as it contained the standard buffet against the wall and a table in the middle of the room, yet both were on a much smaller scale than houses this large tended to warrant. The far wall was lined with windows. The heavy draperies had been pulled back, allowing what remained of the day's light to stream in. The room faced the back of the marquess's house and looked out onto the small but lovely garden. Stacked on the table were the volumes they'd brought from her house.

It gave her a semblance of peace to have that bit of her own household here with her. As it were, her poor Aunt Thea was upstairs, lulled to sleep by a pot of tea laced with more than enough brandy to bring down a grown man. The older woman might have a headache on the morrow, but hopefully her nerves would be settled and she'd have peaceful dreams.

Esme took a seat and once again opened the book she'd been perusing back at her house. It was a translation of an old Italian text purchased just weeks earlier. She'd glanced through it a few times, but she looked forward to delving deeper into the mysteries it held.

Tracing her finger down the page, she tried to concentrate on the text. Ordinarily, this was precisely the type of work she'd find riveting, but it was hard to concentrate with that man sitting in such close proximity. The room wasn't very large, the table only big enough to seat six. And they were in here together. Alone.

She was a scholar, for goodness' sake. Never had she been subject to romantic fantasies. Well, that wasn't precisely true, but over the last several years, she'd become quite accomplished at ignoring fanciful notions. She tried to force herself to focus on the book in front of her. But several minutes later she found herself observing Fielding, admiring the way the sun burnished his brown hair, the way his face changed as he studied the text before him.

Fielding tossed the book aside, then reached for a journal, and when he did he caught her staring. Leaning back in his chair, Fielding steepled his fingers across his abdomen, drawing her eye to the way the fabric stretched across his taut stomach.

Her pulse quickened.

"Esme," he said, her name coming out in a caress. "You warned me I would have to play the gentleman. But I told you that I've never been much accomplished in that." He shrugged, pulling her attention to the breadth of his shoulders. "When a beautiful woman wants me to touch her, I tend to find myself most agreeable."

She tried to speak, but her breaths were coming so quickly she lost her words, and so she merely nodded. Suddenly she wondered what she'd agreed to.

He leaned forward until his face was so close to hers their lips nearly touched. "How am I to deny you?" His cheek caressed her own, the stubble of his beard tickling her flesh.

She swallowed. "My apologies for putting you in such a challenging position."

He moved to whisper in her ear. "This isn't the position I had in mind. I'd much prefer you naked on this table."

She closed her eyes and took a deep breath. "Merely a kiss, 'tis all I request."

"A kiss," he repeated. "Like this?" He trailed tiny kisses across her lower lip.

She sucked in her breath. "More."

His lips moved across hers, tenderly, but with a promise of passion. "How was that?"

"More," she breathed.

And with that he yanked her chair back, pulled her across his lap, and kissed her. His mouth opened slightly and his tongue slid seductively first across her lower lip, then her upper. She opened for him. And his tongue delved inside.

The world around her disappeared. She heard no sound save their breathing and felt nothing but the sensations flooding her body, lighting her nerves like fireworks.

He moved her left leg so that now she straddled him, her skirt bunching up between them.

Desire sparked through her body, igniting every limb, every inch of skin from the roots of her hair to the tips of her toes and radiating in between. Her nipples hardened and pressed achingly against the fabric of her dress. She longed for him to touch them, to rub against them.

As if he read her mind, his hand slid beneath her bodice and cupped her breast. The caress was so intimate, it should have shamed her. But with his warm hand against her aching flesh, she felt a jolt of boldness shoot through her. His mouth left hers and slid seductively down the column of her throat and across her collarbone. Unabashedly, she arched toward him.

She grabbed his shoulders and tried to press herself even closer to him, trying in vain to alleviate whatever the ache was that was building inside her.

Naked on the table.

He kissed her again, so deep, so thoroughly, she thought she would come apart at the seams. Then their kiss ended, and for a moment they sat there holding on to each other, their breath mingling in the quiet air.

"Esme," he said.

"Yes?"

"You must learn to control yourself, as it is abundantly clear that there is no gentleman within me." And with that he sat her back on her chair, then stood and walked to the opposite side of the room.

She tried to concentrate on his words. "This distresses you," she said.

"You are an innocent. I have no wish for some angry family member to come knocking on my door and demand I marry you." He gave her a wry smile. "I am not in need of a wife."

The desire pooling through her body seemed instantly to dissolve, like sugar in steaming coffee. He had no need for *her* was what he meant.

Men always married. It was in them to find a wife to care for them and see to their needs. So it must be that she didn't suit him, and he was trying to be kind.

His words stung to her very core. Yet for all the world she would not have him know how they pained her. She notched her chin up. "I am not looking for a husband either. And you needn't worry about any gallant men in my family tree; I have none."

His face softened. "Gallant men or a family tree?"

"Either." She shrugged. "I have told you, I am my own woman."

"What are you looking for?" he asked softly, and she almost believed he truly cared.

She swallowed and ignored the list of desires that scrolled through her mind. *A husband who loved and adored her. Children.*

She wanted to say that she didn't enjoy being cursed with desire for a man she'd ordinarily never look at twice. Because while that might be true, it had nothing to do with him and everything to do with her. She'd trained herself not to notice attractive men, not to long for that which was unattainable to her.

"I want to get this bracelet off my arm so that I will cease putting you in such an awkward position."

His jaw clenched. "Shall we get back to the books, then?"

"Indeed."

When he returned to the table, he sat opposite her, putting the hard wood of the table between them.

Evidently Fielding had found his gentleman within.

Esme turned over for the hundredth time since crawling into bed. It wasn't that the bed was uncomfortable; it was actually quite plush and warm. It wasn't even that she was wide awake, as her lids felt heavy with sleep, and the yawning was getting to be ridiculous. Yet sleep evaded her, and she couldn't seem to keep her body settled.

Ever since she was a child, she'd been enchanted by the legend of Pandora's box. Her father had regaled her with all the ancient stories and legends when she'd been but a girl. She'd curl up in the nook of his arm and he'd spin the tales long into the night.

When her parents had passed on, she'd wanted only her father's library as remembrance. Not that Elena or Raymond would have given her anything else. As it was, she'd had to beg for the books. She'd taken those books and she'd studied. Formed her own hypotheses and become a scholar in her own right when it came to Pandora and her legendary box.

Despite what Fielding thought, Esme knew she was no dreamer. When it came to her studies, she was quite levelheaded. Why, then, did she become a complete goose around him? Rolling over, she shoved her left leg out of the covers and held up her arm. It was too dark to see anything other than the shadow of her limb, but she knew the bracelet was there. The weight of it rested against her skin. Pandora's curse dangling from her wrist. Something that should have made Esme undeniably irresistible to men.

Only that wasn't how it worked. Instead, she was the one who was cursed. Fielding's touch had left her blood pulsing with desire, her body aching to be caressed. She was filled with lustful thoughts for a man who clearly did not want her. Twice now she'd offered herself to him, and both times he'd resisted. And this from someone who swore he wasn't a gentleman. Yet he was doing a remarkable job imitating one.

Chapter Ten

~~~~~

"How is your aunt?" Fielding asked as soon as Esme stepped into the dining room the following morning. He placed the newspaper on the table.

"Still sleeping soundly." Esme seemed quite determined to look anywhere but directly at him. "I fear I might have slipped her a bit too much brandy last night. But I checked to ensure she's still breathing, and she's snoring quite contentedly."

Fielding couldn't help but notice that Esme looked lovely this morning. Her hair hung loosely down her back in russet-colored curls that looked so soft he wanted nothing more than to run his fingers through them. She wore a plain and rather worn gown of soft lavender that looked pleasant against her fair skin. When she finally looked up at him, her cheeks pinkened ever so slightly.

"It smells heavenly in here," she said.

He motioned to the buffet. "The marquess has spared no expense. Although I do believe our host is still abed this morning. He had a late night."

"I know the feeling," Esme muttered as she piled her plate with smoked fish, eggs, and warm bread.

"Did you not sleep well?" He sipped his coffee. He certainly hadn't, a fact that both annoyed and intrigued him. No matter what was occurring in his life, he'd never been one to fight sleep. But last night as he'd watched Esme slip into her bedchamber, he'd had half a mind to tell her to lock it behind her, so unsure was he about his ability to withstand her temptation.

He'd kissed plenty of women. There was no running tally, no notches in his bedpost, but he'd had more than his share of the fairer sex. And it wouldn't be sympathetic or romantic of him to acknowledge the fact that he'd never shared a more explosive kiss with any other woman. With her willing body straddling his own, he'd wanted nothing more than to bunch her skirts up around her waist and plow into her, yet while he was certainly not above bedding unmarried women, he was fervently against seducing virgins.

It took her several breaths before she answered. "Merely thinking about a solution to our current problem." She sat adjacent to him, placing her plate atop the crisp linen tablecloth. "There simply has to be a way we can get this off. I would suggest we try to saw it off," she said with an impish smile, "but I suspect the metal has been treated for such an attempt."

A saw. He grabbed her wrist, then turned her hand palm up. "I hadn't even thought of that," he said as he ran two fingers along the pale flesh of her wrist. Her pulse flickered beneath his touch, and she uttered a breathy sigh.

He didn't relish the thought of brandishing a saw that close to her perfectly creamy wrist. Drumming his fingers on the arms of his chair, he stopped and reached for the newspaper.

She motioned to the paper. "Anything of interest occurring?"

He looked down at it again. "Mostly talk of the queen's Golden Jubilee."

She chewed thoughtfully. "I'd forgotten that was coming up. Fairly soon too, if I'm correct?"

He nodded, then sipped his coffee. "They're timing the festivities with the eclipse."

She piled eggs on top of a bite of bread, dipped it generously into her jam, then popped the morsel into her mouth. Fielding enjoyed watching her. She, unlike most women he'd encountered, was not shy about eating in front of men. Quite the contrary. It seemed Esme Worthington rather liked to eat.

He sipped his coffee and continued to watch her.

She stopped mid-chew, then swallowed. "Are you not eating?" she asked. Evidently she'd only just noticed that no plate sat in front of him.

"Not this early. I'll have something later."

She nodded. "Is that coffee I smell?" she asked as she closed her eyes and inhaled deeply.

"It is." He smiled. "Would you like some?"

"Oh, yes. I always have preferred coffee to tea," she chatted as he poured her a cup. "But some believe that to be rather uncivilized." Her smile faded a touch.

He placed the cup in front of her. She poured enough cream in it to turn it a nice warm brown, dropped in a cube of sugar, and gave the mixture a vigorous stir. Bringing the cup to her mouth, she inhaled again, then took a slow sip.

Until today he never would have assumed that one

could seductively drink coffee, but Esme managed to do it. And although he knew seduction wasn't her intent, the look of ecstasy on her face and the moan of pleasure that escaped her lips had him shifting uncomfortably in his seat.

"This is divine. Thank you."

He inclined his head.

She went back to eating, interspersing bites with more sips of coffee. Fielding thought she'd never finish, but she was clearly enjoying every morsel, so he didn't interrupt her.

"Do you think those wretched men will find us here?" she asked when she finally pushed away her plate. She dabbed at her mouth with a napkin, but the activity could not hide the tremor of fear in her voice. Her hands shook slightly. Perhaps this was why she'd lost sleep last night. While he'd been imagining her and all the carnal delights he could mentally conjure, she'd lain awake fearing the Raven. Fielding felt like an ass.

"No. They do not know of my association with the men of Solomon's."

She nodded. "You tracked them with such skill to the monastery. I don't suspect I should question your ability to properly hide us."

Although he felt his own cheeks redden with guilt, he didn't correct her. She need not know that Solomon's had led him directly to her.

"Did you know they had me with them?" she asked.

"No, I did not."

"I thought I might die out there, and though I certainly hoped for a savior, I never expected one. But there you were, as if you'd walked right out of an adventure novel."

He noticed her absently fingering the necklace resting against her chest. "Your father gave you that? The key?"

"Yes. When I was a girl." She chewed at her lip. "He brought it back for me from a trip to Greece."

"What made him pick it up?"

"My father was a professor of mythology at Oxford. That's where my extensive library comes from. He and I were quite close, and he taught me much about myths and legends. It was something we shared, something neither my mother nor my sister ever appreciated. So when he was visiting Greece, he happened upon the necklace in a tiny shop, and when he saw it was labeled as the key to Pandora's box, he thought I would enjoy it."

She was so lovely when she smiled it was almost painful to look at her. His own father would have found her delightful, a fact Fielding could not ignore. They would have shared a mutual love of books and history. A good reminder to Fielding of why he couldn't pursue a relationship with Esme. Fielding had never identified with his own father, so he certainly wouldn't ever understand the passions that captured Esme's soul.

"Neither of us ever expected it would actually be the key. He was never particularly fond of the Pandora story the way I was." She wound the thin gold chain around her finger. "Earlier this year I ran across a bit of research that indicated Pandora had worn a key around her neck, and I began to suspect my trinket might be authentic."

"Whom did you tell about your pendant and your suspicion that it was the key?" he asked. Damned if he didn't want to know how the Raven had discovered that little fact.

The brightness in her green eyes dimmed. "I've tried to think of that myself. A few months ago a man approached me at the Guildhall Library, somewhere I frequent, and he seemed fascinated by the pendant. I don't know who he was, but since he shared an interest in Pandora, I did mention my theory about my key. Aside from him, my aunt, my sister, and the two gentlemen I correspond with also know. We share our research."

"Two men?"

"Other scholars." She shook her head fervently. "They would never associate with someone like the Raven. They are far too civilized for that sort of thing."

He wondered momentarily how she'd feel to know he wasn't as civilized as she seemed to believe. Not only had he associated with the Raven, he was related to the man. "Civilized or not, people are capable of all sorts of things if it serves their purposes." Perhaps they would have to pay visits to these two scholars at some point.

"How well do you know these men?"

"Mr. Brown and Phillip," she provided. "I know them very well. That is, I've corresponded with them for quite some time."

Fielding stilled, his coffee cup halfway to his mouth, and gave her a pointed look. "You've never met them in person?"

"I haven't. But I know they would no sooner hurt the box than I would." A blush flooded her cheeks as she looked down at the bracelet on her wrist.

Yes, they would definitely have to visit these gentlemen scholars of Esme's. Indeed, if the men were as "helpful" as she had been, their situation might be dire. "How do you communicate with them?" he asked.

"Through the *Times*. In the advertisement section," she said. "It is not uncommon for scholars to correspond with one another through academic journals or newspapers."

Fielding leaned back. "So, in effect, anyone who reads the *Times* can read your correspondence?"

"Yes, but not in the way you are implying. First of all, I never use my real name; both of the gentlemen know me as Mr. Spencer. That was my father's name. I suspected they would never believe me to be a serious scholar were they to know I was a woman."

He nodded but made no comment.

"Additionally, we use shorthand and riddles in our communications since we're dealing with a very sensitive subject. It's all very secure," she assured him.

But Fielding was not so assured.

"What do you suppose this Raven character plans to do with the box?" she asked.

"He's in the business of hunting antiquities."

She said nothing for a moment, as if she wasn't quite certain what to make of what he'd said. "Well, that's a rather peculiar business," she said. "Does he keep them all?"

Fielding took a sip of coffee. "There is a fortune to be made in antiquities." He went and stood next to the hearth. "The Raven sees to it that he makes more than his share. But no, he doesn't keep them. He usually has a client who commissions him for a particular piece." He leaned against the mantel. "He'll do whatever it takes to get what he wants. Manipulate, bribe, steal; the only thing that matters to him is winning."

When Esme gasped, he turned away from her, staring into the flames. Standing this close he could feel the heat penetrate his trousers, nearly burning his legs; still he made no attempt to move away.

He reminded himself that it didn't matter what she thought. She would never understand him, never understand why he'd made the choices he had and become the man he was.

If he wanted to break that silly spell she was under, believing him to be some honorable hero, he'd have to tell her the truth. He'd have to tell her who he really was, and if she ran, all the better.

"But this isn't merely an antiquity," she said indignantly. "This isn't a trinket to trifle with, something to collect and put on a mantelpiece. This is a powerful box created to punish Pandora," she argued. "It belongs in the hands of someone who will understand and respect what it is."

"Pardon me, my lord, a messenger has come for you," the butler said from the doorway. "He said something about a Raven."

Fielding had sent Esme to the reading room to wait while he dealt with the messenger. She'd crossed the length of the room so many times, it was a wonder she hadn't worn the carpet down. In the short amount of time she'd been waiting, she'd imagined all sorts of terrible things. What would prevent the Raven from abducting her again? And this time doing her serious harm?

When Fielding came into the room, parchment dangling from his hand, he had a heavy scowl on his face.

"He's found us, hasn't he?" she asked. She knew she probably sounded hysterical, so she forced herself into a chair to at least keep from pacing.

He shook his head. "No. He sent this to my home here in London. Or I should say, he left it there after he practically destroyed the place." He cursed and swiped a hand down his face. "He didn't waste any time getting back to your house either. I'll send someone to assess the damage, and if we're lucky, you'll get away with just broken windows."

"Oh, God," she said. She sat on her hands to keep from chewing her nails. "But if the note arrived at your house, then one of your servants must have brought it here."

"My messenger has clear instructions to avoid being followed, Esme. You are safe here."

She nodded. "What does the note say?" Unable to abide her nerves any longer, she stood and walked the length of the carpet.

"Only that he knows I was there in the ruins." He pocketed the note. "And that I have you and the box."

"His men returned to him," she said.

"Thatcher would no matter what. I don't know about Waters, though. I suspect he was probably too afraid of facing the Raven and might be hiding somewhere. Once we figure out the puzzle of removing those bracelets, we'll start with locating Waters."

Esme winced. "I'm afraid we've exhausted my resources. It might be time to call upon one of my friends for assistance."

"You know how to find them?" Fielding asked. "I thought you said they were strictly correspondents."

"I had discussed a meeting with one of the men before I was kidnapped, as he wanted to see my pendant. I have his address."

Fielding inclined his head. "We shall call on him tomorrow."

"It must get tedious for the Raven to have you always come behind him and steal those antiquities from him. But you do the right thing in handing them off to men like the members of Solomon's."

"Is that what you believe I do?" When she nodded, he said, "Esme, sit down."

She did as he bade, but she did not like the expression on his face. His brow furrowed, showing lines deep in his forehead and making him look far older than she knew him to be. She chewed at her lip.

He exhaled slowly, then shifted positions. "You believe me to be some kind of hero who rushes in and saves antiquities from the evils of the Raven," he said. "But that is not the truth."

"Is that not what you do?"

"No," he said.

She felt a frown settling onto her face as she studied him. He looked neither abashed nor proud, and somehow the cynicism of his expression embarrassed her. "No, of course not." She laughed to hide her awkwardness. "I am not a simpleton. Of course it is not your profession to rescue damsels and antiquities. But then, what exactly is it that you do . . . do?"

She waited for him to answer, to offer some reasonable explanation, but he was silent.

"Oh." She stood again. "You are a villain?"

He shrugged. "Perhaps to some. Up until seven years ago, I worked for the Raven. I hunted treasures for him, and he paid me well for it."

She was silent for a moment as she absorbed his words. Had he too kidnapped unsuspecting women in their nightclothes? If he'd taken sacred antiquities and sold them to the highest bidder rather than putting them in a museum where they belonged, why not kidnap helpless women?

But he'd said, "up until seven years ago." She held her breath, hoping he'd add that seven years ago he'd had a change of heart and given up hunting antiques for profit. She hoped he'd say that yet somehow knew he wouldn't.

"Ever since then I've hunted treasure on my own, hiring myself out to clients who are collectors. People who will pay a great deal for me to find their antiquity of choice."

She forced herself to slow her thinking, give him the benefit of the doubt. She knew better than anyone what it was like to be judged and unfairly deemed guilty.

Perhaps he had needed the money, and it had been the only way. There weren't very many opportunities for aristocratic gentlemen to acquire funds if their families were lacking. Then again, his estate had seemed the home of a rather lucrative family.

"Esme?"

She ignored him. He certainly didn't appear to be a villain. Never had he shown her anything but kindness. He had rescued her, although he most certainly hadn't been there for that purpose. And ever since then he had protected her as well as her small family.

Satisfied with her own justification for his behavior, she turned to him. "I'm certain you have your reasons."

"I have earned a lot of money," he said flatly, as if determined to argue with her exoneration.

"Money is not everything."

"No," he said forcefully, "but it is the only thing that will keep you in your house and put food on the table. Money, Esme, not mythical boxes or books."

His words pierced her already worn defenses. He didn't understand her at all. Foolishly she'd hoped he'd be different from other men, had hoped he would appreciate her. Then it occurred to her. He was telling her all of this on purpose, strategically placing a barrier between them. Her lustful advances had gone too far and become, for him, a burden. "Why are you still here with me?" she asked.

"I have to uncover how to get that bloody thing off your wrist and put it and the other bracelets back in the box before I deliver it to Solomon's."

She felt her nostrils flare. "In other words, I am nothing but an inconvenience. And you are nothing more than a bounty hunter?"

"If you wish to perceive me as such." His tone was cavalier. But something crossed over his eyes. Something dark and haunted, as if this entire matter was far more serious than just stolen antiquities and acquiring a fortune. Something deeper and more painful. He'd said something about needing money for a house and food. Perhaps he hadn't always been this wealthy.

Her heart shifted, and as much as she wanted to think poorly of him, as much as she wanted to be angry, her anger would not come.

She sighed heavily. "Then tell me who it is I should see when I look at you."

His jaw was tight.

He obviously didn't want to tell her, but perhaps if she prodded him. "Being a viscount, I should think your family coffers would have afforded you a nice living, but perhaps your family fell on a difficult time?"

He came to his feet. "Don't be so naive, Esme. There are aristocrats all over this country who have no fortune to go with their blue blood." He turned away from her then and stepped over to the door. "I'm going out. I won't be back for several hours." And with that he disappeared into the hall.

Her stomach clenched. That had not gone well at all. His life was none of her concern. It wasn't his fault they were embroiled in this mess together. Perhaps she shouldn't have asked him so many questions.

In wanting to touch that hidden part of him, she might have pushed him too far.

The opened windows overlooked a lush garden. Butterflies fluttered from one brightly colored flower to the next. Birds chirped happily. Such a peaceful contrast to how she was currently feeling.

Fielding obviously didn't believe she could help with their current predicament; in fact, she suspected he believed she made it worse. He didn't appreciate her knowledge about the box or her books on the subject. And to make matters worse, her knowledge and her books hadn't exactly answered any of their questions.

But she could prove to him she had more to offer. Show him her value. That she was a worthy partner.

While he was out today she would make one more pass through the books, see if she couldn't uncover the key to removing this infernal bracelet. She'd always been particularly good at research and puzzles. There was no reason why she couldn't find the necessary information. And with him gone, she should be able to focus completely on the task at hand instead of every inch of his muscular frame.

Part of her enjoyed the physical attention she was able to elicit from Fielding. It made her feel very much the complete woman, attractive and desirable. Esme opened the first book and skimmed the pages. She'd be a liar if she said she was completely ready to remove the cursed bracelet.

Yet, she knew men did not choose women with minds of their own or opinions. They wanted pretty little things who sat by their sides and nodded in agreement. Her mother had warned her of that, had told her repeatedly she needed to learn when to hold her tongue.

Esme had tried for a while, gone to balls and soirees and smiled prettily and tried to be demure, but in the end she just couldn't sit by and say nothing. Other women seemed to do it so easily. Perhaps they simply had nothing to say. But Esme was educated, well read, and she had plenty of opinions. Why could she not share them as men did?

The bracelet had stirred feelings she'd thought long buried. As long as it was on her wrist, she was burdened with the desire to have those things she knew she could not have—a husband and a family. With the bracelet gone, she would be able to forget about those longings and get back to her studies.

In the meantime, she would try her best to keep her hands to herself and off Fielding. A task she knew would be as challenging as finding a way to rid herself of the curse.

Chapter Eleven

———❦❧———

Fielding rang the doorbell, then mentally rehearsed what he would say. He might not be active in proper society, but he'd been raised in it and knew how things worked. These people needed to know that he would not be called upon to marry Esme, regardless of the situation.

For a moment he thought about turning around and leaving, but the door opened before he could turn away.

"Yes?" the butler asked.

Fielding handed over his card. "I'm here to see Lord and Lady Weatherby."

The butler nodded and held the door open. "This way, please."

As he followed the man, Fielding wondered what Esme would think about him calling on her family. No doubt it would displease her, but her opinion was not of consequence in this matter. This was something that had to be done. Esme hadn't exaggerated when she said her sister had married into wealth. The place positively gleamed with money. Every surface shone brightly, and maids were around every corner, polishing and dusting anything that didn't move.

"A Lord Eldon to see you both," the butler said, then with a swipe of his arm, he waved Fielding forward.

The Weatherbys sat in a large parlor decorated in soft blues and greens. Lady Weatherby was perched daintily on a gilded chair and doing needlepoint. Her husband relaxed on the blue sofa with a newspaper in one hand and a cup of tea in the other. Together they had seemingly perfected the life of the English aristocracy.

The couple rose in unison. Though she tried to hide it with a smile, the woman's face perfectly portrayed her confusion. She set her needlepoint aside, then came forward despite not knowing Fielding. The gracious hostess. "My lord, how nice of you to visit," she said.

Her husband moved to stand next to her, newspaper still dangling from his hand. "I don't believe we've met," he said. "I am Raymond Griffin, and this is my wife." His expertly tied cravat and tailored jacket did nothing to hide the man's large stomach. Perhaps he had been handsome at one time, but now Lord Weatherby was rotund with thinning reddish-blond hair.

"No, we haven't. My name is Fielding Grey, and I've come to speak with you about Esme," he said. Fielding steeled himself for an argument and prepared his words to plead his case.

Elena fell back into her chair. "Oh, she will be the death of me." Sitting on the small occasional table next to her were two oval-shaped frames with photographs of young girls. One of them in particular looked very much like Esme, with bright eyes that shone with intelligence and an impish grin.

Fielding could see the slight resemblance between

Esme and her sister. Though Elena was fair of hair and slighter of frame, their eyes were similar. The older sister also boasted more grace; even if she obviously had a flair for drama, her fall into the chair was fluid and lithe.

"What has the girl done this time?" Raymond asked. A beam of sunlight hit the man's bald spot, making his nearly bare scalp glisten.

"The girl, as you both must know, is now a woman," Fielding corrected. "And she has done nothing. She was, however, abducted recently. Right out of her home." When Elena gasped, Fielding sat down next to the woman. Finally, one of them had shown a semblance of concern. "She is safe now. I was fortunate enough to come across her and able to bring her back to London. Aside from a minor injury, she was unharmed."

Elena first looked at her husband, then merely nodded to Fielding.

"I wanted to inform you both of her current situation. I cannot tell you her location, as she is still at risk of danger, but suffice it to say she and Thea are well cared for. And her reputation remains intact." For the time being, although he wasn't certain he could promise it would remain so. He'd already seen her in her nightclothes, with fabric so thin it had left little to his imagination. And he'd kissed her, caressed her, *wanted* her.

"She is prone to scandal." Raymond noisily folded his newspaper and set it on the occasional table beside him. "I'm afraid she's been nothing but trouble."

Elena and Raymond exchanged looks before Elena spoke. "Lord Eldon, I don't know what Esme has told you, but she is not exactly a member of our family," Elena said. "That is to say, we do not have much contact—"

Raymond put his hand on Elena's shoulder to quiet her.

"Esme made her choice years ago, and she now reaps the spoils of her actions. We are, however, very sorry for any inconvenience she might have caused you."

"Esme has always been"—Elena paused as if searching for the appropriate word—"challenging."

"Headstrong," Raymond provided.

She nodded. "Mother always had difficulty with her." Elena picked up the framed photograph that resembled Esme.

"Is that Esme?" he asked.

For a moment confusion marred her features, then, as the realization struck her, she smiled. "Actually, no, this is one of our daughters. Rose. She is very similar to her aunt."

"Headstrong, just like Esme," Raymond said.

"Perhaps it's a matter of understanding her," Fielding suggested.

"There was nothing to understand about Esme," Raymond said. "Women are not complex creatures, though some, like Esme, insist otherwise." He chuckled. "It takes a firm hand to hold the reins on a woman like that, something their father should have done instead of encouraging her behavior and indulging her every whim."

Fielding felt the anger simmering under his skin. "And you agree with all of this," Fielding pointedly asked Elena.

She opened her mouth to respond, but Fielding saw the gentle squeeze her husband gave her shoulder. She pasted on a smile. "My sister and I are very different."

"I can see that."

Angered by their complacence, Fielding stood. "I thought you would be concerned for her welfare, but I see I was greatly mistaken." He scowled down at them.

"Please know that while I am taking responsibility for her well-being at the moment, I will not be called upon at a future date and expected to wed Miss Worthington," Fielding said.

They might not concern themselves with Esme's life, but he could sense immediately that should a circumstance arise that would better the welfare of the Weatherbys, they wouldn't hesitate to use Esme to achieve that goal. Well, he would be no such circumstance.

"Eldon," Raymond said with a chuckle, "we would never impose on anyone of your status or wealth a troublesome girl such as Esme."

"No, of course not," Elena agreed.

He took one more look at Esme's sister. It was hard to believe the passionate and vibrant Esme was related to this simpering fool.

"I believe I've said enough," he said. "And I believe I've taken up enough of your time. Good day." Without allowing them to respond, Fielding turned and left the Weatherbys' presence.

He'd thought only of himself when he'd driven here this morning. He tried to remind himself he'd still done the right thing. There was simply no room in his life for a wife.

What woman wanted to be left at home alone for several months of the year? Or worse, travel with him to sandy, remote locations full of exotic insects and even stranger foods?

A flash of Esme digging in a tomb popped into his mind. She wore a ridiculous hat and was covered in sand. Then she smiled at him. It was a most unsettling image.

*   *   *

Fielding entered Max's home after being gone the entire day. It remained unclear whether his visit to the Weatherbys had accomplished anything of value. He still could not completely comprehend them abandoning her to her own ruin. He supposed if nothing else, perhaps he had a better understanding of Esme.

He knew now that despite the fact that Esme spent more time with her nose in a book than in the reality of the world around her, she was also a fighter. Life had not always been kind to her, perhaps had rarely been, but she'd proven herself industrious. She was a survivor.

Somewhere down the hall a clock chimed the hour, reminding Fielding that it was long past time for dinner. He briefly entertained the idea of going straight up to bed, but decided instead to stop by their makeshift study. On the off chance that Esme was still awake, he wanted . . . He didn't know what he wanted.

Apologize was what he should do, but apologize for what, specifically? For being a complete ass? For having a past full of sins? He rubbed his hand down the back of his neck. He needed to see her.

He knocked on the door but heard no reply, so he turned to go, noticing as he did the soft glow of candlelight flickering from beneath the door. Opening the door, he stepped inside. The room was dark, with the exception of the fire in the corner, which had burned down to a handful of embers, and one candle sputtering on the tabletop.

And there was Esme, asleep on the mahogany wood, her breathing slow and steady.

Books surrounded her, one even serving as her pillow. She did not wake as his steps closed the distance between them. For a moment he stood over her, watching her sleep.

He marveled at the porcelain clarity of her skin, at the plumpness of her lips, which were parted just slightly.

This was a woman of intelligence and beauty. A woman who deserved to be admired, not dismissed as her sister had so clearly done. He reached down and pulled her into his arms, cradling her against him.

"Are you going to ravish me?" she asked against his neck, her voice still heavy with sleep.

Her hot breath streamed against his skin like a feathered caress. His body instantly responded to her, and he inwardly groaned. After years of unscrupulous behavior, why had he decided now to be a gentleman? Because while he might not know her very well, he knew that Esme—with her sharp intelligence and her absolute faith in him—deserved better. Better than a quick tumble on the floor.

"No, I don't believe I'll ravish you," he said. "Tonight," he added.

She nuzzled against him, her lush breasts pressing into his chest. Damn, she was killing him. "Are you certain? Because I can assure you I'd be most willing. You wouldn't even have to seduce me." She released a throaty moan, which reached deep inside him and tore at his resolve. "You smell nice."

"Esme, you are a temptress."

"I hope I remember you said that in the morning," she murmured as he carried her upstairs to her room and placed her in her bed.

She was so tempting, she was distracting him from what he'd planned to do—infiltrate Solomon's. Yet one kiss from Esme, and he'd forgotten all about discovering the identities of the men who had been unable to save his father.

Quickly he pulled off her shoes. He didn't bother with her stockings, as he wasn't certain he could trust himself to touch her bare skin. The memory of how smooth and silky it was had haunted him since he'd rescued her. They needed to get those bracelets off, and fast.

He pulled the covers over her, and she burrowed deep beneath them, curling up on her right side and falling instantly back to sleep. Then, because he simply couldn't resist—or didn't want to—he pressed a kiss to her lips.

Perhaps tomorrow he'd regret not taking advantage of the situation. But toying with Esme's emotions was something he could not afford to do. She might be her own woman, as she liked to say, but she was still a lady and still had a reputation at stake. As much as he'd like to bed her, to taste the full extent of her passion, to teach her the myriad ways of lovemaking, he couldn't take the risk.

Some seductress she was.

Esme eyed her reflection suspiciously. She had a vague memory of being carried to bed, but she was fairly certain that, despite being alone with a man in her bedchamber, her chastity remained intact. It seemed highly unlikely she could have been ravished yet still fully clothed in the morning.

She gave a sheepish laugh when her maid stepped in. "It appears I fell asleep in my clothes last night."

Further proof that while this bracelet might be causing *her* to be filled with lustful desires, it did nothing to enhance her appeal to the opposite sex. Annette bobbed her head and began unbuttoning Esme's dress.

Fielding had kissed her. Twice. And he'd caressed her. Her cheeks warmed with the memory as did the flesh between her thighs. And yet he remained unmoved. His behavior could mean one of two things. Either Fielding had exaggerated his warning and he truly was a gentleman, or she truly was undesirable.

"Annette, do you think I'm pretty?" Esme asked the young maid as she was fastening a fresh dress.

"Yes, ma'am. You are most fetching." She bobbed her head obediently.

Well, that settled nothing. Annette had obviously been taught to be nothing but agreeable to her employers and their guests.

She smiled at the younger woman and watched as she spun Esme's hair up into what looked like a complicated web of curls. Ordinarily Esme wore her hair unfashionably down, but perhaps today she should try something new and allow the girl to fix it in some alluring style.

It wouldn't work, she argued with herself. Fielding wouldn't notice or care how she wore her hair. Or that her gown was the exact shade of green as her eyes.

Plain and simple, he did not want her.

Funny how that thought made her chest ache with regret. Yet her desire for him was fleeting as well, wasn't it? It would dissipate once the cursed band was removed. And last night she'd discovered mention of a diary that explained precisely how to do that. There was only one problem: She didn't know where to find the diary.

She only hoped it would be enough to impress Fielding, to show him that she was useful.

"Do you require anything else?" Annette asked.

"No, that will be all. Thank you."

Esme pinched her cheeks, then went in search of her aunt. Much to her surprise, Thea had already gone down for breakfast. Something that hardly ever occurred at home.

When Esme entered the dining room she was met with great laughter, from both their host and her aunt. Fielding was missing from the table. Which had her wondering and worrying if he'd been the man who'd taken her to her room last night as she'd assumed. How horrifying if instead it had been the marquess who'd done the duty. But there was no way to make such an inquiry.

So she made herself a plate, then sat and waited to see if the marquess passed her a smile that hinted at a shared secret.

"I trust you slept well, Miss Worthington," the marquess said with a broad smile.

The heat of a blush poured over her. Why couldn't she remember what had transpired last night? "I did, thank you," she answered politely but kept her attention on her breakfast.

"Oh, do finish your story, my lord," Thea said, her voice laced with delight. "The marquess was telling me about the time he went looking for a map in the caves of Dover."

Esme was glad to hear the good humor returned to Thea's voice. It had never been Esme's intention to worry the older woman.

"Very well," Max said. "I was there, standing at the mouth of the cave with the renegades not far behind me, and my lantern went out."

"Truly?" Thea asked.

"Indeed," he said with drama. The marquess was adept at storytelling. Esme supposed it was only one of his methods of charming the ladies. "There was no time to relight it, and the cave was far too dark for me to enter without light."

"Whatever did you do?" Esme asked, unable to hide her own curiosity.

Max shrugged. "I waited. I hid myself as much as I could behind a large rock, and I waited. It didn't take long for the men to appear."

"Oh, those nasty fellows." Thea clapped her hands.

"They walked right past me and into the blackness of the cave," he said.

Esme looked down and realized, in the excitement of the story, she'd already cleaned her plate.

"Without seeing you? What did you do next?" Thea asked.

"I followed them. They had three lanterns offering far more light than I'd had, and as long as I kept a measure of distance between us"—he winked—"they didn't seem to notice."

"You have a liking for danger, my lord; I can tell that about you," Thea said, pointing her fork at him. "Did they ever discover you behind them?"

He took a slow sip of tea. "No, they never did."

Max leaned back in his seat, and Esme could see why women found him so alluring. He had an easy way about him, so congenial and fun. But she'd seen on more than one occasion a darkening of his expression. She wondered what it was that lurked beneath his obvious charm.

"As it turned out," he continued, "that particular quest was completely futile, though not without a bit of adventure."

"Oh, goodness," Thea said. "Quite an adventure, indeed. I believe I shall be off to my room for a while. I'm reading a delightful book."

"Enjoy," Esme said. She waited until her aunt had left the dining room before turning her attention back to Max.

"What of the map, my lord? Did you ever find it?" Esme asked.

"In fact, I did. Would you like to see it?"

"Very much," she said. Perhaps she'd get the opportunity to inquire about his membership in Solomon's. She followed him to his office, only a few doors down and across from the parlor in which they'd sat the day of their arrival. It seemed as if that had been a lifetime ago.

"Come in," he said.

He went to stand at the framed map hanging behind his desk. It was unlike any she'd ever seen before. Hand-colored and exceptionally detailed, it was nothing short of beautiful.

She reached up but stopped herself before she touched the aging parchment. "I'm unfamiliar with this country," she said.

He chuckled. "It is not a country, but rather the lost continent of Atlantis."

"Atlantis? Is that the legend you study?" she asked before giving thought to the propriety of the matter. She knew very well that the men of Solomon's kept their studies quite private.

"Yes, it is."

"And this is the map you found?"

"Not in the caves of Dover," he said, "but later in caves on a different coastline." His blue eyes sparkled.

She looked around the rest of his office, noting the texts on Plato and Aristotle. On top of his desk was another map, this one of the world. He'd drawn lines and routes in several of the bodies of water. "Will you tell me more about Solomon's?" she ventured. "Although I realize it might be improper to ask."

"Of course not. Fielding is providing a very important

service to our club, and we know you've been put in danger by the Raven. I should say you've earned the answers to a few questions." He motioned to the chairs across from his desk. "Have a seat." He seated himself behind the desk and with one hand opened a drawer to his left, retrieving a folded letter. He held it out to her.

She opened it to find he'd shared his invitation letter. The flourishing penmanship and quality of parchment spoke to the esteem of the group. Then she noted the date. "My lord, this invitation came fourteen years ago. You couldn't have been more than—"

"Nineteen," he provided. "I was one of the youngest members ever inducted. That will happen when you discover a map such as the one behind me. Up until then, no one had ever seen a map of Atlantis."

"It's beautiful," she said.

"Isn't it?" He looked over his shoulder to glance at the map before he spoke again. "The letter came, then I had a series of meetings with Solomon's. I was reluctant, had never actually heard of them until the invitation arrived. They persuaded me to join."

"I've known about them since I was a girl," she said. "My father was never a member, never invited, but he did provide research assistance to members of Solomon's many years ago. He always said Solomon's was full of the most gallant men in all of England." The tales he'd told her had made her long not only to meet those gentlemen, but to be among them, something she knew was foolish and futile. They did not allow women in their ranks. No gentlemen's clubs did.

"I suppose some of them are gallant, but I could tell you stories about several of our members who could stand to learn a few things when it comes to chivalry."

"But you've saved the crown on more than one occasion," she argued.

His brows rose with surprise.

"I admit to being somewhat of an admirer," she said, her cheeks aflame with embarrassment.

"There have been a few instances when the monarchy has been in danger and a member of Solomon's might have been involved in the solution," he said modestly. "But we are mostly scholars, such as yourself. While Her Majesty is certainly aware of our existence, she relies on her own soldiers and guards to protect her."

The compliment warmed her, yet somehow she wished the words had come from a different man. "Where did the name come from?"

"Solomon's mines. Our charter member studied the ancient legend until he died. As you might have guessed, he never did find the mines."

"Is it true that King Henry VIII was involved in the Solomon's club?" she asked.

He smiled. "No, but people do favor that story. In fact, Solomon's came about a hundred years after good old Henry."

The door opened behind her. "Max, have you seen . . . Ah, Esme."

She turned to find Fielding staring intently, and for an unknown reason she felt guilty sitting here with Max. Abruptly, she rose to her feet. "The marquess was merely sharing some of his research with me." And Fielding had been looking for her. That notion pleased her immensely. After his departure yesterday, she'd worried their congenial way with each other had disappeared. But he'd sought her out.

"Might I have a brief word with you?" Fielding asked.

She nodded, then turned back to Max. "Thank you for sharing this with me." She handed the Solomon's invitation back to him.

Fielding turned on his heel and left the office, and she followed him to the room they'd set up for their research.

"What is it?" she asked once he'd closed the door.

"You mentioned something last night," he said, leaning against the table, "something that wasn't quite coherent. I thought perhaps you might remember it this morning."

So he had been the one to carry her to bed. As attractive as the marquess was, she was glad it had been Fielding's arms she'd nestled in and not her host's.

His eyes lit upon her and scanned her appraisingly. She fancied she saw a bit of possessive interest in his gaze. Perhaps he was not as immune to her as he seemed to be. The thought made her bold.

She sauntered up to him and trailed one finger down his shirt. "Might I ask you a question, then?" she asked.

"Yes."

"How does a woman go about seducing a man? Obviously, it can be somewhat complicated." She flattened her hand on his stomach, and she felt his muscles twitch beneath her palm.

"Are you planning on seducing the marquess?" Fielding asked.

If she didn't know better, Esme would have sworn she detected a hint of jealousy in his tone. It fueled her boldness. "You know very well who I have my eyes on."

His voice lowered to a sultry tone. "You want me to tell you how you can seduce me?"

"Yes." She ran her hand over his torso.

"Esme, you are treading dangerous waters." He grabbed her wrist and stilled her hand.

"There is nothing dangerous about you." She met his brown eyes, the golden flecks in them shimmering like amber. "I would like to know should the need arise," she said.

His brows rose, and a slight smile played at the corners of his mouth. "What sort of scenario would make it a necessity for you to seduce me?"

"Well, I don't know." She pointed a delicate finger at him. "But you never know about these sorts of things. And I prefer to be prepared."

"Esme, I don't think this is an appropriate conversation."

"Why? Because I'm a virgin?" She leaned into his hard, lean body, pressing herself against him. "I know all about what goes on between a man and a woman. I am no green-behind-the-ears girl."

He tried to hide his smile. "I believe the phrase you're looking for is 'wet behind the ears.' Or simply 'a green girl.'"

"No matter. I am a woman of seven and twenty years. I have lived on my own for quite a while now." She looked directly into his eyes. "I am perfectly capable of deciding to take a lover should I desire one." She punctuated the last four words by poking him in the chest. "And I desire you." Unfortunately, her bravado failed her and her voice wavered with her next words. "I thought, perhaps, you desired me as well."

"You need do nothing to seduce me," he finally said. He grabbed her hand and pressed it to his groin. "Do you feel that?"

Esme gasped at the heat she felt beneath her palm and curved her hand around him.

"That is my desire for you. You need only sit there the

way you do and look at me with those eyes and smile with that perfect mouth of yours, and I want you." He grabbed her arms with more force than she anticipated. "I'm out of my mind with want for you, but that doesn't change anything. I cannot have you."

Her pulse quickened at his words until she thought she heard its thundering in her ears. She had to swallow before she could speak. "You are promised to another, then."

He shook his head. "No."

Confusion hit her. He desired her, and yet he claimed he could not have her. Which was ridiculous, since she'd offered herself to him. He had listed her physical attributes with a heated hunger that left no doubt about his interest in them.

Then it had to be her very soul he found unappealing. Her personality, her manner, her intelligence. She stepped away from him. Suddenly she felt very foolish that she'd allowed Annette to put her hair up in this concoction.

She clamped her hand down over the band, as if covering it would somehow diminish its hold over her. It was the bracelet, she reminded herself. She wouldn't always feel this way.

She cleared her throat. "I have found how to rid myself of this bracelet. Well, not precisely the solution, but a possible way to find the solution."

She flipped open a journal, then handed it to him. "About three-quarters of the way down the right-side column," she said, her serious tone almost convincing her she was in control of her emotions.

His eyes scanned the page, and he looked ready to close the book, perhaps convinced she'd found nothing useful, but then . . . He looked closer.

"Have you ever heard of this Biedermann Diary before?" he asked.

She shook her head fervently. "No. I thought on this for quite a while last night, and the name doesn't sound familiar." She handed him another book. "I dug around, and it appears this Biedermann had been working on a translation of a particular Greek text."

"It says here," Fielding began, still perusing the journal, "that the Biedermann Diary holds the key to undoing all the curses within the box." He looked up at her. "At least that's what"—he glanced back at the article—"George Winthrop claims."

Her back straightened and she smiled. "George Winthrop is a foremost scholar of Pandora's box. He lives in America, and his 'claims,' as you say, would be considered directly on the mark. If we can locate this Biedermann fellow, we should find our answers." She leaned forward and poked him in the arm. "Aren't you impressed with what I found?"

"Most impressed. Any ideas as to how we can locate Biedermann?" Fielding asked.

"As a matter of fact, I do. I suspected it might be time to pay a visit to my friend Phillip, as this seems precisely the bit of information he'd be helpful with. In fact, I took the liberty of sending him a note this morning notifying him that we would be stopping by."

Chapter Twelve

Esme tugged at her sleeve, pulling it firmly over the gold band that dangled from her wrist. "If you would, please allow me to do the talking. Judging from our correspondence with each other, Phillip is a delicate sort. Although he's quite intelligent."

She looked pretty today. Not more so than usual, yet he couldn't help but notice. The color of her dress matched her green eyes perfectly, which were so bright with her enthusiasm he had a difficult time looking away from her. "I like your hair better when it's down," he said.

She self-consciously reached up to touch her hair.

"I didn't say it looks bad, Esme. It looks rather nice, actually. But personally, I think it looks rather seductive when it brushes against your shoulders."

She moistened her lips. "No doubt Phillip will have an extensive library." She clasped her hands together. "How I do wish we had more time to peruse it if that is the case," she said.

"But we don't," he reminded her.

Again she fiddled with her sleeve, attempting to cover the bracelet.

"Esme, what are you doing?"

Pink settled in her cheeks, and she looked away. "I do not wish Phillip to know how foolish I was, how weak. I only want to inquire how one might remove or reverse a curse, not this specific curse. Or perhaps we could tell him we know the Raven's men have two of the bands." She shook her head, and Fielding could have sworn a stray teardrop slid down her cheek. "But I should have known better."

He wanted to tell her not to cry, but he wasn't certain what should come after that. He was not in the practice of consoling women. So he merely nodded. "I won't say anything." He squeezed her knee.

"Thank you."

Fielding pulled the bag closer to him. "We're not showing him the box until I am certain he's not involved in any way with your kidnapping."

"I can't see how it would be possible for Phillip to work with the Raven."

"Anything is possible," he said.

She shook her head, clearly unconvinced. "No, not Phillip. He's far too honorable a man for that. Besides, an intelligent man like Phillip wouldn't be taken in by a nasty villain like the Raven, who—"

She broke off short, her cheeks burning, as if she'd only just realized she'd implied that he himself was neither honorable nor intelligent.

"I didn't mean—," she began.

He didn't give her the chance to finish. "The Raven is a very charming man when he chooses to be. He's convinced stronger men than your scholar to do his bidding."

She said nothing, so it was unclear if she believed him or not.

Fielding felt his own irritation with Phillip, the scholar, growing. So what if this intelligent, *honorable* man was exactly the sort Esme should end up with? He was, no doubt, a pasty-skinned weakling. And he'd be completely unable to protect Esme from the Raven.

However, the thought did little to raise Fielding's spirits. Was that why she'd taken such care with her hair today, because she'd known she would see her scholarly friend? No matter how Fielding tried to convince himself that he wasn't jealous of Phillip, he couldn't shake the suspicion that he was lying to himself.

A moment later the carriage stilled. "I believe we're here," he said.

Together they walked up the steps to her friend's corner redbrick townhome. Fielding knocked on the door, and few moments later they'd been led into the study and seated in worn but comfortable leather chairs.

The curtains had been pulled back to allow the day's light to pour in. The room was small, or perhaps it only felt that way because of the towering columns of books that lined three of the four walls. Esme had been right to assume Phillip had an extensive library.

Esme's face lit up at the sight of so many books. The moment the servant left, she popped out of her chair to stroll among them, her fingertips trailing their spines like a lover's caress.

Fielding wanted to growl with frustration. It was bad enough being jealous of her anemic scholar. He would not be jealous of the man's books.

When there was a sound at the door, Esme started guiltily and returned to her seat.

"Oh, we shall finally meet," a man's voice sounded from the hall.

Esme fidgeted with her skirt.

The man stepped into the study with a small calico cat draped in his arms. He stopped suddenly. "Mr. Grey, whatever are you doing here?"

"Mr. Nichols is your scholar correspondent?" Fielding asked. The relief that surged through his body annoyed him. It was relief only because he knew for certain Mr. Nichols wasn't the one who'd told the Raven about Esme's key. Fielding knew the reason behind his shoulders relaxing had more to do with the fact that Mr. Nichols didn't warrant jealousy on Fielding's part.

Esme frowned. "You know each other?"

"Mr. Nichols is part of the group of men from Solomon's who hired me for this job," Fielding said.

Nichols placed the cat on a chair.

Esme stepped forward and clasped both of Mr. Nichols's hands. "It is such a pleasure to finally meet you in person."

"Dear girl, indeed a great pleasure. And this is Pandy," he said, leaning down to stroke the kitten. Then he looked over at Fielding. "And you, sir, have chosen a perfect intellectual guide for this quest to secure Pandora's box. This lovely woman has dazzled me with her grasp of theories both ancient and new."

Fielding didn't bother correcting the man. There was no need to bring up Esme's kidnapping, unless she wanted to do so herself.

"Now, then, what can I do for both of you?" the older man asked.

Fielding could still see the nervous man from that day in Solomon's, but Mr. Nichols was doing an admirable job of hiding his anxiety for the time being. No doubt that was for Esme's benefit. Evidently the man wanted to hide his fear as Esme wanted to hide her bracelet. Still, it was hard to miss the older man's twitching hands and sweaty brow.

"Phillip," Esme began, "please call me Esme now that we've met in person." She sat on the edge of her seat, careful to keep her right wrist and the band hidden. "In my readings I've come across reference to a Biedermann's Diary. Have you heard of it?"

The cat had settled on the older man's shoulder. "Biedermann's Diary," Mr. Nichols repeated. "Well, now, that does sound familiar." He scratched his chin. "Let me think. Perhaps I'll take a peek in my own notes." He grabbed several small books from a nearby secretary and flipped through them. "I've seen the name, know I have. I only have to find it." He moved to a second book and stopped flipping pages halfway through. "Ah, yes, here we are."

Esme smiled at Fielding, her excitement shining brightly in her eyes. Were he not the man he was, he could see how easy it would be to join in that enthusiasm. Esme's passion was contagious. But Fielding was immune.

Mr. Nichols's chubby finger pressed against the text as if he were holding the words on the page. "Biedermann, a German scholar of Pandora's box who moved to London about forty years ago." He kept skimming his finger down the journal. "Yes, yes, he was in possession of the only copy of an ancient text regarding the legend, and his life's work was translating it." He looked up at Esme. "Thus the diary detailing his efforts."

The man went back to the book. "Evidently Biedermann died a couple of years ago," he read, "and all of his belongings, including his diary, were donated." He turned the page, the paper scraping across his shirt. "To the museum."

"Which museum?" Fielding asked.

Mr. Nichols looked up. "Why, the British Museum. Evidently Biedermann had quite a collection, and his nephew, who inherited it all, had no use for his uncle's research and didn't want to pay to have the books shipped back to Germany. A couple of months ago he simply gave it to the museum."

"So the diary should be there as well?" Fielding asked.

"I suppose." He frowned. "Although I wouldn't think it would be on display. If I had to guess, I'd say they probably have translators working to complete Biedermann's work before they put the original text and its translation in the exhibits."

"But they don't allow patrons to see items that are not on display," Esme said. "How could we view it?"

Mr. Nichols shrugged. "I suppose you could go in after hours and take a peek." He smiled broadly.

"Break into the museum?" Esme shrieked. "Absolutely not. We couldn't." She shook her head. "No, there must be another way to . . ." But Esme didn't finish her thought. She eyed Fielding cautiously.

"Another way to access the diary," Mr. Nichols said. "No, I don't suppose there is. You could try to set up an appointment with the curator, but the new one they recently hired is an addle-brained twit."

Mr. Nichols continued complaining about the museum curator, but Fielding wasn't listening. He'd brought the box with them, upon Esme's request, only because he'd given her the benefit of the doubt that her scholar friend might be able to help them. Fielding had hoped the man would be able to take one look at the box and immediately figure out how to remove those bloody bracelets. Then, when they'd arrived here and Fielding had seen that it was in fact Mr. Nichols, he'd had second thoughts.

Despite not wanting to keep Solomon's abreast of his every move in this situation, and despite not trusting Solomon's, Fielding could not deny that Mr. Nichols might be able to help them. Help Esme. She was ready to rid herself of the curse, and Fielding couldn't blame her.

He leaned forward and held out the bag to Mr. Nichols. "We found it."

Mr. Nichols stopped speaking and eyed Fielding in confusion. Then recognition lit his aging face. "The box?" Mr. Nichols's eyes rounded and quite instantly filled with tears. "Oh, sweet heaven." He pulled the box out of the bag and for several moments simply stared at it. "You succeeded, boy!"

"Not completely," Fielding corrected. The cat circled Fielding's legs, purring loudly.

But Mr. Nichols was too involved in examining the box to make note of Fielding's words. The man ran his hand reverently over the top of the box. Closely, he examined every side, following the engravings with his fingertips.

Fielding nudged Esme.

She sighed but nodded. "If one wanted to rid themselves of a curse, how could one do such a thing?" Esme ventured.

"Oh, curses—such nasty things." He laughed at his own joke, then unfolded a pair of spectacles and perched them on his nose. "Now, then, what sort of curse are we talking about? The sort you find on the outside of a mummy's tomb? Or perhaps one that releases a biblical plague?" He paused and looked up from the box, "Oh, dear, this is about the box, isn't it? I'm so daft. Someone has opened it, then?"

"The Raven's men," Fielding said. From the corner of his eye, he saw Esme relax.

"What has happened?" Mr. Nichols asked.

"Nothing," Fielding said.

"As of yet that we know of," Esme corrected, "but certainly it is affecting them. It appears the box holds cursed bracelets, and the wearer of a bracelet becomes the victim of its curse. We know that both of the Raven's men reached into the box, and each received a bracelet for his efforts."

"Indeed?" Nichols reluctantly set down the box and moved to his worn desk. He opened a massive book and began to skim through several pages. "So a curse that afflicts the individual. Those are tricky, I can tell you that."

"But it's possible to break the curse?" Esme asked.

"Dear girl, anything is possible." Mr. Nichols smiled. "As Mr. Grey here has proven by rescuing the box. Of course, with these cursed bracelets released into the world, there is still much work to be done." He nodded toward Fielding.

Fielding and Esme exchanged glances. He nodded; trying to encourage her, give her hope. Still, he knew the whole ordeal was beginning to take its toll on her. While she still looked lovely, exhaustion had settled behind her eyes. She held up such a brave front, but the edges were beginning to crumble. He longed to comfort her but made no move to do so.

"Ah, yes, here we are. An ancient gypsy tradition of ridding oneself of an evil spell." His finger followed along the page. "Yes, yes, the art of tattooing."

"I beg your pardon?" Esme said.

"Tattooing. Well, in this case, simply painting one's body. Not to worry, dear; they are not always permanent. For some it takes only inscribing the body with an anti-curse to rid the person of their affliction."

"What sort of inscription?" Esme asked.

Mr. Nichols grabbed a piece of parchment and scrawled out a note. He handed it to Esme. "It would need to go on the persons' centers, their lower backs, and lower abdomens, as well as across their hearts and at the base of their heads."

"What sort of tools would one need for this process?" Esme asked.

"I believe I still have some of the paste I used for this very thing." He opened a cupboard and began rummaging through the contents. "About twenty years ago, I was in Rome with a friend, and we came upon a tomb." His voice was muffled as he talked into the closet. "In any case, we were both plagued with a skin disease, but this method did the trick, and we soon were good as new. Good, I found it."

He came over to Esme and handed her a small clay pot, the sides stained with what looked to be dried ink.

"I would simply use a quill," the older man suggested.

"And write the inscription on the person's body?" Fielding asked.

"Directly onto their skin," Mr. Nichols said.

Fielding watched Esme swallow. "How long will the ink last?" she asked.

"It's temporary, but it does last a good two weeks," Mr. Nichols said. "I suspect the most difficult part will be catching those two thieves and holding them down long enough to apply the paint."

Esme released a nervous laugh. "That will be challenging."

"If the ink is twenty years old," Fielding said, "will it not be dried out?"

"That's not ink, my boy; well, not standard ink. It's a type of herbal paint, and it should be in perfect condition." To prove his point he took the pot from Esme, opened it, and showed the black liquid to Fielding. "As it should be," he said, then handed it back to Esme.

Mr. Nichols returned to his seat and again picked up the box. "There are so many theories on the curse of Pandora's box, it's hard to know what will happen to those men. I don't suppose it should be our concern as far as them injuring themselves, but if the curse afflicts others . . . Wait a moment." He leaned over to the secretary and retrieved a large magnifying glass. "What have we here?"

"What is it?" Esme went and stood next to him.

"An inscription, here on the bottom," he said.

"How did I miss that?" Esme asked.

Mr. Nichols read aloud in what Fielding assumed was ancient Greek.

The older man frowned. "Essentially it says that once the box is breached, you have until the next lunar eclipse before those who opened the box are destroyed."

"Lunar eclipse?" Esme asked. Her face paled as she wandered back to her seat. "That's not even—"

"A week away," Fielding interrupted. He may not believe in this curse, but it was clear Esme feared for her life. He must find a way to remove the blasted bracelet before the eclipse.

Fielding stood and said, "It appears we have work to do." He placed the box back into the bag. "Thank you for your time and suggestions." When Esme still hadn't risen, he held out his hand to her. "Esme, we need to go."

Her green eyes met his. In that moment he longed to be the hero she believed him to be. He would *have* to be that hero. He could not allow anything to happen to her.

Chapter Thirteen

Esme, are you absolutely certain about this?" Fielding asked. She'd come to his room wearing nothing but a robe and carrying a quill and the paste Mr. Nichols had given her.

"It's the only way. We cannot break into the museum. It simply wouldn't be right." She took a deep breath and stepped into his room.

"What about your aunt?" he asked.

"No," she said firmly. "She mustn't know about the curse." She closed the door behind her. "Thea's nerves have been rattled enough; I don't want to worry her any further."

He shook his head. "You know this isn't going to work," he said, more to himself than to her. And perhaps it wouldn't, but what if the damned inscription on the box was right, and they had only a handful of days to get that band off her wrist before she died? The thought sickened him. Regardless of how he normally felt about curses and the like, this time he wasn't taking any chances.

"No, we don't know that. Mr. Nichols said it worked for him once before," she said.

Fielding held up his hands in surrender. "If you want me to paint your body, I won't argue with you. Where do you want to start?"

"My back." She held a dark blue sheet in her hand. "I thought this might help to keep most of my body covered."

Her modesty mixed with her prior brazen behavior toward him was an alluring combination.

With a shuddering breath, she turned her back to him and dropped her robe.

It occurred to him he probably should turn away, give her some privacy, but he didn't. And there she stood in her full glory. His eyes took in the length of her, a narrow waist flaring out into generous hips and then her bare bottom, so rounded and full. This was going to be a long evening. The sheet came around her, covering her tempting body.

He retrieved a wooden chair from the corner of the room and set it in front of her. With a forced cough, he tried to clear the desire out of his voice. "Sit on it backward."

Esme straddled the chair.

"Drop the sheet farther down." Fielding tugged on the material at her back.

She let the fabric fall to her waist.

"This will probably be cold," he said. He scrawled the first word of the inscription.

She sucked in her breath and arched away from him. "It's actually quite warm. How strange." Her back relaxed.

He wrote another word and then another. The quill slid across her pale skin, leaving behind a dark engraving that marred her perfect flesh. Yet something about it—the roundness of her bottom peeking up from beneath the dark blue sheet and the black ink staining her back—was intensely erotic.

Word for word, he copied the phrase onto Esme's back. He reached out to test how wet the first words were. Her flesh was warm beneath his fingers, and he found the writing had completely dried. "It dries quickly," he said.

"I suppose we should do the base of my head now." She gathered up her chestnut hair, clearing the nape of her neck.

His mouth went dry. Right in that moment he'd never seen anything as seductive. He'd had women all over the world, experienced women, exotic women, and yet, here in this borrowed bedchamber, this woman, with her incessant chattiness and bright innocent eyes, was the one who stole his breath.

He tried to ignore the muscles tightening low across his abdomen and the blood pounding through his body. He tried to pretend she wasn't driving him mad with desire, but he was failing miserably. As quickly as he could he wrote the first word on her neck. He glanced back at the piece of paper on which Mr. Nichols had written the inscription. As ludicrous as this whole scenario might be, Fielding wanted to do it correctly. He released a heavy breath, scattering gooseflesh across her neck and back.

She sighed.

He swore under his breath.

She turned to look over her shoulder. "What's the matter?"

The matter was he should have more bloody control over himself. He wasn't a ruddy schoolboy. He ran his hand down her back, and she closed her eyes in response. "You're driving me to distraction, woman."

She said nothing and did not move.

"Hold still and let me finish." He inscribed the words as fast as he could. He'd had to write much smaller on her neck, but he managed to get the entire anti-curse in place. "Finished."

She dropped her hair.

"I think you'll have to lie down for me to do the rest," he suggested. He walked away from her then, uncertain that he'd be able to keep his hands off her were he to take in the full length of her naked backside again. Attempting to regain control of himself, he took several deep breaths.

Once she was in the bed waiting, he made his way over to her side. There she lay, partially covered by the blue sheet, her pale limbs a stark and lovely contrast to his masculine bed.

She maneuvered the sheet so that the top edge lay across her pubic bone. He could see the tiniest hint of her soft curls. She crossed her arms over her breasts.

He crawled onto the bed next to her and smoothed his hand across her bare abdomen. Chills followed in the wake of his touch. "Are you cold?"

"No." Her eyes were tightly closed.

Fielding dipped the quill into the paste and then touched it to her belly. The skin here, less taut than on her back, gave and moved beneath the ink, making his writing messy and uneven. He pressed his hand to her abdomen to try to tighten the skin in an attempt to better his penmanship. She was soft where a woman should be soft, and he wanted nothing more than to tear that sheet the rest of the way off and spend the night running his fingers, not a quill, across her flesh.

He finished writing the phrase as she looked up at him. "Only one more," she said, her eyes glassy with pent-up desire.

"Across the heart," Fielding said.

She visibly swallowed. "That's what he said." Then her eyes fluttered closed as she unfolded her arms and placed them firmly by her sides.

Inwardly Fielding swore. Esme's breasts were neither large nor small, but rather perfectly sized to be cupped in his hand. Pouty and round with a creamy shade of pink darkening the middles, they had exquisite jutting nipples. Already primed for arousal, it was no surprise when he hardened immediately. He released a deep breath.

"Low enough so that you won't be able to see it when I'm fully clothed," she said. "Please."

He'd memorized the phrase now so there was no need to refer to the piece of paper, but he found himself checking every word. With as much speed as he could manage, he wrote the inscription across her left breast. Her mouth opened and she arched toward him. He moved his hand carefully away from her breast and set the ink and quill on the bedside table. Then with one swift movement she was upon him, her mouth covering his in a flurry of kisses.

Before he could fight her, she had him pinned to the bed, her naked body writhing across him. Fielding gave where she took and met her passion for passion. She kissed him deeply, her tongue sliding against his own. One arm wrapped around her, he moved the other down her body, eager to feel her passion. She was hot and wet for him, and when he touched her flesh she arched back and cried out.

He plunged his finger inside her. Though he could not afford to lose control of himself, he knew what she wanted, what she *needed*. His mouth settled on her breast while he moved his finger deep within her. Her folds, slick with desire, tensed around him.

With his thumb, he found her center. Esme's release was immediate. She shook and shuddered while whispering his name again and again.

In that moment, he knew if they went any further, he wouldn't be able to stop. With one movement he slid her off him, then stood.

"I don't think this was the outcome we were trying for," he said.

Esme's eyes were still darkened and hooded with desire. She looked so small and delicate clutching the sheet to her chest. "No, I don't suppose the procedure worked." With a deep, heartfelt sigh, he came to her feet. "Tomorrow night," she said, her chin rising slightly, "we will go the museum and find that diary."

More than anything Esme wished her father were still alive. Certainly he'd know what to do in this situation. Granted, Esme wouldn't tell him about her improper behavior, but he could help with the curse; she knew he could.

He'd always known what to do. As a girl, whenever she'd argued with her mother he'd been there, always her champion and advocate. On more than one occasion she'd overheard him telling her mother to leave Esme alone. "Not all men prefer brainless females," he'd tell her. "Some of us enjoy clever banter. I should think you would remember that."

She'd believed her father, and for a time thought she'd

find one of those gentlemen, the ones who chose girls not only for their dowries or their pretty faces, but also for their minds. But then he'd died, and it seemed that her dream of finding such a man perished with him.

Esme knew it was late and that Thea was probably already sleeping, but she needed to talk to someone tonight, needed the comfort of a friendly face. Before leaving her own bedchamber, Esme made certain all the inscriptions on her body were completely covered. She didn't bother knocking, just entered Thea's room and found her cat snuggled up on the bed, nestled in the crook of her aunt's bent knees.

"Traitor. I'm only in the next room," she told him.

Horace eyed her sleepily, then laid his head back down on the brown velvet coverlet.

"Esme?" Thea said groggily.

"I'm sorry to wake you."

"Don't be foolish. Come and sit." Thea scooted up so her back leaned against the great wooden headboard.

Crawling up into the bed, Esme suddenly felt as she had as a child, when she'd climbed into bed with her father and he'd tell her tales of myth and legend. She knew she was on the verge of tears, so she swallowed hard to dissolve them. Her throat felt as if it were full of ground glass.

"What's bothering you, child?" Thea asked.

"Nothing," she said, forcing the sadness from her voice. She smiled and tilted her head to the side. "I'm probably only feeling homesick. It's strange being in another's house."

Thea frowned. "Is that all?"

Esme thought for a while before continuing. It was a battle between wanting to tell Thea everything and not

wanting to frighten her with talk of ancient curses and
illicit love affairs. "I don't suppose it is."

"Esme, you know you can tell me anything," Thea
said, her voice brimming with love.

Esme finally settled on a simple question. "Did you
ever take a lover?" she asked, trying to focus on scratching Horace behind the ears rather than embarrassment at
her brazen question.

"No," Thea said with a light chuckle.

"I didn't think so," Esme said.

"But I almost did. Once."

Her frank answer surprised Esme. Over time Thea
had become a dearer companion than Esme could ever
have imagined. Yet there were still things she didn't know
about her aged friend. Thea had family from which she
was estranged, yet Esme had no idea why. In her more romantic moments, she always imagined Thea as the heroine of a tragic love affair, though Esme had never inquired
about it before. Tonight she needed to know.

"Tell me about him," Esme requested.

"Oh, it was so long ago. Though I suppose I remember
it all as if it were yesterday. I was two and twenty. And he
was so handsome, so strong." Thea's expression took on
a dreamy look, her smile winsome. "Albert Moore was
his name."

"Were you in love?" Esme asked, but instantly she
wished she hadn't. Part of her didn't want the answer to
that question. *Don't be foolish*, she reminded herself. She
was not in love with Fielding. She was merely suffering
the effects of a curse.

"I believe I was, although I didn't recognize it at the
time." Then Thea frowned. "Well, that's not precisely
true either. I did know it was love; I simply didn't realize

how rare such a love is. I was young and foolish and believed love abounded around every corner." She gave a sad laugh. "I never would have imagined how wrong I could be."

"Then you did not marry?" Esme asked.

"No, but not for lack of asking on his part." Thea absently scratched Horace's fur.

Esme's heart broke for Thea. "You didn't want to?"

"No, I did. Desperately. But my mother didn't think he was good enough for me. He didn't have a fortune, and therefore she believed him to be beneath us." She leaned forward and scratched under Horace's chin. "She convinced me another suitor would come along, one I'd love even more, and foolishly I believed her. It didn't take me long to realize that I should have fought for him, should have run away with him, but by then it was too late."

"Did he marry another?" Esme asked.

"I don't know. When I went to find him, I discovered he'd left for Egypt." Then she smiled. "He'd been a student of antiquities when we met. I suppose he finally decided to quit reading about them and headed off to see them himself." She was quiet for a moment and then said, "It was why I was so often at the Guildhall Library. I thought for so long that I was looking for him, but I know now that I was there simply so I could find you." She tweaked Esme's chin.

Esme's eyes filled with tears. "Oh, Thea, I wish I'd known."

"We all make our choices, Esme. Choices that might not change anything—and then there are those that seem so simple at the time, yet end up altering every aspect of our lives."

"Have you ever tried to look for him? Contact him?"

"No. I've seen his name in the newspapers from time to time. He's become an accomplished explorer. Found all sorts of exotic artifacts for museums all over the world."

"Then he has made his fortune," Esme said.

"Ah, yes, the great irony in that story, I suppose. It goes to show that you should always follow your heart."

They sat in silence for several minutes, and Esme searched for the right thing to say, but before she could, Thea spoke again. "You should get some sleep, Esme. You look tired." Thea's familiar smile returned. "And you know how much sleep I require to maintain my youthful beauty."

Esme stood and kissed her aunt on the cheek. "You are the best family I've ever had," she whispered.

On her way to her bed, Esme contemplated Thea's lost love. If Thea's Albert was often mentioned in the papers, then chances were he had connections to London. Surely he would want to see Thea again, provided he wasn't married.

Esme made a vow to try to locate him. If he was that well known, it shouldn't be too challenging, provided she didn't get arrested tomorrow for breaking into the British Museum.

Chapter Fourteen

I cannot believe we're going to break into the museum. Do you realize this is a royal institution?" Esme asked. Even in a whisper her voice sounded shrill. "It will probably be considered treason, what we're doing tonight. Treason is punishable by death."

"We're here," Fielding said.

She was still gazing out the window, trepidation written all over her face.

"Listen to me." He tilted her chin so that she would look at him. "We're going to go in and walk around as standard patrons." He flipped open his pocket watch. "They close in an hour. Before that time we need to find somewhere secure to hide, then we wait."

"Wait for what?" she asked.

"For everyone to leave. Then we'll find the diary."

Her cat-green eyes narrowed. "You have this all figured out."

"Of the two of us, I have more experience with theft. Unless you have something you wish to share with me."

He folded his arms and raised his eyebrows. "Perhaps you have a better plan you'd like to propose?"

She eyed him silently for a while, then her lips pursed into a tight bud. "Of course not."

He managed to control the laughter he felt brewing inside him. "Very well. Do you wish to remain in the carriage or perhaps go back to the marquess's house?"

She looked completely affronted. "Absolutely not." Without another glance, she opened the carriage door and stepped down completely unassisted. "It has been so long since I've visited this museum, I should very much like to see their new exhibits," she announced perhaps too loudly. Subtle, she was not.

He matched her pace and held his arm out to her. She cautiously took it, meeting his eyes for more than a moment. They used the entrance off Montague Place and walked quietly through the hall.

No sooner had they entered the museum than he heard his name.

"Oh, Mr. Grey," the voice called.

Fielding turned to his right and found James Silsbee, a former client, standing there. The older gentleman held his hat against his chest with one hand while he used the other to maneuver his cane.

"Mr. Silsbee," Fielding said. "A pleasure to see you again. Allow me to introduce Miss Worthington."

The man nodded to Esme. "You've certainly hired the best, madam. Mr. Grey here is responsible for unearthing the Great Library of Alexandria." His eyes glistened when he smiled.

Esme whirled around to face him. "You found the library? *The* library?" she asked, her voice entirely too loud.

Fielding squeezed her arm. "Mr. Silsbee here provided me with extensive research; I only filled in the holes and did the actual digging."

"Where did you find it?" She shook her head in disbelief.

"Beneath the Temple of Isis," he said simply. "I'm afraid we're in a bit of hurry," he said to Silsbee.

"Oh, certainly, the museum closes soon. I may be in touch," Mr. Silsbee said. "I believe I may have found a reference to Homer's lost texts."

"Very good," Fielding said. He pulled Esme away. "This way," he said.

"I cannot believe it," she said. "What other treasures have you found? When you told me you hired yourself out to find antiquities, I assumed you were unearthing pottery and perhaps a gold staff or jeweled-handled blade every now and again. But this . . ." Her voice trailed off.

Her awe made him uncomfortable. He dropped her arm and shoved his inside his coat to check his watch. "We can talk about this another time," he said. "Right now, we have other tasks to attend to."

Fielding proceeded to the museum guard and showed him a card.

"Where are we going?" Esme whispered.

"To the reading room."

The guard moved aside to let them pass, and soon they had stepped into the grand reading room. Book-lined shelves filled the space, from the floor to the dome-shaped ceiling high above their heads.

Esme gasped, her hand finding its way to her necklace.

Her obvious joy pleased him. "I thought you might like

the reading room." Fighting his desire to kiss that smile from her luscious lips, Fielding shifted away from her.

"They're not generous with passes, so I've never been in here," she said, her voice filled with wonder. Her eyes never for a moment left the shelves in front of her. "I thought once to send in a request for a pass, but expected that a single woman would not be given much courtesy."

He'd suspected as much, which was part of the reason he wanted to bring her in here before they had to hide themselves away. She was utterly transfixed, her eyes darting from one shelf to another. He found it difficult not to watch her.

Her passion for books tugged at something deep inside him. There had been a time so long ago when he'd loved books and history and the promise of adventure. Things had changed, though, and he'd had to face responsibility and be an adult, earn money to pay off his father's debts.

She walked straight up to a shelf and bent to read the titles. Then she trailed her hand against the spines as she walked to another shelf. Standing up on the tips of her toes, she perused a row of books above her head.

Seeing the room through her eyes, it was as if he too was seeing it for the first time. The tiers of shelves led up to great windows that surrounded the bottom half of the copper dome, and the early evening sky was already lightly dusted with stars. Several men sat at the rows of desks that jutted out from the walls of the room like spokes on a wheel.

"How much time do we have?" she asked, her voice laced with awe.

He checked his watch. "Twenty minutes," he whispered close to her ear.

She stood looking from him to the shelves, obviously conflicted.

"You have time to look around a little before we go. And we can always come back another time."

Her genuine smile lit her face so quickly, he didn't have time to prepare himself for the effect. What was he doing making promises for a future outing with her?

Fielding took the opportunity to browse the room, looking for somewhere they might safely hide until the museum employees left for the evening. He kept one eye on Esme while she browsed the shelves, stopping periodically to pull down a volume and flip through it.

He'd walked the circular perimeter of the room, seeking a closet or cabinet that would conceal them, but so far he'd found nothing.

"Ten minutes," a guard said as he walked through the room to give a warning that closing time was near.

The men working at the desks began packing up their belongings. Fielding made his way over to Esme.

"There's nowhere in here for us to hide," he whispered. "Follow me." They stepped out of the reading room and into a hall, going deeper into the museum until they came to a darkened room.

"Egyptology," Esme said with interest. "I haven't been here since they expanded this exhibit."

"Indeed," Fielding said.

Footsteps sounded in the next room. It was two men, judging from their voices.

Fielding grabbed Esme's hand and pulled her through the exhibit. The only other door besides the one through which they'd entered led to the location of the voices.

That's when he saw it. An Egyptian coffin flanked by cat statues stood upright, leaning against the wall. The stone sarcophagus had the likeness of an Egyptian woman painted on the front, and though the image was chipped in some places, it was still a thing of beauty. No doubt he could have fetched a pretty penny for something like that.

"We can hide in there," he said, pointing to the sarcophagus.

"Are you mad?" Esme stopped and stared at him. "We cannot hide in a coffin. You won't even be able to shift the lid to open it. That stone must weigh twice as much as you."

A pair of gentlemen lingered at the other side of the room, reading the plates by a display of canopic jars. One of them made a note in a small book he carried, then he nodded to his friend and together they walked away. Fielding waited until they'd disappeared into the hall before he spoke again.

"We don't appear to have any other options." He once again scanned the room, looking for another place to hide. "Perhaps I should have better planned this," he muttered.

She gave him a wry smile.

"We can come back another time," he suggested.

She looked down at her wrist, then shook her head. "No, I need to remove this bracelet as soon as possible."

Esme was desperate to rid herself of this curse, of her lust for him. Granted, she also believed her life was in danger, yet he still suspected her desperation had more to do with her feelings for him.

Moving the lid was indeed a challenge, as she'd predicted, but not one he couldn't manage. He was able to slide the lid to the side without completely removing it from the base.

"Since you're so desperate to be rid of me," he began as he stepped inside and felt the cold stone permeate his clothes, "come here." He held his hand out to her. "Let's do this."

Footsteps drew closer.

"I swear I saw two people go into the Egyptian room," a male voice said.

She eyed Fielding warily but moved quickly to join him.

Facing him, she pressed herself against his chest as she joined him inside the casket. This plan would never have worked had Esme been a larger woman.

Maneuvering the lid back into place proved more difficult from the inside, especially with the delectable Miss Worthington nestled against his body. He was able, though, to shift it to an almost closed position. There was no way to know if he'd be able to get the lid off if he shut it completely or if they would be able to breathe.

"It's very tight in here," Esme whispered.

"Yes, it is," he said, and in doing so managed to suck in a mouthful of stale air. It smelled and tasted of ground sand.

He shifted, trying to move her away from him so that her hip wasn't pressed quite so intimately against his groin. But he failed miserably, succeeding instead in moving her in such a way that should he become aroused—which seemed imminent at this point—there would be no way for her to miss his growing erection.

"Did you know that the word *sarcophagus* means 'flesh eater'?" Esme whispered.

He could not see her, but he could clearly imagine her

wide eyes gazing up at him with that inquisitive look she so often wore. And it was hard enough for him to concentrate with the lack of air, let alone with fighting the sensation of her tight little body pressed against his.

Before he could answer, the guards entered the room. Fielding put his hand over Esme's mouth, her hot breath coming in short puffs against his palm.

"Chesterfield, you should come with me," the first voice said. "My sister has plenty of silly friends. One of them is bound to find you passable. Not Marie, though. I'm claiming her. Sweet Marie, plump in all the right places."

"Can't. I'm going to Suffolk on the morrow to visit my ailing aunt."

"Next week, perhaps," his friend suggested.

"For a willing lass," Chesterfield said wistfully. "If it weren't for my aunt, and her small fortune," he added with a laugh, "I'd be there."

"I don't see anyone in here, Chesterfield. They must have left."

"What about over there?"

If possible, Esme pressed her body farther into Fielding's.

"The cupboard? No, it's always locked."

Footsteps passed right in front of their hiding place and stopped. "You know, I've always found this old thing a bit frightening." The man tapped on the sarcophagus with his toe. The sound echoed around Fielding and Esme.

Esme flinched and her breath caught.

There was a long pause before they heard, "Come along. We have three more wings to patrol."

Fielding's hand left Esme's mouth, while the other rubbed gently against her arm. It would do them no good if she panicked and alerted the men to their hiding place. Having her this close, though, was wreaking havoc on his body. And supposedly she was the one suffering from the curse of lust. It seemed he was equally afflicted.

A door closed and the voices faded away.

Esme relaxed into his body. "I thought for certain they would discover us," she said.

The faint scent of lilacs wafted to him and for some reason gave him a measure of calm. He breathed her in, her hair tickling his nose.

She shifted and in doing so rubbed her breasts against him. Desire surged through his veins and pooled in his loins. This was bloody perfect.

"Fielding?" she asked, her voice lined with panic. She poked him right in the ribs. "Are you still breathing?" Her finger continued to jab him in the side.

"Yes." He grabbed hold of her hand.

"Oh, you frightened me." She relaxed against him. "I believe this is the sarcophagus of the priestess Amon-Ra. I read about it not too long ago. Many people who have had contact with it have died. So it is thought to be cursed," she whispered, then paused as voices from the hall drifted by.

"In fact, the owner of this sarcophagus, who won it in a wager in Egypt," she continued a moment later, "simply donated it to the museum in an attempt to remove the curse from his life." She took a deep breath. "And when you didn't answer immediately, I thought maybe . . ."

"That the curse had done me in?" he supplied.

"Honestly. The two travel companions of the man who owned this died shortly after returning to England. Then he gave the sarcophagus to a friend as a gift, and that friend's mother died. Then there was all this very peculiar business with a photographer—"

"Esme, you're going to use all of our oxygen," he said.

She shrugged her delicate shoulders, which only ended up rubbing her breasts against him again. He groaned.

"Are you all right?"

"Yes," he answered through gritted teeth. "It will only be a few more moments before everyone leaves for the night and we'll be able to get out of this tomb."

"You smell rather nice," she said.

They needed to get out of this bloody box. There was only so much temptation a man could take.

She nuzzled against him.

Desire shot through him. *Damnation*. There was no way to reach her mouth for a kiss; there simply wasn't enough room. So he did the next best thing. He brought her hand to his mouth and laved her wrist and fingers with kisses. Bloody hell, he'd never craved a woman the way he craved her.

She'd finally felt his arousal pressed against her and had tentatively brushed her hand across the front of his breeches. They needed to get out of this box. Now.

He reached around her, pushing at the lid. The lid scraped against the stone as he tried to shove it to the side. "Can you squeeze out?" he asked once he had managed to create a small opening.

She tried to ease out of the sarcophagus sideways, rubbing her hip against his groin in the process.

"If we don't get out of here soon, I'm going to take you on the museum floor," he said.

"Open it a little more," she said.

He complied, although it was much more difficult to move the lid from inside the sarcophagus.

She wiggled herself out, then stepped aside for him to step through. "As it turns out, not a terrible place to hide, but I don't suppose I ever want to do that again," Esme said brightly.

As soon as he stood next to her, she grabbed the front of his shirt and pulled him to her. "But I have no objections to your proposed plan for the floor, by the by." She kissed him firmly.

Fielding kissed her in return. It occurred to him it would be impossible not to. He gently pushed her away to end the kiss before he did toss her skirts up right there and then. A cold wooden floor was no place for a seduction.

He moved the lid back into place, then took a cleansing breath and shook his arms at his sides. "We need to find that diary," he whispered. He gave her a quick kiss on the nose before he pulled her to the door.

"I suspect we should start in the curator's office. It might not be in there, but we should find cataloging records regarding where the diary is," she said.

Finding the curator's office proved more difficult than Fielding had hoped. They made their way through the Egyptian room and on to the Grecian room, past the Roman room and the special exhibit on prehistoric animals, then the newspaper library in addition to two other offices before finally locating the correct one.

The curator evidently wasn't a very tidy man, as his office was practically dangerous to walk through with all the boxes and books on the floor. Likewise, the man's desk was completely covered so that you could not even determine what type of wood it was made from.

"We should make quick work of this," Fielding said. "The evening guards will be here in less than thirty minutes."

Esme glanced at the large grandfather clock in the corner.

"I'll look for documentation of Biedermann's dona-tion," he said. "That should indicate where his papers are housed in the museum. You could look for the diary itself, on the off chance that it's still in here."

She made her way across the room and began going through the boxes stacked in the corner. "I still cannot believe I am doing this."

"Remember, it was your scholar friend who suggested it," Fielding said. "And it is for a good cause."

She nodded and went back to digging through the boxes.

Several minutes later Fielding asked, "How well do you read ancient Greek?"

She looked up from the pile of books she was flipping through. "Fair at best. Why?"

"I found the Greek text Biedermann was translating." He held up the book. "The diary has got to be in here. There's a note attached about a translator coming in next week."

Esme checked the clock again. "Fielding, we have less than ten minutes."

"We'll find it."

She moved to a stack of books on a windowsill and had looked through nearly all of them when she picked up a small leather volume. "I think this might be it," Esme said.

Fielding came and stood beside her as she flipped through the book.

"I think this is actually papyrus," she said, fingering the pages. "He must have specially ordered it." Her voice was filled with wonderment.

Biedermann's handwriting was tight and small and completely illegible in the dim lighting.

"What do we do?" Esme asked. "We can't very well read it in here without turning on the lights and thus alerting the guards to our presence. Nor does it appear to be the sort of book one can quickly flip through in hopes of landing on the right page." She fanned through the bulk of pages to prove her point.

"Take it with us," he suggested.

"Steal?" She pressed the book against her chest. "From the museum?"

"Do you have any better ideas? As you've pointed out, our options for reading it here are grossly limited."

She eyed him, then the book, looking unconvinced.

Fielding pointed to the pile of materials from which the diary had been uncovered. "It doesn't appear to be on their list of most valuable items."

She chewed at her lip.

Damn, but she was attractive and seductive in a way that only innocent women could be.

"Esme, I'll take it; you'll be nothing more than my accomplice. They'll likely never miss it, provided we get it back to them before the new translator arrives."

She took a deep breath. "I suppose we don't have a choice. I'm really rather desperate to get this cursed thing off my arm."

"Indeed. Otherwise you might continue to act the brazen woman and take advantage of my weaknesses." He gave her a toothy grin.

She frowned. "That's not funny."

The clock chimed the hour.

"We are out of time," he said.

Chapter Fifteen

———✦❧ ❧✦———

Two hours later, safe from the museum guards, Esme and Fielding sat huddled over the diary back in their study room at the marquess's, reading through the handwritten pages—which included drawings and diagrams Mr. Biedermann had evidently thought important—but so far they had found nothing of use.

Fielding stood to stretch his legs. It seemed as if they'd been looking through Biedermann's diary forever, and all they'd read was a retelling of the mythological structure of Mount Olympus.

"This is all quite fascinating, but it doesn't help in the least," Esme said as she flipped through another few pages. Her brow furrowed in concentration. "We must keep reading. I know we shall find something."

Fielding leaned against the hearth and watched as she read a page, then turned to the next. Again and again, finding nothing. "We don't have to read through the entire thing tonight."

She waved her hand dismissively. "That journal

specifically mentioned this diary," she said as she turned yet another page. "And Mr. Nichols knew of it as well." Another page. "Where is it?"

"Esme, go to bed. We can continue in the morning."

She fanned the book's pages and placed her hand randomly inside the diary, then perused that page. "Nothing."

"Esme," Fielding tried again.

Her right index finger landed on another page and followed the text to the bottom and then to the top of the next page. She sat taller in her chair and looked up at him with a smile. "I do believe I might have found something."

"Finally." He shoved off from the fireplace and walked toward her.

She began reading: " 'The vices will appear as golden bands encircling the flesh of those bold enough to breach the box.' " She looked up at him. "The Greek text was obviously right about that."

"Obviously."

Her forehead wrinkled. " 'Until all those who wear the cursed bands reunite with one another in the presence of the box, they cannot be removed. If the bracelets are not returned to the box by the eclipse of the full moon, those enslaved will surely perish.' " She bookmarked the spot with her hand and looked up at him. "It does appear my mortality is still at risk."

He grabbed another chair and angled it across from her. "Esme, you're not going to die. I'll make certain of that." He leaned his elbows on his knees and exhaled slowly.

She released a shaky laugh. "Somehow I don't think you can prevent an ancient curse from taking its toll."

Fielding could only look at her in silence. Perhaps his fair maiden was finally beginning to understand that he was no hero.

"What about the Raven's men? Should we locate them and try to warn them? Can they be reasoned with?" she asked.

"I don't know. Thatcher has never been particularly steady. I do know that the Raven would never be so fond of an employee that he wouldn't use them as leverage."

"Surely they would see reason if we explained to them the seriousness of the curse."

He wiped a hand down his face. "These men are unscrupulous, Esme. They can be cutthroat and dangerous, and they are not to be trifled with. And they are not afraid of curses. Or death. More than anything, though, they are loyal to the Raven. Without hesitation."

"But you said Waters was most likely afraid of the Raven," she countered.

"Oftentimes fear and loyalty go hand in hand."

"You are not taking into consideration the bands they wear." She fumbled with her own as she spoke, the gold twinkling as it twirled around her wrist. "The strong pull they have. The way they can make you do things you will only regret later." She met his eyes as she spoke.

Her words were well deserved, but they hurt nonetheless. He had gone out of his way to prove to her he was not the hero she made him out to be. Evidently his hard work had paid off, as she clearly wished she'd never let him touch her.

"Where will we find Waters?" she asked.

"We?" He shook his head with a chuckle. "Oh, no." He stepped over to the window.

"Oh, no, what?" Esme asked. "If you think to leave me behind, you are quite mistaken."

"Damnation, Esme, I will not argue with you about this." He turned away from the window to face her. "The places I'll have to go to look for Waters are not fit for a lady. It's too dangerous in those parts of the city."

"Fielding, I'm going to die in less than a week if I do nothing. I hear your argument, but in light of my circumstances, it's weak." She slowly made her way over to his side and smiled sweetly. "I'll be right by your side, and no harm will come to me. Would you allow anything to happen to me?" She tentatively touched his chest.

He gritted his teeth, then rolled his eyes. "That is a ridiculous question. But whether or not I would protect you isn't even the point." He grabbed her arms and looked into her eyes. "Putting you in a position where you could get hurt would be grossly irresponsible of me."

"Ah, but I managed to get myself kidnapped without your help. So it is not as if you'd be introducing danger into my life for the first time."

He exhaled in frustration and dropped his arms.

She straightened, her slight height gaining at least an inch. "I am a grown woman." She frowned as she pointed a delicate finger at him. "I certainly do not need you to tell me"—she jabbed him in the chest—"what I can or cannot do. If you won't allow me to go with you, I'll simply hire a rig and follow you."

He eyed her for several minutes, hoping his glare would make her back down, intimidate her, but it didn't work. She was quite serious; he could see it in the firm set of her chin and the unwavering look in her eyes. She would follow him, and then if she got lost or too far behind he wouldn't be able to protect her.

He swore loudly, which only made her smile as she recognized her triumph.

"I am not happy about this," he said.

"Duly noted." She slanted him a mocking frown.

"I'm serious, Esme. This is not a part of town you've ever been in. It's dangerous; it's dirty; it smells terrible. I cannot prepare you for what you might see on the street."

"I know about prostitutes," she said defiantly.

"I'm only trying to warn you."

"Consider me warned. I'll try not to be too shocked by anything we see. Or smell." She did nothing to hide her impish grin.

The following evening, Fielding and Esme sat in a darkened corner of a less-than-reputable tavern on the edge of the Thames. Fielding had insisted she wear a cloak and keep the hood up around her face, which made seeing anything around her rather challenging. He himself had worn a greatcoat, and together they kept to the shadows.

Esme did not want to touch anything, so she folded her hands in her lap. As it was the floor was so filthy, it stuck to the soles of her shoes. She kept lifting her feet, simply to assure herself she wasn't permanently glued into place.

Since discovering the bands had to be reunited in order to remove them from their wearers, Fielding had been using his sources to try to locate Waters. If the man was hiding from the Raven he wouldn't be visiting his regular haunts, so they'd had to look elsewhere. The informant had been lucky and found the man at a dirty little pub near the St. Katharine Docks.

They'd been told that every evening for the last five days, Waters had come into this pub and stayed for nearly three hours. Tonight, though, Waters had yet to arrive.

Fielding decided they should not approach Waters here but rather wait until the man left, and then they'd follow him. A perfectly crafted plan wouldn't matter, however, if the nasty man didn't show. So for the time being they sat in silence, surrounded by the filth and the noise. And there was plenty of both. For someone more accustomed to the quiet halls of museums and libraries, this pub's crowd of rambunctious men was an assault to Esme's senses. It seemed every word spoken merited applause or cheers. At least they were a mirthful bunch.

Her cloak prevented her from seeing much farther than the end of their table but did nothing to impede from reaching her the foul stench of wretched body odor mixed with the smells of tobacco and whiskey. Her eyes watered.

"Where is he?" Esme whispered.

Fielding scanned the room once more. "I don't know."

A bar girl made her way over to their table.

"Evening," she said and bobbed a deep curtsy clearly designed to display her tightly corseted breasts, which currently threatened to fall out of her dress. "Can I get you and your lady friend something to drink?" She smiled widely, revealing several blackened teeth.

Fielding waved his hand. "No."

She turned to go. Before she could reach the bar, a man with long, beefy arms reached out and pulled her onto his lap. Immediately the man began to fondle the girl's breasts. She squirmed and fought, trying to get off his lap, but never lost her forced smile.

The offending man snaked one hand under the girl's skirt. "Hold still, Minnie," he growled. All the men around them cheered.

Esme came to her feet, unsure of what precisely she could do, if anything, but she was feeling rather incensed by the entire display.

"Enough," Fielding said, his deep voice carrying across the noisy pub.

The large man didn't remove his hands from the girl's body, but he did turn in Fielding's direction.

"Who the 'ell are you?" the man growled, then came to his feet, dropping poor Minnie onto her bottom.

She scrambled to her feet and slugged the big man in the stomach, then turned to Fielding. "I can take care of myself," she said, her voice etched with bitterness.

"Esme, we should leave," Fielding said as he pulled her close to his side. As he and Esme crossed the crowded pub, he turned to the oaf. "When the girl says to stop, she means it." He tossed a small coin purse to Minnie as they left the door.

Once safely inside the brougham, Esme found that despite the chill in the air, her cheeks felt warm. Her hands still shook with indignation.

"I should never have taken you in there," he said quietly.

"Fielding," she said, placing her hand on his knee, "I am unharmed."

"You shouldn't have had to witness any of that."

"Why? Do you believe I am so naive that I'm unaware of how some girls make their living? I can assure you that while I'm an innocent, as you say, I am not ignorant."

"I never suggested you were naive or ignorant," he said defensively.

"Minnie is trying to make as reputable a living as she can by serving those oafs, and they only want to take what she's not offering. I feel sorry for her." She twisted her hands into the folds of her cloak to steady them. "Sorry for the fact that she'll probably never know a man's kindness or gentleness. Every day she has to live with the groping of disgusting men or risk losing her position."

He said nothing in response.

"Look at us. I've done everything save ravish you myself," she said quietly. "Yet, you have been able to withstand my temptations. You are a good man." Or maybe that wasn't it at all, the little voice inside her head suggested. Maybe it had little to do with Fielding's temperament and everything to do with her appeal. Regardless, she knew he was a good man.

"Although I'm unable to completely ignore your temptation," he began, "I will not take advantage of you."

"But—"

"I know you believe it won't matter. But Esme, you don't know what you ask of me."

"I don't know what you think I'm asking, but it's certainly not for a commitment," she said.

"Damnation, woman." His voice was lined with frustration and something else. Something dangerous. Before she knew what was happening, he'd pulled her onto his lap and began to kiss her passionately. His lips moved firmly against her own, and she didn't care if he was angry or trying to prove a point. She wanted him, plain and simple; it mattered not what excuse he gave himself.

Desire pooled between her legs as his mouth and tongue moved against her own. She wanted to feel him beneath her. Feel his desire pressing against her, but her infernal dress was in the way.

He deepened the kiss, locking his fingers in the back of her hair and tugging ever so much. Not painful, but noticeable, firm, possessive. It only fueled her desire for him. She clamped her fingers into his shoulders and ground herself against him, needing release.

"Esme," he whispered. He touched his forehead to hers. "We can't." Gently, he placed her on the seat next to him.

She looked away from him, hiding her flaming face. "You are a bastard. Always teasing me then withholding your affection."

His jaw tensed. "You're right. I am a bastard. I will fight it no longer. If you decide you still want me, tonight you shall have me. I've tried to protect you, but if you are not concerned, why should I be?"

She said nothing in response.

"Now, though, I must go back in and look for Waters. You'll be safer in here," he said.

"You're going to leave me in here alone?"

"Yes, but only for a moment. I'm going to ask a few questions. I shouldn't be long."

"Are you quite certain I can't come with you?" she asked.

"Stay here, Esme."

She nodded in the darkness, then closed her eyes when she felt his lips brush her cheek. His speech hadn't been particularly romantic; still, she quivered with desire for him. If she had any sense at all, she'd sequester herself from him until this bloody curse could be broken. But she knew she'd never do that. Part of her questioned whether she'd ever be able to walk away from him.

What, precisely, was he trying to protect her from? Even if she foolishly fancied herself in love with him, which she didn't, then what harm would that cause? People had their hearts broken all the time and survived.

The carriage door opened.

"That was quick," she said. "Did you already find him?"

"Hello, Miss Worthington." A match struck, and an unknown man sat across from her lighting his cigar.

Cold fear spread through Esme's body, slowing her pulse down so that it felt as if warmed molasses were traveling through her veins. She forced herself to breathe deeply. Fielding would be here soon. She would be safe.

"Who are you, and how do you know who I am?" she asked, hoping she sounded angry rather than terrified.

"They call me the Raven." He took a drag on his cigar, his lips curling in a devilish smile. Something about that smile looked strangely familiar, and a deep gnawing bit at her stomach. "I'm sure you've heard of me."

"I have." She crossed her arms over her chest, partly in an attempt at appearing formidable, but more to hide her trembling. "Nothing good, mind you," she said tartly.

His deep chuckle resonated through the carriage.

"What do you want?" she asked.

"I want what you want, Miss Worthington." He leaned forward. "I want Pandora's box."

His presence took up so much space in the small carriage, her very breath felt threatened. She shifted in her seat.

"We can make a deal, you and I," he said, his smooth voice slicing through the darkness.

Though the dimness prevented her from seeing much in the way of details, Esme could clearly see the Raven was a conventionally handsome man. His chiseled features and silvery-gray hair would certainly make him a desirable companion.

"I'm sure we can find a way that we are both satisfied." His emphasis on the "s" sounds conjured the image of a slithering serpent. Perhaps this was how Eve felt in the garden before she took that first bite.

"I will make no such deal with you," she said.

"Are you so certain?"

"I am."

His voice softened. "But you don't even know what I have to offer in exchange." He took another drag on his cigar, then smiled.

She glared at him.

He grabbed her wrist; his rough grasp pressed the bracelet into her flesh. "What have we here?"

She tried to jerk her hand free, but his grip held firm.

"I see my worthless employees weren't the only ones who answered Pandora's siren call." He tsked his tongue. "Miss Worthington, I would have expected more restraint on your part."

Aha, so at least one of the men had returned to the Raven. Not only that, but they'd been honest about the bracelet. She felt her fear give way to curiosity. Perhaps if she could coax some information out of him about the other two bands, she might give Fielding the upper hand. Then he'd see how useful she could be.

"How are your men faring with their curses?" she

asked. "Have you noticed anything peculiar about their behavior?"

One eyebrow slowly arched; then he smiled. "Curses?" he said slowly. "What is it that you're afflicted with, Miss Worthington?" A spark of interest reflected in his gaze.

He might have thought he'd given her nothing, but now she knew that up until this moment the Raven had not sought the box because of the rumored powers within it. "Oh, you didn't know." She chuckled. "So I don't suppose you know about the second curse either. Pity. Tell me, why is it that you seek this box?" she asked.

He shrugged. "It is a client, not I, who wants the artifact. Now, about that deal."

She scoffed to hide her glee. He couldn't fool her. There was no client. Or if there had been, now that the Raven knew about the curses, he would have no intention of fulfilling his end of the bargain. That's how the villain's plan always played out in her adventure novels. "Nothing *you* could offer would possibly interest me."

"I can be awfully persuasive, Miss Worthington." His tone was low and dark.

It occurred to her that she might be playing cornered mouse to his clever cat. A drop of perspiration slid down the center of her spine. "And I can be equally stubborn." She feigned bravery.

He laughed heartily. "You are a charming woman. Very much like your aunt."

As if he'd reached across and squeezed her throat, Esme's windpipe seemed to close. She eyed the door, wishing Fielding would burst in.

"What do you know of my aunt?" she whispered.

"I know plenty." He exhaled slowly, the smoke from his cigar curling toward her. "She favors an upstairs corner at the Guildhall Library every Tuesday. And she excels in conversation, though I find talking with her can become tiresome. She does like to prattle on."

Oh, God. Esme fought the urge to flee, but she needed to hear what else he had to say, what else he knew about Thea. She clamped her hands to the edge of the carriage bench, anchoring herself down.

"You stay away from her," Esme said through gritted teeth, knowing full well her threat would not be taken seriously. Still, she'd needed to say the words, and if it came down to it, she'd find a way to protect Thea.

Again he chuckled, but his mirth was short-lived. "Perhaps now you will see my way of things, Miss Worthington. The box in exchange for your aunt's safety. Things could become quite messy from here on out."

He trailed one finger over her wrist.

She shivered with revulsion.

"It's better not to fight me. The box will be mine; it's merely a matter of time." He grabbed her hand again, but this time he pressed a kiss to her palm. "I lost something once. I've never made that mistake again. Suffice it to say, I always get what I want." Then he opened the door and stepped out of the carriage.

Fielding had said he wouldn't be long, but she could not wait for him any longer. Especially with the Raven skulking about. Glancing down both sides of the street to ensure the nasty man was gone, she stepped from the carriage and darted across the road. She had to fight her way through a crowd before she was able to step back into the pub.

A large man grabbed her by the waist, his meaty fingers cutting into her flesh. "Back for yours, I see."

*   *   *

Fielding rolled his eyes when Esme stepped into the pub. His annoyance swiftly changed to anger as the nasty man who'd fondled the barmaid pressed his filthy body against Esme. Her frame seemed impossibly small engulfed in the man's arms. His grubby hands roamed all over Esme, smashing her breasts and trying to reach beneath her skirt.

She landed a firm kick straight into her offender's shin, which doubled him over in pain.

"How dare you, sir," she said indignantly.

The man reached for her again just as Fielding finally made it to her side. Fielding punched the brute square in the nose. Blood sprayed from the man's face. He yelped in pain and reared back to hit Fielding, but before the man could land his blow, Fielding had knocked his fist hard into his stomach. The oaf fell to his knees.

"You ever touch her again and I'll kill you." He turned to Esme. "Did he hurt you?"

"No. I am unharmed."

But Fielding could tell that wasn't precisely true. Her eyes were glassy with fear. He draped one arm over her shoulders and led her outside. He shouldn't have left her alone. Shouldn't have even brought her with him. They were halfway across the street before he spoke.

"Why didn't you stay in the carriage?"

"He found me," she said. "And he knows Thea. Knows where she sits at the library."

Fielding helped her into the carriage. "Esme, what are you talking about? That man doesn't know Thea."

Shakily, she met his glance. Though no tears fell, her moss-colored eyes swam. "The Raven. He came here." She tapped on her seat, then looked around the small enclosure as if she still expected him to be inside.

He swore. He'd been a fool. Fielding had been too careful for the Raven to have successfully followed them, but obviously he too was trying to locate Waters, which was undoubtedly how the Raven had stumbled upon them tonight. How could he have forgotten how ruthless and cunning his uncle truly was? Fielding squeezed Esme's hand. He'd gotten careless.

Fielding gave instructions to the driver to take a long and winding trip back to Max's. Hopefully, they'd lose anyone trying to discover their hiding place.

"What did he say?" Fielding asked once they were under way.

"He wanted to make a bargain. Said he knew there was a way we, meaning he and I, could both get what we wanted." She shook her head. "I don't see how; it's not as if we can slice the box in half." Her brow furrowed. "He threatened Thea's safety if I didn't give the box to him."

"Did he hurt you?" He ran his hands up and down her arms as if to prove to himself she was unharmed.

"No. Do you think we should leave Max's house? Do you think he's found us?"

Fielding shook his head. "No. We've been very careful, so it's unlikely. Besides, if he'd found us he would have made a move, made his presence known."

"I want to check on Thea. I need to make certain she's all right." She rubbed her wrist and winced.

"He did hurt you."

"A little. He grabbed me, right at the band." She shook her head and offered him a small smile. "It's only a bruise."

Fielding held her hand up to his chest.

"I did learn something new," she said. "You were right

that at least one of the men has returned to him, as the Raven knew about the bracelets. I was trying to uncover which of the other bands had been removed from the box, and although he didn't intentionally give me anything worthwhile, he didn't appear to realize they were cursed."

"If he didn't know about the curses, then why would he want the box?" Before she could offer her guess, he continued. "I'd wager it's not him who wants the box, but rather a client."

"So he claimed. Any idea who?" she asked.

"No, and I'd imagine the list of possible buyers would be rather long." Fielding held Esme in place as they took a particularly rough curve. "All of that might have changed, though. If he now believes the box to have actual power, he will at the very least change the price for his client. I suspect that he'll decide perhaps it would be in his best interest if he kept the box."

"That's what I was thinking as well," Esme said.

"The bad news is if he wants the box for himself, he truly will stop at nothing until he claims it."

"You won't give it to him," Esme said.

"Not without a fight," Fielding replied.

"And you'll protect us," Esme said with certainty. "Thea and me; you'll do everything necessary to keep us safe."

It was time for her to know the truth about him. Time for her to stop fancying him as some sort of knight destined to rescue her. He'd certainly proved otherwise tonight. Fielding wasn't even sure why he'd kept it to himself for this long. Perhaps some part of him had hoped that his family lines didn't matter, that someday he could be the man Esme thought he was.

If only her lustful curse would be expunged by his simply telling her the truth.

"You should not rely so heavily on my protecting you," he began.

"What are you talking—"

"Did the Raven frighten you?" he interrupted.

"Yes, he did. Very much so."

"Then know this, Esme: That man's blood, the very man you fear, runs through my veins. He is my uncle."

Chapter Sixteen

───────※∞∞※───────

*Y*ou are the Raven's nephew?" Esme asked, certain she must have misheard him.

"I am," he answered, his voice clear and slightly defiant.

"And you didn't think to tell me this before now." Their carriage had stopped, but she remained in her seat. She thought she saw a flicker of regret pass over his face, but he made no verbal apologies.

"Go check on your aunt. We can talk about this later." Exhaustion lay heavy in his voice.

Once inside the marquess's home, Esme climbed the stairs as quickly as she could, making her way to Thea's room. Although Esme knew the older woman was probably sleeping, she didn't bother keeping quiet as she flung open the bedchamber door. The thought of the Raven and his charming demeanor cornering her poor unsuspecting aunt had Esme's veins running with ice water.

Her cat perked up as she entered the room, but Thea's soft snores kept their steady rhythm. The older woman's eyes were covered with a sleeping mask, and she had one leg kicked out from beneath the heavy covers.

Seeing her aunt resting so peacefully, Esme resisted the urge to wake her, to ask about her visits to the library. Her questions could wait for the morning.

Quietly, she sneaked into her own adjoining room. She poured tepid water into the basin and scrubbed at her face. There were so many offenses she wished to remove from her person. With the sponge she washed her arms too, noting a flicker of pain as she passed over the bruise blooming on her wrist.

Certainly Fielding owed her some explanation. Or perhaps he didn't. They were nothing to each other outside this Pandora's box business, she reminded herself. She was not his lover or even his friend, not truly, though she had thought they were developing a friendship of sorts.

Whether or not he was related to the Raven honestly meant nothing to her. She knew what it was to share blood with those who were different from you, those who didn't understand you. It seemed blood was the only thing she'd had in common with her own mother.

No, what she wanted to know more than anything was why he'd told her in the way he had. As if he'd intended to frighten her, as if he wanted her to be afraid of him. Perhaps this was what he'd been trying to protect her from. But she'd felt Fielding's touch enough to know there was nothing to fear. He was far too tender, too gentle.

Even tonight, as he'd kissed her in the carriage, told her how much he'd wanted her, he'd stopped himself so as not to hurt her. Feeling a sudden undeniable urge to see him, Esme slipped out of her bedchamber and went in search of him. He was not to be found anywhere downstairs, so she made her way to his room.

One knock and he opened the door. He'd removed his coat and unbuttoned his shirt. Although the white folds gaped open, it still was tucked firmly into his trousers. His naked chest revealed dark hair covering a taut and muscular abdomen.

Now was not the time to succumb to the curse. She wanted information right now. But not more than she wanted to run her hand down that tightly corded stomach of his. She closed her eyes.

"Come in, Esme. I'll tell you what you want to know." He poured them both brandies, and she took a seat in the plush wingback in the corner. He took a seat next to her.

"How is Thea?" he asked.

"Sleeping soundly. I worry about her, though." She waved a hand in front of her. "That isn't why I'm here."

He nodded.

"The truth," she reminded him.

He took a healthy swallow of his own brandy, then leaned back in his chair. His long legs stretched out in front of him, crossing at the ankles. She'd never fancied a man's legs before, but she knew how strong his were, how firm they felt beneath her.

"My father was a member of Solomon's," he began.

She'd always detected a slight resentment in his tone when he spoke of Solomon's, so it wasn't a surprise to hear this revelation. Immediately she wanted to ask questions, but she knew she shouldn't rush him. Interrupting him might cause him to neglect a detail, and she wanted every detail.

"My sister and mother and I were used to traveling around with my father while he chased after his treasure. The Templar's Treasure, you might want to know."

"The legendary gold the knights supposedly hid after returning from the Crusades," she said.

"Correct. It was like a game when we were children. Digging in the dirt and going on adventures. But then we got older." A dark shadow crossed his face. "We settled at our estate in the country, and I was sent away to school. My sister and mother were left behind while my father continued his obsession."

He drained his brandy, then leaned forward, placing his elbows on his knees. "In addition to his absence, my father proceeded to whittle away the family fortune while chasing that damned treasure."

Still nothing about his uncle, but she bit her tongue.

"Of course, none of us knew this until he got himself killed. He was digging in some cave up north by Hadrian's Wall, and there was a cave-in." He bit down on his lip. "Then the creditors started paying calls, sending notices. He'd lost everything. Our estates, my sister's dowry. All of it." He met her eyes then and gave her a wry smile. "I was seventeen. I quit school and went to work for my uncle.

"It seemed simple at the time." He paused for a moment before continuing. "Though my uncle and my father had never really gotten along, I didn't believe I had another choice. Who else was going to employ a penniless viscount?"

He stood and went to the window, looking out into the darkness and saying nothing for several minutes. "I never knew precisely what their conflict was, though I always suspected it had to do with my uncle's success." He shook his head as if shaking off a bad memory, then faced her.

He was looking in her direction, but it didn't seem as if he saw her, but rather that he looked through her.

"My uncle would never admit it, but I know how he longed for entrance into Solomon's. He'd asked my father to nominate him, which he did. The membership, however, refused my uncle an invitation to their secret club because he studied no specific legend and instead seemed more interested in those items that were worth the most money. He was furious. Believed my father had intentionally sabotaged him."

Esme said nothing, but she couldn't help hearing the familiarity in his words. They'd argued about this very thing just the other day. She could see now that Fielding's interest in locating antiquities solely for profit was grounded in something far deeper than a shallow quest for funds.

"I suppose he took his own kind of revenge. It wasn't too long after that my uncle became known as the Raven." He shrugged, and for a moment he looked at ease, as if he were merely telling her a humorous anecdote. Then the darkness permeated his eyes once again. "I only know what I was told, as I was born about this time. 'A ruthless treasure seeker, hunting and stealing antiquities for profit,' that's what my father always called the Raven."

Esme set her still-full glass of brandy on the table beside her and leaned forward.

"My father abhorred my uncle's profession and the way he used antiquities to find fortune. Father was quite clear on that front. 'Antiquities are to share with the world, not for profit,' he said. You see, my uncle rarely went about acquiring the antiquities in honest ways. There tended to be a great deal of bribery, conniving, and theft involved." Fielding gave her a half smile. "I suppose I took my own revenge against my father." The bitterness was heavy in his voice. "Punishing him for losing our fortune by earning it back through the very means he would have despised."

He'd been shielding her from the ugliness of his past. Esme felt her heart soften.

He poured himself another drink and returned to his seat. "My uncle—his real name is David, by the way—came to visit me at school. He was the one who told me about my father's death and our financial problems. He seemed to have the perfect solution for me to save the family." Fielding gritted his teeth. "So I went back with him to London, to his grand estate, and he plied me with food and women until I was trained and ready to go out on my own dig."

He looked so lost, so broken sitting there. She could almost picture the young man he'd been—hurt, abandoned, and overwhelmed with the financial burden of caring for his mother and sister.

"It's understandable, Fielding, what you did. You were a young man, and your uncle manipulated you. Used your anger toward your father against you."

"Don't you see, Esme?" He looked at her then. For the first time all his defenses were stripped away, his heartbreak and betrayal shining clearly in his eyes. "I became one of them. I cheated people. I tricked them." He took a breath. "I *stole* things that did not belong to me."

She wanted to go to him, to pull him into her arms and erase all the horrible memories from his past. "That's not what you did. You worked for him, and you were nothing but a child."

"That may be, but had I still been in his employ, it would have been me abducting you that night. Not rescuing you. Have you ever thought of that?"

"But you did rescue me," she said. "Everything you've

done, every decision you've made, has been for the sake of your family. To save them. People have done worse for lesser reasons." She smiled. "And you succeeded, didn't you? I saw your family estate; it was glorious. You did that with the funds you made."

His face tightened. "Yes, but at what cost?"

It wasn't really a question, so she said nothing more.

"Seven years I worked for him, and I paid off every one of my father's debts. Then I went into business on my own."

"And you no longer steal?" she asked.

"With the exception of that damned box, and the diary," he added with a weak smile. "No, I don't."

"What of your family?" she asked.

"They live here in London. We don't have much contact since I travel so often." He held his glass up in a mock toast. "My mother never did approve of my work."

She stood and walked to him. Placing one hand on his shoulder, she said, "You did what you had to do."

In the swiftest of movements, he rose and pressed her against him. His hungry kiss tore through her, pleading for everything she had to give.

Did it matter to her if he wanted her, truly wanted her, or if he was simply needing the touch of another to cleanse himself of the harsh memories?

Esme told herself no. That she was a woman of the world. She'd survived kidnapping and was currently living with an ancient curse. If she was ever going to take a lover, it had to be now. It had to be Fielding. When would she ever again have the courage to do such a thing? Besides, she had less than a week before she might die. Before she *probably would* die.

Pretty words of love mattered not. She wanted him

only to warm her bed, to make her a woman in every sense of the word. And in this moment she wanted to be what he needed.

He continued kissing her, his mouth at times angry as he pressed into her. She fed off his urgency, clung to him as desire shook through her.

His mouth left hers and began raining kisses down her throat, across her collarbone, and onto the gentle swell of her breasts.

With her right hand, she ran her fingers against his chest hair, its prickly texture tickling her palm. She outlined his stomach muscles.

She wanted to touch him everywhere. Memorize every hard line of his body.

He tugged on the back of her dress and she heard the buttons pop, the fabric giving way as seams tore and material fell open. Gently, he pushed the sleeves off her shoulders.

His voice came out ragged. "I'll buy you another. I need to see your body again."

She removed the rest of the dress and slipped out of her shoes, and then she stood before him in her shift and stockings.

He knelt before her and picked up her right foot. With a satin-soft touch, he rolled the stocking down her thigh, over her calf, then slid it off her foot. He did the same with her other stocking.

Wet desire trickled between her legs in response.

A day's growth of whiskers had settled onto his face, darkening the shadow on his cheeks, making him look dangerous and so handsome her knees went weak. The makings of his beard scraped against her sensitive flesh.

Again he stood before her. Nuzzling into his neck, she

inhaled deeply, trying to forge his scent of sandalwood soap, and what she knew only as Fielding, forever in her memory. Gently she kissed the skin there, loving the taste of him and the feel of his skin against her lips. He groaned softly and ran his hands down her arms. Goose bumps followed his touch and her nipples hardened.

With one hand he slid the straps of her shift down her arms until the flimsy material pooled at her feet. He traced the words inscribed on her left breast and then those on her stomach.

"There's something positively erotic about these tattoos," he said. "Exotic etchings on such well-bred flesh."

He placed his hands on her waist, then slowly caressed his way to her breasts. His warm hands kneaded the sensitive flesh, his touch only fueling her desire. But she didn't want to rush him. She wanted to feel every sensation there was to be felt in lovemaking. Her hand again slid down his torso to rest on his flat, hard stomach.

He pulled her to him and kissed her fervently, his tongue sliding against hers in a passion dance that nearly made her climax.

He gripped her bottom and pressed her to him. "You have a wonderful bottom, Esme Worthington."

That only made her smile.

His erection pushed hard against her bare stomach and she longed to wrap her legs around him, to put that part of his body firmly against her core. She lifted one leg in instinct, wrapping it around his waist. He picked her up and cradled her to his chest, then carried her straight to the bed. She'd been naked in his bed before, and he'd stopped just short of making love to her. Esme knew tonight there would be no such interruption.

"Esme," he breathed. He leaned over her, bracing both arms on either side of her.

It was all the encouragement she needed. She reached between them and unfastened his trousers to free his hardened length. She needed to touch him, needed him to be inside her.

With some assistance, his pants slid off him and then his shirt and the rest of his clothing. He lay atop her, his hot skin against hers. Nothing was between them. She hugged him to her and soaked in the sensations; his weight pressing onto her, the crispness of his hair tickling her legs, his erection lying firmly against her stomach.

"It will hurt," he told her. There was such honesty in his eyes, but pain was the last thing on her mind.

"I don't care." She opened her legs, making room for him.

He kissed her cheek. "I don't want to hurt you." His mouth met hers in a tender and vulnerable kiss that came close to bringing tears to her eyes.

Desire slid through her like molten lava. With one swift movement he pushed into her. Pain pierced her, but she fought the urge to flinch. She wanted to be strong for him.

Several breaths passed before he moved within her, slow and shallow at first, then tentatively he pushed himself deeper inside. Instinctively she encircled his body with her legs, taking him in even deeper still. Pleasure shrouded the pain as he drove into and out of her, made love to her.

"Yes," she breathed.

He nibbled her shoulder, nuzzled her neck. The climax bloomed within her, curling into a tight spring she knew was seconds away from exploding. He kissed her then, deep, sweet, and full of tenderness.

And then spirals of pleasure burst through her. She tightened her legs and grabbed onto his shoulders as it rocketed through. A moment later she felt his abdomen stiffen, and then he released a guttural moan as he lost his seed within her.

For several moments they stayed in that position, sweaty, out of breath, and clinging to each other.

He withdrew himself and rolled over. She was unsure of what to do next, but she didn't have to wonder long before he pulled her into the crook of his arm.

She said nothing, merely snuggled up against him, relishing the smell of him, the scent of their lovemaking permeating her skin. His hand absently stroked her back.

"No one would blame you for working for the Raven," Esme said softly.

He only squeezed her closer to him in response.

She longed to say more. To say something that would ease the guilt she knew ate at Fielding, but she found herself at a loss.

They lay in silence for so long Esme would have guessed he'd fallen asleep.

"So tell me, Esme," he whispered. "What secrets are you hiding?"

"Secrets?" she asked. "Tit for tat, I see. Well, I don't suppose it will hurt to supply you with the details of the Worthington family secrets." She still lay in the crook of his arm, snuggled against his chest.

"Worthington family secrets. Sounds intriguing. Tell me, why is it that you refer to yourself as a woman without a name?"

Her right hand made lazy circles through the hair on

his chest. She was not in the habit of revealing her own humiliation. But she had claimed to be forthcoming with him; she couldn't very well make herself out to be a liar. And he'd shared something with her, something he evidently was not proud of.

"Obviously I do have a name, although it is a name with no protection, as it were," she began. "My father was a baron, but we lived a comfortable life. He and I were quite close; it is from him that I inherited my extensive library."

"You mentioned he was a professor, but a landed *gentleman* professor." He released a low whistle. "That's interesting. I would wager that caused quite a stir among his peers."

"Yes, and with my mother as well. It was not what she'd agreed to, she always told him. He came to teaching only after my sister and I were born. My mother, well, she and I never did see eye to eye on much of anything. She and my sister, Elena, were very much alike, though. Both beautiful and charming and able to persuade men to do their bidding with little more than a flutter of their eyelashes."

As much as she'd hate to admit it, the pain was still there, pinching her like a broken corset bone.

"Spoiled and tiresome," he muttered.

She merely smiled and kept going. "Elena is five years older than I am, and as a little girl I wanted nothing more than to be just like her. She was so pretty and graceful. I couldn't wait until I grew up and had my coming-out so that I too could be courted by a line of suitors.

"I can still see her coming down the stairs in our small townhome, her soft curls pulled up in an intricate coiffure decorated with jeweled hairpins, her rose-colored ballgown brushing the rails of the stairwell as she left for a night of dancing." Esme paused a moment to enjoy Fielding's fingers as they traced haphazard patterns on her back. "It wasn't until later," she continued, "that I realized blood was the only commonality Elena and I had. In any case, it only took her one season, and she married one of those suitors."

"Lord Weatherby," he provided.

"Yes. The wealthiest and perhaps the most handsome of all her suitors. I was all of fifteen. Shortly thereafter, our mother and father both fell ill and died. Scarlet fever." She tried to speak quickly so the tears wouldn't come. "My father left no other heir, so my brother-in-law took immediate control of our household and became my legal guardian. Very quickly, he sold my parents' home and all our belongings, save the items my sister wanted, and my father's books." For which she'd had to beg.

"Your sister's handsome, rich husband turned out to be a scoundrel," Fielding said.

Esme shrugged, trying to appear as if she didn't care. As if the last twelve years had meant nothing to her. "Oh they're quite happy with each other. Both looking pretty in their big house with their expensive furnishings and hordes of servants. I'd wager their children are perfect as well."

"And what of your own debut?" he asked. "Why did you never marry?"

She exhaled slowly. "My debut was a disaster. My mother had spent the better part of ten years instilling in me the teaching that I should not flaunt my education around men. She reminded me time and again to hold my tongue, and that if I could do so, I might make a decent match."

Fielding had already started to chuckle.

Esme frowned. "What's so amusing?"

"I can sense trouble coming," he said. "There's no situation in which you could keep your opinion to yourself."

She could have been offended, but instead Esme warmed under his assessment. There was no judgment in his tone, but rather a matter-of-fact understanding of who she was.

"What happened?" he asked.

"After an extensive lecture from my sister, reminding me to heed all Mother's advice, I went with Raymond and Elena to an exclusive dinner party hosted by the Duke of Devonshire. For most of the evening I managed to smile and nod and be the perfect dinner companion. I nearly survived the entire meal, but as they were bringing out the seventh course his lordship was touting his knowledge of all things Egyptian. Then he boldly, and foolishly I might add, claimed that Cleopatra had never been pharaoh. I saw Elena shake her head, but I could not abide his ignorance. So I corrected his facts."

Fielding tilted her chin so she looked up at him. "You corrected the duke in his own house at his own party?"

"I did," she said slowly. "And I paid dearly for it."

He kissed her forehead.

"It was a scandal I could not recover from. No matter how much Elena and Raymond apologized on my behalf, they knew better than to ask me to do so. After that dinner, no man would have me; they were far too concerned with the stigma marrying me would carry. A woman with opinions of her own." She sighed. "A month later they gave me my dowry and told me to go live in the country. I was given three estates to choose from. I chose to stay in London."

"On your own?" Fielding sat up. "Where did you go?"

She kept the sheet tucked under her chin. "To the only place I knew and the only friend I had," she said.

"Your aunt?"

"Yes and no. I went to the Guildhall Library. I had always spent so much time there; it was like a second home to me. Thea was there often, and we'd spoken on more than one occasion, but we didn't really know each other. She caught me crying that day, and I told her the whole story. I was surprised to learn that she too, in some ways, had been turned out by her family. So we pooled our money and bought our home, and we've been there ever since."

"You've lived on your own since you were but a child." It wasn't a question, merely a statement spoken with a touch of awe and pity.

She did not want his pity. "I've done rather well for myself, wouldn't you agree?"

"Yes, you have," he said. "So then Thea is not truly your aunt?"

"She is the only family I have."

"Are you not angry?" he asked, his own voice full of anger on her behalf.

She could not lie. "Certainly I am. I think my sister is the most selfish creature in all of London. But I enjoy my life, my freedom. I'd be a liar if I said I didn't lament the opportunities I never had. The dancing and the courting. The chances I should have had to become someone's wife." She was quiet for a moment. "But I can't blame them for everything. It was my mistake, my scandal. And had it not been that evening, it would have been another. You said yourself, I can't keep my opinions to myself."

She picked a piece of lint off the sheet. "I don't suppose I would ever have gotten along well with proper society; they tend not to favor women who speak their minds."

"True though that may be, you should have been given the opportunity. There are some men who admire women with thoughts of their own."

She ignored the flip her heart made. He had said "some men"; it was not a personal admission.

He was quiet for a moment, and then he said, "You and she favor each other, but the similarities are slight."

She sat up. "Elena and I? How do you know?"

"I went to see Elena and her husband."

"When?"

"Shortly after we arrived here at Max's." He smiled. "Evidently you have a niece who is rather similar to her aunt Esme and is causing quite a stir with her parents."

She shook her head. "Why? Why would you do that?"

"I wanted them to know you were safe."

She crawled from the bed and tossed her shift over her head. One by one, she gathered up the pieces of her clothing. Clutching it all to her chest, she faced him. "You had no right to do that." Now they would know everything, all the trouble she'd caused. It was humiliating.

"Esme—"

But she didn't wait to hear what he had to say.

Chapter Seventeen

———✦———

Esme waited until she'd heard the first stirrings before she opened the adjoining door to Thea's room. She found Thea sitting bleary-eyed in the bed, talking to Horace.

"If I didn't know any better I'd say you weigh two stone." The cat turned his head for a better scratch. "But you do keep my legs warm, so I suppose I'll let you stay."

"Good morning," Esme said from the doorway.

Thea smiled warmly. "Good morning, yourself. You're up early."

In truth she hadn't slept much at all. She'd returned from Fielding's bed sometime after three and hadn't gotten any sleep after that. Truth be told, she wasn't completely certain why she'd been so angry. She didn't like him going behind her back, but she realized her anger was not truly with Fielding.

In fact, it was more humiliation she'd felt than fury. The idea of Elena and Raymond knowing about the kidnapping had Esme's stomach in knots. They already be-

lieved the very worst of her; there was no need to confirm
it or provide them additional fodder for judging her.

"I wanted to speak with you," she said to Thea. There
was no sense thinking on other matters at the moment.
She had much more pressing things to handle. "I believe
you might have met a gentleman at the library."

Thea patted the bed beside her, and Esme edged herself onto the mattress. "I don't know that I've met anyone
recently."

"Perhaps you've spoken to him before. It's quite important, Thea. Think," Esme said, trying not to lose her
patience.

"You seem most grave," Thea said. She picked at the
nails on her right hand. "I speak to plenty of people at
the library." She shrugged. "You know me; I am rather
social."

"Yes, I know." Esme squeezed Thea's shoulder. "There's
nothing for you to worry about; I only need to know about
one gentleman in particular. A tall man with graying hair
and nice-looking features. He would, no doubt, have been
very friendly and charming." When Thea still hadn't said
anything, Esme added, "Perhaps he mentioned me?"

Thea's pale blue eyes brightened with recognition.
"Oh, yes, there was that handsome fellow. You know, I
don't guess I actually got his name." She frowned. "But
we have spoken on several occasions. In fact, earlier this
week we had a lovely conversation. And you're right, he
is exceedingly charming. I had actually thought to introduce the two of you at some point."

Esme's stomach tightened. "And he asked about me?"

"He didn't precisely ask about you. No, more or less,
he knew things about you. I fancied him as an admirer
of yours. He said he'd heard of your studies surrounding

Pandora's box from two other scholars whom you correspond with."

Esme fought to keep her breathing steady. She did not want to frighten Thea, though fear was certainly coursing through her own body. Somehow the Raven knew about Mr. Nichols and Mr. Brown, and that meant the two of them were in danger as well. She needed to contact them as soon as possible to alert them to take all precautions necessary to protect themselves.

Thea continued to peel at her nails. Esme stilled the older woman's hands. "Thea, I need for you to cease visiting the library for the time being. Please restrict yourself to the marquess's library while we are staying here. He has a grand collection; I'm sure it will suffice."

"Esme, what are you hiding from me?" Thea frowned, her bright cherub face creasing. "Are you in some sort of trouble?"

"Nothing like before—I can assure you I am finished with scandals." Esme laughed, hoping it would soothe Thea's worries. She might indeed be done with scandals, but curses were another matter entirely. "But that gentleman you've spoken to is certainly attempting to cause trouble for me. It is most important that you stay away from him. Charming though he might be, he is not a nice man."

Her face relaxed. "Oh, poppycock; that man is too kind and handsome to cause any harm. Perhaps it is another man you are referring to?"

"I don't think so. Promise me you'll stay away from the library?"

"I promise." Thea nodded. "And you stick close to that Mr. Grey. Allow him to watch over you, my dear."

Esme had turned to Fielding last night, and her body

still hummed with the pleasure he'd given her. His love-making had been so passionate, so possessive, she feared she'd lost a bit of herself to him she'd never regain.

"I know you are used to standing on your own," Thea continued. "But on occasion one needs to lean on someone stronger."

Ah, but what if that stronger person did not want you leaning on him?

Esme had put aside her anger with him long enough to solicit his help.

"I'm sure both men are perfectly fine," Fielding said.

"I sent a message for Mr. Brown to the *Times* today; they'll print it tomorrow. But Mr. Nichols—I need to be certain he's unharmed."

When Fielding said nothing, Esme's shoulders deflated.

"The Raven mentioned them to Thea, and he knows who the men are and my connection with them," she said.

"I'll drive you over to see Mr. Nichols. Because I know if I don't, you'll simply go without me." That should have earned him a smile, but instead Esme simply nodded. He longed to touch her again but feared if he did, even just to graze her hand, he'd lose control and make love to her again. He wanted to regret last night, even knew he should; yet he felt no remorse.

They had been in the carriage for ten minutes before Esme spoke again. "I'd like to locate a lost love of Thea's. A man she almost married."

"What brought this on?" Fielding asked.

"I can't protect her. I need someone who can," she said. "If the Raven got to her, I'd never forgive myself."

"What is the man's name?"

"Albert Moore. I'd intended to contact him after this business with the curse was completed."

"He is an old man now," Fielding said. "Not much protection."

"Perhaps, but Thea said he was an adventurer. Surely that means he has some experience in dealing with unsavory situations." She swallowed hard. "Besides, it occurred to me today that this might not end so positively for me. That perhaps I should try to find him sooner. And someone looking after her, regardless of their age, would be better than her being alone."

. "You will survive this, Esme," he said.

She eyed him warily, disbelief shining in her eyes. He said nothing else for the remainder of the ride.

Twenty minutes later they were standing on Mr. Nichols's front stoop.

"Ring it again," Esme pleaded.

Fielding did so and again there was no answer.

"Something has happened to him. I know it, Fielding," Esme said, dread thick in her voice.

"Stay close," he said. With one great shove he managed to get the front door open. Heeding his warning, Esme practically attached herself to Fielding's side. "Mr. Nichols," Fielding called.

But there was no answer.

They stuck close to the wall as they crept along the hallway. The first room they checked was the room in which they'd met Mr. Nichols on their previous visit. It looked much like it had that day, quiet and tidy, but today it was empty.

The next room was much the same, although it appeared to have been unused for quite some time. White sheets covered the chairs, and the rest of the furniture was sparse.

Two more rooms and no sign of Mr. Nichols. "Perhaps he went out of town," Fielding suggested.

"What of his servants?" Esme asked. "Someone would be here."

They found the kitchen, which appeared empty except for a loaf of bread sitting on the counter. Mold ate at the corners. Two dirty pots sat near a drain bin.

The bottom floor was empty. Together they climbed the stairs, then entered the first door on their right. It was completely dark inside, and the windows were shuttered from the inside. Without them open, the room had no light save that which leaked in from the hall.

"Stay here so you don't stumble," Fielding told her. Carefully he maneuvered through the room until he could open a pair of shutters. Cloudy light from outside dropped onto the floor, providing some visibility, though it remained dim.

"Oh, no," Esme whispered.

Fielding followed her gaze to a chair and table behind him. There, slumped over in the chair, was Mr. Nichols. His small calico wound around the dead man's legs and mewed. "Esme, wait in the hall."

She shook her head, then her fingers found their way up to her necklace. "What if they're still here?"

Fielding touched his hand to Mr. Nichols's neck. "I believe he's been dead a while, love. Go ahead and step out so I can look around in here."

"Come here, Pandy, kitty-kitty," Esme called, though her voice cracked. The cat flipped her tail in the air and darted straight for Esme. She bent and cradled the crying creature. A few scratches behind the ears and soothing words soon quieted the mews to purring.

Once Esme no longer stood in the doorway, Fielding moved to Mr. Nichols's body to take a better look. Blood covered his white shirt, and a hole straight through the fabric indicated a gunshot wound. He'd been a kind man, and no matter Fielding's conflict with Solomon's, Mr. Nichols had not deserved this.

There was no note, no written message, but Fielding knew this was a warning meant for him. To remind Fielding that neither Esme nor anyone else he knew was safe. It had nothing to do with Mr. Nichols, and now the poor old man was dead.

Damn the Raven. Damn him straight to hell.

He made his way through the room, looking for anything that seemed out of the ordinary, but since he hadn't truly known the victim, it was hard to tell. In the end he decided this was best left to the police detectives, so he stepped into the hall and found Esme leaning against the far wall. Her eyes were still wide with shock.

"I'm sorry," he told her.

"I tried to warn him," she said. "But I was too late."

"You did what you could," Fielding told her.

She scratched under Pandy's chin. "I'm taking her with me."

He nodded.

"The Raven killed him, Fielding. And he could get to Thea or me. Or you." The eyes that looked up at him were completely washed in fear. "How can we be safe?"

"I'll take care of everything. Right now I need to notify the authorities. And Max, so he can inform Solomon's about Mr. Nichols's death."

* * *

Once back at Max's home, the marquess had assured Fielding that Solomon's had taken care of everything, though Fielding knew from his own experience that there were some things Solomon's wouldn't dirty their hands with. Namely, a widow and her children surrounded by debt. Then they simply walked away.

When he and Esme had returned from Mr. Nichols's, a message had been waiting for Fielding. This time it had come directly to Max's. The Raven had found them.

Five words were scrawled on the parchment: *I can find her anywhere.*

It had given Fielding only one option. He grabbed the heavy handle of the knocker and slammed it against the cumbersome double doors of his uncle's stately home.

Officially it was called Black Manor; his uncle had always jested that Grey just wasn't dark enough for him. It was a far cry from the small home he'd started with, before he'd become the Raven and earned his fortune. Everything about this house was a gross overstatement of wealth; from the sheer enormity to the gilded ceilings and elaborate moldings.

Fielding remembered as a child he'd always wondered why his uncle had lived in a larger home than he and his own family had, considering it was his father who had been the viscount. As a boy, he'd been impressed by the grandeur and envious of the obvious wealth. Now Fielding had his own money, all earned by his own hand.

The large doors opened with a creak, and his uncle's butler appeared. The short, crooked man looked the same as he had the last day Fielding had been here. The day he'd told his uncle that he would no longer work for him. Fielding had thought that was the last day he'd ever darken this doorstep, but evidently their business was not yet complete.

Dark, beady eyes looked at him from above a sharp beaklike nose. Fielding had the unsavory impression the man was not surprised to see him. As if the butler had always known Fielding would one day be lured back to the Raven's lair.

After Fielding was directed to his uncle's office, he had barely stepped into the room, had not even fully crossed the threshold or made a sound, yet somehow his presence was known.

"Fielding," his uncle said without turning around to greet his nephew. "I can always tell it's you by the sound of your gait. You walk exactly as your father did. Methodical, and with intention."

"I did not come here for your parlor tricks," Fielding said, his hands clenching into fists at his sides.

The Raven spun around in his thronelike chair, his face expressionless. His black eyes revealed nothing, and his silver hair was slicked back, accenting his widow's peak. "You never did enjoy the sleight of hand." He flicked ashes onto a small silver tray.

"What do you want?" Fielding asked.

"You've made an alliance with the enemy," he said. "I will admit, very little surprises me these days, but that"—he paused—"I wasn't expecting."

"Solomon's? They are a client, nothing more."

"Of course, merely a client." He paused for several moments, then continued. "What of your association with Miss Worthington and her aunt. Are you protecting them?" He tsked his tongue. "That's not like you." His fingers drummed on the desk.

Esme's aunt. "Is that how you found us? Through Thea?"

The Raven gave a wolfish grin. "She's really quite talkative once you get her going. Thea and I have been visiting every week for a while now. She's a fount of information."

Fielding forced his breathing to slow. He stood behind a chair and gripped the back with shaking hands.

"Come now, Fielding, you know very well what I want." He waved a hand flippantly. "There is no need to make me play these silly games. I have no use for the girl, or her aunt. Although I do want that key." He picked up his cigar and took a long, thoughtful drag. "And of course, the box."

"Do you honestly believe I'll simply hand it over to you because you asked nicely?" Fielding replied. He mentally counted to ten. It would do him no good for his uncle to see him lose his temper. "Perhaps you don't recall our history together, but I no longer work for you." Fielding did nothing to hide the loathing in his voice.

"I remember everything," he said slowly. "You would not be where you are today were it not for me."

"Leave Esme alone. Your fight is with me."

The Raven stood, leaning over the ornately carved desk. "What is so special about this woman? You've never given a damn about anyone but yourself."

"It doesn't have anything to do with her," Fielding said.

"That's not true, though, is it?" The Raven chuckled. "You care about her, don't you? But let me give you a piece of friendly advice: Don't be so naive." He rose to his full height. "Simply because you happened upon Miss Worthington and played Galahad to her Guinevere does not make you a hero. Honestly, Fielding, you don't wear it well."

His uncle was, of course, right. He was no hero, and he had proved as much last night. Taking Esme to his bed when he had no intention of marrying her.

Fielding stood his ground and said nothing.

"If you think I don't know what you're up to, boy, you're an even bigger idiot than I imagined." He jammed a finger onto his desk. "Don't believe for one moment that I don't know every decision you're going to make before you make it."

Fielding took a step back. He never should have come here today. This meeting was nothing more than an opportunity for his uncle to toy with him as he'd always done. Fielding was a grown man now, and he no longer had to play the manipulated nephew for his uncle's games. "You know nothing about me," he said, his voice so forceful he barely recognized it. "And I owe you nothing."

"Ungrateful," the Raven muttered. "Just as Waters is ungrateful. Should that man ever come crawling back to me, he will find himself on the wrong end of my temper." He took his seat again and lit another cigar.

So Fielding's suspicions had been right: Waters had not returned to the Raven.

"Do you know who hired me to find that damned box?" The Raven's tone was once again calm.

Fielding remained silent.

"The nephew to the king of Prussia. Evidently one of his advisers told him if he secured that box, he could rule all of Prussia." The Raven laughed. "So the fool contacted me to find it for him."

"What is he paying you?" Fielding asked.

"That's the beauty." His uncle leaned forward as if

they were as they used to be, friends sharing a conversation. "Once he's king, he'll grant me an island off in the Caribbean where I can rule as I so choose."

"An island," Fielding repeated.

"It was an agreement I made before I knew the box actually had powers. I do believe I'll have to renegotiate our settlement," the Raven said.

"What are you planning to do?" Fielding asked, knowing full well it was a futile question.

His uncle flashed a smile. "You'll have to wait and see."

"I'm not giving you the box."

"I don't want to hurt her, but I will if I have to. Let's see—" He scratched his cleanly shaven chin. "What curse does she wear?" He pretended to read through some notes on his desk.

"If you come anywhere near Esme again, I'll kill you." Fielding turned to go.

The Raven's dark laughter filled the room. "Don't be so dramatic, Fielding. You and I can come to an agreement."

Fielding stopped; his hand remained on the doorknob. But he said nothing.

"How about you come back to work with me. It will be as it used to be, you and I traveling all over the world. Together we can make new fortunes. And we can uncover what truly happened to your father that fateful day. I know you long to know, long to make someone pay."

Fielding's hand tightened on the knob as he fought the urge to turn back and wrap his fingers around his uncle's throat.

"Come back to me, and I'll leave Miss Worthington unharmed." The Raven's voice was slick.

It would be so easy. Make a deal with the devil and protect Esme.

"My offer won't last forever," his uncle said.

"Go to hell," Fielding said. He didn't bother closing the door on his way out.

He had the driver take him back to his own house instead of Max's. He needed some time to himself. Time to decide what to do next. His house was deserted, which suited Fielding's foul mood.

Though his servants had done their best to restore his home and clean everything, there were still signs of his uncle's men having been there. Broken windows were covered, yet not repaired. His father's collection of Roman urns, which had taken Fielding four years to track down after they'd been sold to pay off debts, had been destroyed. Bits of the broken pottery lay scattered in the open hearth.

Fielding collapsed onto a red-velvet Chippendale sofa. He'd been a fool to think he could ever dissuade his uncle from something the man wanted. Somehow, though, Fielding had hoped there was enough humanity left in the Raven to keep Esme safe. It appeared that Fielding had grossly underestimated him.

To make matters worse, it had become abundantly clear that despite his efforts to the contrary, Fielding was more like his uncle than he cared to admit. The Raven had guessed Fielding's plan to make Solomon's pay for his father's death because that's exactly what the Raven would have done.

Perhaps revenge was wrong; perhaps he would go too far. But Fielding needed to know what happened to his father. More important, he wanted to know who was responsible. There had been two other members of Solomon's with him that day; both of those men had escaped the cave unharmed.

Fielding had been given an opportunity to discover their identities through his new association with Solomon's, and he'd allowed Esme to cloud his mind. He'd almost lost sight of his goal. But he'd ignore it no longer. Tonight he would go to Solomon's and uncover the information he needed, but first he would try once again to locate Waters.

Chapter Eighteen

A tankard crashed to the floor. The noise shattered Fielding's thoughts. Once again he sat in the dank pub, watching and waiting for an opportunity to find Waters. It wasn't his prime reason for going out tonight. No, that would happen in another hour when Solomon's closed for the night and Fielding could sneak inside. He knew from previous conversations with his father that Solomon's kept meticulous records on their members. Somewhere in that club, he would find out who was responsible for his father's death.

Fielding had left Esme at home, and to prevent her from following he'd enlisted Max's help. As it turned out, the man was rather useful. The marquess had agreed to host a dinner party in Esme's honor—thus forcing her to oblige the invitation—and he'd invited several would-be suitors. As much as that thought left a bitter taste in Fielding's mouth, he'd reconciled himself to the situation. Courtship was an experience she'd never had, and he wanted her, if for only one night, to experience it.

He suspected right now she was sitting with two wealthy gentlemen on either side of her, complimenting her on her beautiful ivory complexion and her eyes the color of clover.

But none of them would see the intelligence glimmering in those green eyes. They would dismiss her witty comments as silliness. Not notice the way she quietly smiled when she found something amusing but didn't want to laugh.

Just then the serving girl stopped by his table with a drink. He'd ordered it when he arrived, although he had no intentions of drinking anything here. There was no reason, though, to draw unnecessary attention to himself, and a man sitting without the company of either alcohol or women would most definitely draw attention.

As the girl set down his mug, Fielding recognized her as the girl from the other night. "Where is everyone?" he asked. The pub was close to empty with the exception of a scattered few.

When she turned to him, he could see weeping sores along her cheekbone and another cluster on her neck. "Everyone is sick. Best you leave here, mister." She glanced around. "Something ain't right in here no more." She moved away from him, scuttling behind the bar and disappearing.

At that very moment, Waters stepped into the pub. He glanced around the room, then rapidly made his way to the bar.

Fielding pulled his hat farther down on his face and shifted his stool deeper into the shadows.

Waters took a seat at a nearby table where he could watch the door. No doubt the man was on constant alert waiting for the Raven to appear. "Minnie," he yelled. "Get me a tankard."

The girl brought him his ale, then quickly returned to the back room.

A man sitting at a table in the middle of the room screamed. He grabbed at his face and screamed again. Boils covered his weatherworn skin and then started to appear on his forearms. The man stood and ran from the pub, still yelling.

Fielding pushed his glass of whiskey away from him and tightened his coat.

Another man erupted into a coughing fit that ended with him vomiting blood into his tankard.

The girl had warned him that everyone was sick. From the looks of it, they were covered with pustules and full of disease.

Fielding looked back at Waters, who appeared to be in excellent health as he absently sipped his ale. The gold bracelet shimmered against Waters's sleeve.

Greed, disease, hope, and lust, Fielding repeated to himself. *Disease.*

Waters wasn't sick, though; instead he seemed the very picture of health.

Fielding wasn't ill yet either, but no sense tempting the fates. He made his way out of the pub and into his rig.

Esme's research had indicated the bracelets would curse the person wearing the bracelet. However, what if the books had been wrong, and the bracelets instead plagued everyone but the wearer?

Years and years he'd hunted antiquities; he'd walked into tombs that promised certain death and caves from which no one had ever escaped before him. Nearly every legendary antiquity or hidden treasure came with some kind of warning or curse, none of which he'd ever seen come to fruition.

But the bands from Pandora's box—they were real. They had to be. He'd seen it with his own eyes.

Had he too been affected by the curse? Was that why his desire for Esme ran so strong, why he couldn't resist her charms? He'd tried. Tried not to respond to her wanton behavior, but he'd failed miserably every time.

Slowly she'd worn away at his defenses, shown him that he could be a better man. He'd even begun to understand his own father more after seeing Esme's passion for Pandora's box. Fielding knew he didn't deserve her, but perhaps she'd have him regardless. Perhaps it was time for him to marry.

Or perhaps he was merely the victim of a centuries-old curse.

The twenty-minute ride to Solomon's ended abruptly, jarring Fielding from his thoughts. He had the driver drop him off a block away in the alley behind the club's buildings.

Fielding pulled his black coat closer to him, both to ward off the night chill and to shroud himself in darkness. The alleyway was empty save for a stray cat that took one look at him and bolted in the other direction.

When Fielding came to the back entrance of the club, it took him only a moment to work his way around the lock and crack open the door. He stood in the entryway for several breaths, allowing his eyes to adjust to the darkness within.

Quietly he made his way through the back of the building and up to the room where he'd first met with Jensen and the others. Without light, the room seemed much larger, like a cave beckoning. Fielding searched the space, looking for the club's records book, but found no trace of the log.

Perhaps it was kept behind the closed door at the opposite end of the room. Fielding found the door unlocked. He had taken two steps into the room when a light flickered on.

"Good evening, Mr. Grey. I've been wondering when you'd come for a visit."

Esme knew that Fielding was behind tonight's impromptu dinner party. He was trying to keep her occupied while he went off on an adventure, blast him. But as the guest of honor she could do nothing about it. His underhanded way of keeping her home was vexing, but she supposed he was only trying to protect her. Yet what use had she for dinner parties and social engagements? Such things had never interested her, even before the debacle with the Duke of Devonshire. Attending one now, when she was the victim of a curse and it seemed as though the fate of the world hung in the balance, seemed even more futile.

Still, she had to attend, so she'd donned her new gown and Annette had styled her hair. Though the girl had tried her best to convince Esme to wear her curls up, Esme had won; a proper dinner party was no place to showcase her tattoos, temporary though they were. She had allowed the girl to weave in a hairpin with two plumes that perfectly matched the blue in her gown.

Thea met her on the staircase as they made their way down to the dining room.

"This is a lovely surprise," Thea said. "And you look beautiful, Esme. Simply stunning."

Esme had to admit she did feel particularly lovely

this evening. She didn't think she'd ever owned a prettier dress. The marquess had seen to it that she and Thea both had new gowns for the evening, including all the matching accoutrements. The cerulean satin of Esme's gown matched with white netting looked perfect with her skin tone. Beading lined the scooped neckline and was further accented by a string of tiny blue flowers that just covered the inscription on her left breast. The tightly cinched waist and full skirt accentuated her best features, and she'd finished everything off with elbow-length white satin gloves.

"Thank you," Esme said as they descended the staircase.

The parlor attached to the dining room was abuzz with servants and early arriving guests. It was not a room Esme had visited since her arrival at Lord Lindberg's townhome. Lovely green wallpaper covered the room, accented by the cream-colored molding and two large columns. But the true showcase was the great, swooping chandelier. Crystals draped together like lovely necklaces hanging from a woman's neck.

Despite the circumstances—despite *herself*—something deep inside Esme awoke. The sight stirred those girlish dreams of beautiful ballrooms and darkly dressed suitors whisking her away while romantic music swelled in the background. Fantasies she'd long since forgotten until Fielding had awoken that part of her and made her yearn for more.

She couldn't have more, she reminded herself. Especially with the man she wanted. He thought her a dreamer, and he'd never see her as anything but.

"There you are," Max said, jarring her thoughts. He

approached with an older gentleman beside him. "I'd like to introduce you to someone."

"Albert?" Thea whispered. Her eyes brimmed with tears as the tall, gray-haired man approached. She looked over at Esme. "How?"

Esme said nothing, merely watched the older couple embrace after what must have been twenty long years. Her own heart stumbled clumsily as she witnessed the reunion.

"My sweet Thea," Albert murmured. "You look as lovely as ever."

Thea's burgundy gown was accented with cream-colored lace that not only flowed out of the neckline in two lovely swags, but adorned the three-quarter-length sleeves and peeked between the split skirt in four ruffled layers. Annette had even done Thea's hair up in an elaborate confection of curls that took at least ten years off Thea's face.

But none of that enhanced her appearance the way her beaming smile did.

"Thank you," Esme whispered to Max.

He shook his head. "I'm not responsible for this." With one last look at Thea and Albert, Max held his arm out to Esme. "May I escort you to dinner?"

"I'd like that." Esme never took her eyes off her aunt. Even as Max introduced her to several people, she couldn't help being distracted.

Fielding had done this for her. He'd paid attention to her concerns about Thea's safety and had taken it upon himself to find Albert Moore. Perhaps this was his peace offering for going to see her sister.

Now as Thea listened to Albert's every word and

giggled like a young schoolgirl, Esme wanted more than anything to thank him. Yet Fielding was not here.

Max led Esme into the dining room and seated her at his end of the table, but between two gentlemen she did not know. She smiled warmly at each of them, but made no attempt to converse. Their first course was served, and Esme was tempted with the rich aroma of fish stew. She took a bite with a nice plump piece of cod.

"Miss Worthington," the young man next to her said. "Lord Lindberg tells me you and your aunt are visiting for a short while. How are you enjoying London?"

Esme caught Max's wink before she answered the man to her right. Evidently the marquess had been kind enough to weave a story explaining her presence. "I find it quite exhilarating, actually. I've barely been able to catch my breath from all the activities." She didn't even have to lie. "It seems to have been ages ago that I was last outdoors."

"Being a champion croquet player, I find myself outdoors quite often," the young man replied. He was a bland-looking fellow with sand-colored hair and a pale countenance. Esme seriously doubted the man had ever been outdoors.

She smiled politely and went back to her soup. She'd barely swallowed a spoonful before the man across from her gave her a toothy grin.

"Ever heard of Darwin's *Origin of Species*, Miss Worthington?" he asked. The portly man looked to be about her age, with ruddy, freckled cheeks and muddy-brown hair. He wore a purplish-blue coat with a wide velvet collar, looking very much like a portrait she'd seen of the newly popular writer Oscar Wilde.

"Of course," she said. "I'm rather well-read."

He nodded knowingly. "Though he refuses to acknowledge the affair," the man began, "he and my mother had quite the tryst. And I"—he motioned with his hands—"am the product of their love."

Esme nearly spit her soup back into the bowl. She caught herself and covered a cough behind her napkin. "Is that so? How very interesting."

And what a horrific conversation opener. And to think, people at her previous society dinner parties considered *her* ill-mannered. She tried to catch Max's eye again, but he was otherwise engaged in conversing with the older woman next to him. Though Esme wondered from his sly smile if he hadn't intentionally bookended her with these two fools.

"Croquet, did you say?" the fat man asked of the pale man. "I dare boast I am quite accomplished at that myself."

"Indeed . . . ," the pale man answered.

But Esme was no longer listening. Instead she was caught up in watching her aunt. Thea was deep in conversation with Albert. It was as if those two were utterly isolated from the rest of the dinner party, so affixed were they on each other. A lump settled in Esme's throat, and she found it difficult to continue eating.

Perhaps it meant nothing, but to Esme, Fielding could have made no grander gesture. He might always argue with her, insist he was no hero, but Esme knew better. She knew there was no man more honorable, more noble, than Fielding Grey.

Conversation abounded across the table of sixteen. She continued to answer any question aimed directly at her, but for the most part, she concentrated on her food. She was most eager for the evening to end. She looked down at her dress and fingered the small flower nestled between her breasts. Her vanity longed for Fielding to walk in and see her in the pretty blue dress. But as she bit into her baked cherry pudding, he still had not arrived.

Three courses and four hours after the dinner began, she and Thea climbed the stairs to their bedchambers.

"That was a delightful evening," Thea said, her voice lyrical. "So thoughtful of the marquess to plan such an event in your honor."

"I do believe it was more in your honor," Esme said.

"How did the marquess know about my past with Albert?" Thea asked.

"Fielding must have told him. I mentioned it to him once before." And he had remembered. She squeezed Thea's hand. "Are you going to see him again?"

"He's taking me to a poetry reading tomorrow night," Thea said dreamily.

Esme almost warned her that it would better to stay here, where it was safe. But Albert Moore was an acclaimed adventurer; he was older, to be certain, but still fit and conditioned. He would be able to protect Thea. Esme relaxed a little.

"I'm glad you found each other again," Esme said. "You deserve happiness."

"I was already happy, Esme. This is a nice addition, though." They made it to Thea's room. "Are you going to stand in the hall all evening, or come in?" Thea asked.

Esme nodded and stepped into the room. "I apologize. I'm a little distracted."

"Indeed? I hadn't noticed at all," Thea teased.

"I apologize. I wasn't a complete dolt during dinner, was I?"

"Even if you had been, I wouldn't worry overly much." She paused, thoughtful, then continued. "That was an interesting collection of men the marquess invited."

"A motley crowd, indeed." Esme found herself at the window, staring down at the barely lit walkway leading to the townhome. No sign of Fielding. She had to admit she was a little nervous about the fact that he hadn't yet returned.

"I feel as if I'm on holiday," Thea said. "Living in an expensive hotel with anything I want at my fingertips. I could get used to a life like this." She smiled mischievously.

"Perhaps you can have a similar one with Albert."

"I don't want to get ahead of myself." Thea slipped out of her shoes. "You've made a good choice, Esme. I think he is rather dashing, all things considered," Thea said.

Esme turned from the window, feigning ignorance. "The marquess? He's handsome, I suppose, but I would never be so presumptuous as to—"

"No, you goose. Mr. Grey. Unless I am mistaken and you do not fancy him?"

"Yes, Mr. Grey is rather dashing," Esme said.

"Then why the hesitation? You can't convince me you are not interested in him. Even tonight, with plenty of men paying you all sorts of attention, all you could do was watch the door." She dropped her shoes in a corner. "Granted, most of those men were nothing more than silly fops." She paused in front of Esme. "Don't end up an old maid like me." Her tone turned somber. "If you want him, you should have him." She walked to her dressing table.

Plain and simple logic. It made sense to her too, Esme realized. But she also acknowledged that life wasn't quite so simple. Wanting Fielding did not mean she would have him. One must be wanted in return. Her mind flashed to his hands on her skin, his mouth on her body, and she smiled from the memory. Perhaps he did actually want her as well. But for how long?

Still, the scenario seemed much more complicated than mutual want. She and Fielding had been thrust together in extraordinary circumstances. Ancient curses with a death warrant and a desire so strong for him she could barely catch her breath.

"Are you suggesting I offer myself to Fielding as his mistress?" Esme asked.

Thea stopped moving, her jewelry in hand. "Most certainly not. I was thinking of something more permanent," she added with a tilt of her head.

"Marriage?" Esme asked, unable to hide the wistfulness in her tone.

"Why not? You sound as if the notion never crossed your mind. I've seen the way you look at him." Her aunt smiled knowingly.

Truth was, Esme hadn't thought about it; she hadn't allowed herself to. The desires Fielding had awakened in her—not merely the sensual desire, but the heart-wrenching need for a family of her own—were dangerous, and she'd done her best to swallow them at every turn.

"There is nothing to keep you from making a good match with him. He seems fond enough of you as well," Thea said.

Fondness was nice, but would it be enough? Sure, there was desire as well. She'd felt Fielding's hot and demanding desire for her in the way that he kissed her and the way his hands caressed her skin. She shivered with the memory.

"And who wouldn't be?" Thea added. "You are, after all, the most charming girl in all of London."

Esme snorted. "Charming, perhaps some might agree. But none would call me a girl. I am well past marriageable age."

"Poppycock." She turned her back to Esme and pointed at her buttons, which Esme promptly began to undo. "I see announcements in the *Times* of brides twice your age."

"No doubt after burying husband number one, perhaps even two," Esme said, patting her aunt's back to let her know she was done.

Thea stepped out of her gown. "Always an answer for everything, child. Listen to your old aunt; I know love when I see it. And you'd be a damned fool to walk away from it when you have it in your grasp."

Fielding glared at the man behind the large desk. Jensen picked up a glass and took a sip of the amber liquid. "Would you care for a brandy?"

Fielding rubbed the back of his neck. "No."

"You might as well take a seat," Jensen offered.

"How did you—"

"Know you were coming?" Jensen interrupted. "I didn't; I was already here sorting through a stack of membership recommendations." He bent and withdrew a massive leather-bound volume from a drawer and set it on top of the desk. "But I do suspect I know why you're here."

Fielding sat. "I want to know who was there with him."

"The day of the cave-in?" Jensen provided.

"Yes. I know there were two other men with my father. Two other members of Solomon's. But we were never told who."

Jensen inclined his head. He cracked open the book and turned the crisp pages. "Here we are." He turned the book to face Fielding. "Right there," he said, pointing at a section on the left page.

In flourishing penmanship was a recounting of all the steps Fielding's father had taken to research and locate the Templar's Treasure. The final entry, dated September 4, 1873, detailed the trip to Hadrian's Wall his father had taken, and listed his companions on the trip: William Higginsworth and Stephen Piper.

"As you've already been informed, there was a cave-in," Jensen said. "William and Stephen did what they could to pull your father out. When they finally retrieved his body, it was determined that he'd died when a particularly large rock hit his head."

The two names stared up at him. Fielding recognized one of them, Higginsworth; even remembered that he'd been his father's closest friend. And yet after his father had been killed, Higginsworth hadn't bothered to inform his friend's family of exactly what had transpired in that cave.

He'd imagined this moment over and over. It seemed he should feel . . . something. Anticipation or perhaps satisfaction.

Yet for the first time he felt himself questioning his own motives. Would making these men pay for encouraging his father's futile quest really bring Fielding any contentment?

Before he could search his conscience for the answer, Jensen spoke. "I can give you the men's addresses."

"No, I can find them myself," Fielding said.

"It was an accident." For the first time since they'd met, Jensen's voice had an undercurrent of compassion.

He sipped his brandy again. "Going after those men will not bring your father back, nor will it answer all of your questions."

The kindness didn't soothe Fielding; instead it seemed to fuel his anger. "You don't know anything about me," he said.

"I know that you were but a boy when your father was killed, and suddenly you were the man of the family. In one swift moment you had to learn to live without your father while taking on the duty of caring for your mother and sister," Jensen said. "'Tis a lot of responsibility for a boy of seventeen."

Fielding glared at him. "No more than any other heir takes on."

Jensen shrugged noncommittally but then added, "I understand there were some financial difficulties as well."

"It was my father's fault he couldn't pay the bills." It made Fielding uncomfortable to learn how much this man seemed to know about his life. "I didn't see anyone here discouraging him from continuing to spend money we didn't have to chase that bloody dream of his."

"You'll not find the answers you're looking for here," Jensen repeated.

"Far be it for the great and mighty Solomon's to take any responsibility."

"For that, I suggest you look closer to home," Jensen said.

Fielding met the older man's gaze. "What is that supposed to mean?"

"When was the last time you spoke with your mother?"

When Fielding didn't respond, Jensen closed the book, in effect shutting the door on the conversation. "I've treated you fairly, despite the fact that you've entered our facility unlawfully." Gone was the brief flash of compassion, and back in its place was cool indifference. "I will not alert the authorities, Mr. Grey, but I do suggest you depart immediately."

Chapter Nineteen

Fielding wasn't accustomed to taking advice from others, but the very next morning he found himself in the entryway of his mother's home. He'd been unable to dismiss Jensen's suggestion that his mother might have had something to do with their financial ruin. Fielding knew his mother to be a lady of taste and discrimination, yet she lived modestly. There was no chance she'd spent them into ruin.

"Lady Beatrice is in the dining room having her breakfast," the housekeeper told him. "Follow me."

Fielding followed the tall woman down the hall to the back of the house. He remembered from when he'd lived here that his mother preferred to have her morning meal in the east corner of the small home. She enjoyed watching the sun rise.

He entered the room, and immediately his mother rose to her feet. "Fielding, what a surprise. I would not have guessed you'd be up this early."

He kissed her cheek. "You look well, Mother."

She returned to her seat but motioned to the sideboard behind her. "Have some breakfast with me."

"Coffee?" he asked.

"Mrs. Jarvis, please make some coffee for my son." The housekeeper bobbed and withdrew herself through a back door.

"What could possibly bring you out to see me at this hour?" Beatrice asked. "As much as I'd prefer to believe you've come simply to call on me, I know you better than that." His mother was aging well. Her brown hair had grayed around her face and lines mapped out the years of her life, but she was still very much a beautiful woman. "What has it been, Fielding, six months, longer since we last saw each other?"

"I've been out of the country," he said. Although he'd been back from Egypt for nearly three months, he'd been otherwise engaged for most of that time.

She smiled. "Always."

"Mother, I wanted to speak to you about something," Fielding said.

His coffee was delivered by Mrs. Jarvis, and then they were alone again. Despite his reservations about his plan for revenge, he knew someone needed to pay for the hardship his mother had endured. Losing her home and all her belongings had been humiliating. She'd never been the same. Even after Fielding had earned the money and bought back their homes and all their belongings, she'd stayed in this small house that her family had owned. Fielding had always thought she'd in a way been punishing herself.

"I know who was there." Fielding sat beside her and took her hand. "Who was with my father when he was killed. We can finally make them pay for what they did."

Beatrice's delicate features hardened in confusion. "Fielding, what are you talking about? Your father was killed in an accident. It was a cave-in; no one was responsible."

"No. They were there, and they encouraged him to go into that cave."

"As he'd gone into many caves before then." Beatrice looked down at her hands. Hands that had once been smooth and graceful but now were lined and stiff. She shook her head in sadness. "Is this what you've been after this whole time, trying to find someone to pay for your father's death?"

He ignored her questions. She'd simply forgotten what their life had been like before they'd lost everything. "Yes, he'd gone into other caves, had searched this entire bloody continent for a treasure that does not exist." He leaned on the table, willing her to understand. "Those men, the ones who pretended to be his friends, pushed him to do that. To spend every last pence in our accounts."

She was shaking her head. "No," she said firmly. "That isn't true."

Fielding swallowed, his saliva seeming to harden in his mouth. He pulled back from her. "What is it that you've been hiding from me, Mother? Jensen told me to look closer to home; what was he talking about?"

"Yes, yes, Jensen told me you'd accepted a job from them. It would appear the man talks too much." She gave a weak laugh as she reached across the table and covered his hand with hers. "You've been so angry for so long, and I've allowed you to believe what you wanted instead of telling you the truth." Her expression softened. "If you need to be angry with someone, my love, you should be so with me. All of this is my doing." She pushed away from the table and stood.

She gathered her own plates and set them on a tray in the corner of the room. "Your father didn't lose our fortune through his travels and research. He lost the money because he was being blackmailed."

"I don't understand," Fielding heard himself say.

"He was protecting you as well as me." She worried the lace trim lining her neckline. "We should have simply told you the truth." She returned to her seat and took a steadying breath.

"My father never thought of anyone but himself." Fielding stood, determined to leave. There was no need to listen to his mother as she canonized his father. Fielding knew the truth; the man had been selfish.

With her jaw set and her eyes held firm, suddenly she was the mother who'd raised and sometimes chastised him. "You will sit here and hear all I have to say; after that you may decide to leave and not return." She tapped on the table defiantly.

Fielding sat, then drained his coffee and poured himself another cup. He did his best to fend off the restless waves that rocked through his stomach.

"There was once a time when your old mother was thought to be a perfect bride. I was attractive, polite, and I had a sizable dowry. My parents gave me much instruction on making a good match, and I thought I'd found the right one. At least my heart told me so.

"We were passionate about each other, and he was from a good family. It stood to reason that my father would say yes when he went to ask for my hand. I was such a foolish, foolish girl. I believed I was secure. I believed we would be married within months. That–"

She broke off, pressing her hand against her mouth as if to hold in her emotions. "It seemed, though, that my father had already promised me to another earlier that day."

Fielding felt dread skitter along his nerves. It was the same feeling he'd had when he was excavating a tomb and a booby trap was seconds from being triggered. The floor was about to give way.

"Two brothers had been wooing me, and they were both good men. But I was young and foolish, so I of course set my heart for the younger, more dashing and adventurous of the two." She'd gone to stand by the window and had pulled the wispy drapery aside.

Her actions seemed casual. The kind of thing she no doubt did every morning, but her movements couldn't disguise the faint tremble in her hands or dull the importance of her words.

Two brothers, she'd said. And she'd loved the *younger* one. Every cell in his body rebelled against the thought. How could his mother—his delicate and refined mother—have possibly once loved the vile man now known as the Raven?

"Oh, the life we'd planned," she said wistfully. "We'd talked about buying a ship and sailing from one end of the earth to the other, stopping in every exotic port so he could buy me gems and perfumes from every corner of the world."

Fielding listened the way a child would who dreaded the scary bits in an adventure novel, squeamish and un-settled. Part of him wanted to yell at her to stop, but he could not. Fielding knew what was coming, but he had to hear it for himself.

"My parents preferred the more responsible, staid

brother, so when he came and asked for my hand my
father readily agreed. The wedding plans began that af-
ternoon. I'd tried their patience enough, rebelling in the
small ways I could, so when they set me down to inform
me of my pending nuptials, I knew I had no choice. It was
time I accepted my responsibility." She laughed softly,
then turned to face Fielding.

"Besides, I knew your father would be a good husband;
he was so kind and steadfast. I didn't even have the courage to tell David to his face; I sent him a note and hoped
your father would smooth out the rest. But the day our
engagement was announced, David left England. And by
the time you were born, I had grown to love my husband."
She returned to her seat and gathered Fielding's hands in
her own. "Neither of us could ignore the timing, though;
your father was smart enough to do the mathematics."

"I am David's son." *The Raven's son.* Everything inside Fielding seemed to stop moving. His breath stilled;
his heart ceased beating; he was numb.

"Yes," she whispered. "When David returned, he knew
immediately. He came to the house and threatened your
father. I could hear them yelling downstairs and I tried"—
she spoke through her tears—"to speak to him to make
him understand, but the man I'd loved, the man I'd known,
was gone. In his place was an angry, bitter, and frightening man I no longer recognized. He vowed to make your
father pay, and he made good on that promise.

"Two days later the first blackmail letter came." She
swiped at her tears angrily. "That's how we lost all the
money. Your father lost every cent trying to protect you
and me from a scandal that would have robbed you of
your birthright."

"No," he argued futilely. "He spent our fortune hunting

for the Templar Treasure. That's where the money went. He was obsessed."

"Yes, and no. Your father was a scholar; he loved history and the legend of the Templar's Treasure. Truthfully, I believe he tried to become someone he wasn't for my benefit, tried to make me fall in love with him by being more adventurous and daring. I tried to convince him that I loved him as he was, but by the time the blackmail started and we needed the money, he would not listen to reason. He was certain he'd find it and he would be able to pay off his brother, but, well, you know how that ended. And then you went to work for David . . ."

"I didn't know," he said. "But in doing so I bought everything back; I purchased every last thing that we'd lost."

"The only reason you were able to purchase those things was because I made David promise he'd allow you to."

"I don't understand," Fielding said. "I paid the bank for those properties."

"Yes, but David owned them," his mother explained. "He'd bought up everything before your father died, planned to continue to control us by that means once the blackmailing funds ran out. But I didn't want you to know. I convinced David to sell you everything through the bank. I thought I was doing the right thing," she said softly.

Fielding flinched as if she'd struck him. He grabbed the table and felt the edge of the wood dig into his palm. All that time he'd spent working for his uncle. When he'd come to Fielding's school to get him after his father had died. Memories flashed through his mind, curdling his stomach and flaming his anger.

"I know you've blamed your father for years for the

financial problems, looked to Solomon's for an explanation; but the truth is, they were never involved. Those men were friends to your father. They even gave us money, bought this house that I live in." She squeezed his hand. "Do not go looking for revenge with any of those men."

When he and his mother and sister had moved into this smaller house on the edge of Mayfield after they'd lost everything, his mother had told him it had been her family's. Another lie. Everything he'd been told, everything he'd ever believed—it was all lies.

"Do you ever see him?" Fielding asked, unsure if he actually wanted to hear the answer.

"No." Her voice was soft, barely more than a whisper. "I went and saw him after your father died, when you started working for him. But that was the last time." She grabbed Fielding's hand. "And that was only because of you. It's all been for you."

Fielding slid his hand out from beneath hers. She slumped against the back of her chair, folded her hands in her lap. "I'll be here if you have any more questions."

He made no move to stand, to leave. But there was nothing else he wanted to ask.

"Jensen tells me you've met your match with Miss Worthington," his mother said.

"You're right, Jensen does talk too much."

A part of him *had* thought he'd met his match with Esme. Hell, he'd been ready to marry her. But now, with all of this, he was more certain than ever that Esme deserved so much more than he was: a bastard masquerading as a viscount.

Chapter Twenty

❦

Esme wasn't accustomed to bathing in the morning, but she had gone to bed so late last night, lying awake waiting for Fielding to come home, that she'd fallen asleep on the window seat in all of her clothes. This morning she'd awoken to find herself quite chilled and sore. When Annette had suggested a warm soak, Esme hadn't been able to say no.

With a sigh, Esme settled into the soothing warm water, relishing the scent of lilac that stirred around her.

Thea had warned her not to walk away from love. *Love.*

But she did not love Fielding, did she? Admittedly, he was handsome. She would, no doubt, have thought that regardless of the bracelet. She respected him. Perhaps admired him. She certainly found him most agreeable. And though it had only been one evening, she'd missed him terribly last night.

One by one, memories flashed through her mind: Fielding rescuing her from the dungeon, traipsing all over

London looking for a way to remove her curse, finding Thea's lost love, even his visit to Elena and Raymond to let them know she was safe, touching her, making love to her . . . He'd been more than her rescuer.

Her hand flew to her mouth.

Oh, no!

She sank under the water. She *had* fallen in love with him.

She came out of the water sputtering.

What was she supposed to do now?

A knock sounded from her bedchamber door. Annette was eager to please, which was very sweet, but annoying when one needed private time. Like now, when Esme was currently having a bit of a crisis.

A knock again, then the door opened.

"Annette, I don't need—" Her words died in her throat as she saw Fielding standing there.

His eyes darkened as they took in her naked body half immersed in water. "I didn't mean to interrupt your bath." He turned as if he meant to leave, but he made no further movement. Standing there, Esme watched some sort of battle play across Fielding's features.

"Fielding?" she asked.

He met her glance, and again she could see pain shrouding his eyes. Without a word, he shut the door, then locked it.

Her heart sped, beating so loudly she couldn't think clearly.

"I should get out," she said, leaning over the tub to reach for the waiting towel.

He stilled her arm. "Lean forward." He knelt beside the tub, paying no mind to the water droplets that would dampen his pants. After pushing up both sleeves, he reached in behind her and grabbed the sponge. "Close your eyes."

She did as he bade. Thick currents of warm water slid down her back. Again and again he squeezed the sponge over her skin. He lathered the sponge, then gently slid the suds across her back. Ever so slowly, he moved over her shoulders, down her arms. Esme felt the tension ooze from her body. In its place settled intimate awareness, and with every pass of his hand her flesh craved more.

"What has your maid said of your tattoos?" he asked. His finger trailed across the words imprinted on her lower back.

"She has not seen them. I won't allow her to assist dressing me until I have my shift on. And I haven't worn my hair up since."

His soft chuckle whispered across her skin like a caress.

"Lean back," he urged.

She rested her neck against the tub's copper edge, all the while keeping her eyes closed.

He picked up her right leg and ran the sponge down the length, stopping short of her mid-thigh. The left leg received the same treatment. Esme's pulse quickened and desire coiled through her, warming her and melting her blood.

The sponge slid between her breasts, leaving a trail of sudsy water across her skin. A droplet slid across her left nipple and it hardened instantly. The next touch came from his hand instead of the sponge.

Esme opened her eyes, but he was not looking at her face. Instead he was intently focused on her body. She knew it couldn't be true, but in that moment what she saw etched in Fielding's features was not desire. His glance was much softer as he stroked his soaped hands across her abdomen.

He swallowed, then licked his lips.

Was it possible that Fielding loved her too? Without thought, she reached up and cupped his face. Smoldering brown eyes met hers, and then he leaned in for a kiss. A second later she was dripping water across the floor as he carried her to the bed.

Since girlhood she'd believed her bookish ways would be unappealing to any man. She believed she lacked some basic element of femininity. But with Fielding, a lifetime of doubts simply dissolved.

No woman could have felt more beautiful or more desired than Esme did in that moment. Gently he placed her on the bed, covering her with his own body.

"I want you." His hot breath teased her ear.

"I want you too," she said.

His arousal strained against his trousers, pressing into her stomach. She tugged on his shirt, and in answer he stood to remove his clothing. Once before she'd seen Fielding's body, but this morning she took a moment to fully appreciate him.

Broad shoulders with clearly visible muscles that flexed as his arms moved. Dark hair sprinkled over his chest, then tapered to a thin line that trailed down the center of his abdomen and ended in the curls surrounding his erection. Long, strong legs slipped the rest of the way out of his trousers.

"You're staring," he said.

"Perhaps. You're worth such close inspection."

He crawled into the bed next to her, the warmth of his skin covering hers.

She pulled his head down for another passionate

kiss. She could drink from him for hours. Their mouths mated, increasing the arousal within her. Her body sang with sensitivity as he trailed his fingers down her waist to her hip.

His kiss moved from her mouth, down her shoulder to her breast. He laved the swollen tip until she arched with need. Still he did not stop his sweet torture. His wet, seductive tongue made quick work of her stomach, dipping once into her navel, before licking down to her waist. She clamped her hands onto the bed, grabbing fistfuls of the sheets as he nipped over her waist and across her hip until he hovered over her center.

With his fingers, he parted the curls at the juncture of her thighs and thumbed the sensitive nub hidden there. She cried out.

"Shhhh," he whispered.

Even with the light streaming in through the windows, she'd forgotten that it was morning and that people were awake and moving about in the house.

Again he flicked a touch over her aching center. Before she could respond, his mouth was on her. Hot, wet, and so sinfully delicious she forgot her name. Her mouth fell open as she pressed her head into the pillow beneath her. He suckled her, then slid one finger inside. Pleasure surged through her.

The rhythm of his mouth and hand were lost to her as she stopped paying attention to what he was doing and focused on how his touch made her body feel. Tension climbed inside her, and every part of her tightened as if she was bracing for a strike. Then the pleasure boiled over, starting in her center and shooting through her body.

Before the waves had ceased he was inside her. She was slick with desire and felt none of the pinch or discomfort she had experienced the last time they made love. Her body still shook with release as he built her up again, stroking and pulsing inside her.

The cords in his neck tightened. Low, guttural sounds came from his throat. One more thrust and his eyes squeezed shut. His release pushed her right over the edge again, and together they rocked with pleasure.

"I love you, Fielding," she whispered.

He stilled and rolled off her. Instantly, air wafted across her naked body, cooling her skin. But it was his words that chilled her to the bone.

"No," he muttered. "You can't love me."

Her eyes flared with anger. She sat and held the pillow to her chest. "What do you mean, I *can't* love you? I'm a grown woman; I should think I can do what I choose."

Fielding stood and pulled on his trousers. He was the worst sort of ass. He'd come here to tell her about the reversal of the curse, but he'd taken one look at her in that bathtub and lost his mind. Suddenly all he could think about was what his mother had told him. He was David's son. *The Raven's* son. And he'd needed to forget, needed to lose himself in Esme's light.

Now Esme fancied herself in love with him. In love with a man he could never be. He was no better than the Raven. They were cut from the same cloth; the Raven's blood ran through his veins.

She looked so small huddled in the large bed, clutching a pillow to her chest. Her still-damp hair lay in soft curls around her head. God, she was so beautiful, so fragile. But he knew that no matter how much he tried, he could never be the man she wanted him to be.

He'd wanted to believe he could, but his mother's

revelation had confirmed otherwise. How could he settle down and be a good husband, when neither the man who'd sired him nor the one who'd raised him had been able to make his mother happy? He had to end this now, before he did more than break Esme's heart.

"I don't love you," he said. Though as he said the words, his heart seized in his chest.

She forced herself to swallow the tears forming in her eyes. "Why did you come here this morning?" Her voice was brittle.

He cleared his throat in hopes that he could dissolve the emotion clinging there. "The diary is wrong. About the bracelets and their curse." That's not what he wanted to say. He longed to tell her the truth about who he was. But he was too afraid of her reaction. He was revolted by the idea himself. Esme, with her scholarly ethics, would be repulsed by the knowledge that he was the Raven's son—that she had just made love with the spawn of the devil himself.

Her expression pinched as she looked down at the bracelet. "I'm wearing this thing, and you can attest to the fact that I can't remove it."

"Yes. That isn't the part I was referring to," he said.

She pulled the heavy coverlet up around her, creating more of a boundary between them. "Please say what you came to say, then leave me with the only shred of dignity I have left."

He started to take a step forward, but he stopped himself. "I found Waters last night."

"Is he here?" she asked.

"No." He shook his head. "But I noticed something. Something perhaps we should have considered before." He rubbed his forehead. "Everyone in the pub was ill.

Then the moment Waters walked in, their illnesses became even worse. Visibly so."

Her frown deepened.

"Even the serving girl, Minnie, said something about business being slow. The crowd had thinned considerably from the last time we were there. When I asked her where everyone was, she said they were all sick. She looked rather ill as well." He shook his head, trying to rid his mind of the memory of what he'd seen.

"I don't understand." She shook her head. "Fielding, what are you trying to say?"

"The bracelets don't curse the wearer, they curse those around them." When she said nothing, he sat on the edge of the bed. "Waters must be wearing the band of disease."

"That can't be," she whispered. Her eyes had widened with shock, her skin gone impossibly pale.

"Do you know what this means?" he asked.

"I do," she said quietly. She did not move, simply sat there staring down at her own bracelet as if looking for an explanation or confirmation. "It means that all the while I was losing my heart to you, all the times you let me touch you, that you touched me in return . . ." Her voice hitched. "When you made love to me, you only did so because you were under some sort of spell." She looked up at him, her eyes filled with tears and sorrow, but when she spoke her voice was steely with resolve. "Get out."

He hadn't even denied it. Esme flung herself back on her bed and stared up at the painted ceiling. Fielding didn't want her, at least he wouldn't want her once she took off the bracelet. And she'd professed her love to him. Her cheeks flamed with humiliation.

She truly loved him. After all, she had not been affected by the curse. She had no other excuse for her behavior.

All the things she'd done. Pressing herself against him, kissing him, sitting on his lap, all with no provocation on his part.

It mattered not that she had honestly believed herself to be under the power of the bracelet, unable to control her inner desires. Had she been using the curse only as an excuse to behave as badly as she wanted? Had it been nothing other than some secret wanton behavior she'd hidden away for years? Thank goodness she didn't wear a band of anger; no telling what she would have done.

She'd told him she loved him, and despite his reaction, despite the curse, she meant it. For a moment, she'd thought she'd seen love shining in his eyes, but that had been nothing but a cruel trick of the fates. It had been nothing but his reaction to the damned curse.

And that reaction did beg a certain question: Why had Fielding responded so strongly to her band, yet none of the other men she'd encountered, such as Max or the men from the dinner party, had a similar reaction? Granted, she hadn't acted the wanton with anyone else; still, their lack of response was curious. Putting her bare feet to the floor, Esme contemplated what she knew she had to do.

It was beyond time to remove this bloody band. Not only had she lost her heart, but with the upcoming eclipse, she was dangerously close to losing her life as well.

Chapter Twenty-one

~~~~~~

Fielding tightened his coat around him, making sure the diary was well hidden as he climbed the steps to the British Museum. This time he had no intention of breaking in or staying past business hours. He could very well have simply sent the diary back to them by post, anonymously, of course, but for Esme's sake he wanted to return the book himself. Make certain it was put back where they found it.

Using a fictitious name, he'd scheduled a meeting with the curator to discuss a potential donation. The diary weighed heavy in his inner coat pocket. All he needed to do was cause some sort of distraction so he could deposit the book unseen.

It was the least he could do for her after he'd treated her so shabbily. He wanted to believe that she truly loved him, but he knew it was only something she'd convinced herself of because of their circumstances. Hurting her now would be far better than causing her pain every day over a lifetime together.

*   *   *

Esme was unsure of where Fielding had gone today, but his absence made her own plans all the easier. Mr. Nichols's death meant Mr. Brown was most certainly in danger. She'd received correspondence from him in this morning's *Times*, and currently she was on her way to their meeting destination.

His note had suggested she go to the east corner of Hyde Park. She scanned the park benches but found no one who seemed to be looking for her.

"Miss Worthington?" a voice came from behind her.

"Yes." She turned to find a young man wearing a red-and-black livery standing there. He was fresh-faced and smiling warmly.

"I have your carriage ready," he said. "Mr. Brown sent me."

"He was supposed to meet me here in the park." For one second she paused, uncertain if she should go. Mr. Brown had approached Mr. Nichols regarding his research. Their correspondence had proved so mutually helpful that eventually Mr. Nichols had invited him to join his ongoing cryptic discussions with Esme via the *Times*. If Mr. Nichols could trust him, then so could she.

"Yes, but my employer suggested it might be safer for you to discuss these delicate issues in a more private place." The young man gave her a sheepish grin. "I believe he's actually too afraid to leave the house."

Of course he was; he had good reason to be. It pleased her that he was heeding her warning. She nodded, then followed the boy to the carriage. Two large steeds stomped impatiently.

Nearly twenty minutes later they traveled through two large iron gates on a drive that circled in front of a sprawling estate just on the outskirts of London. Far enough from the city to take up more than just vertical space, it was as high as it was wide. With its parapets and sharp towers, it looked ominous and foreboding as it stretched up to meet the heavy morning clouds. Gargoyles watched over the grayish-green stone like little demons waiting to pounce.

She'd had no idea Mr. Brown was so wealthy. Or had such Gothic taste.

The carriage door was flung open, and a chilled wind swirled around her. She clutched her cloak tighter.

"Miss Worthington." The driver held his hand out to her.

He ushered her safely inside a second before the clouds opened and rain fell in heavy sheets. "Thank goodness we made it inside safely," she said. But the boy had disappeared. In his place stood an elderly butler.

He gripped her arm and pulled her forward.

"Unhand me, sir." Esme jerked her arm away from the short, crooked man. "I am quite capable of walking on my own."

The old man gave her a disgusted look but allowed her to walk freely. She followed him through a long hall until they came to some double-wood doors that opened into a large room. After she stepped inside, the nasty little man closed both doors behind her. They shut with an echoing thud that mirrored the dread lying heavy in her stomach. Perhaps she should not have come alone.

The plush Persian rug softened her steps as she walked farther into the room. Ornately carved chairs with more swirls and curves than she could count sat scattered throughout the space. Their embellishments were enhanced by the garish blue-velvet upholstery.

Slowly she walked the perimeter, scanning her environment. A mahogany desk, as ornamental as the chairs, took up most of the back quarter of the room. Hanging directly behind the large piece of furniture was what looked to be a medieval sword; the blade shimmered as if recently sharpened. A collection of smaller knives and daggers flanked the sword on every side. Evidently her host had an appreciation for old weaponry.

She had just taken a seat when she glanced at the crest above the fireplace.

A large black bird on a red background.

Oh, God. What had she done? She stood and started for the door.

"How nice of you to join me, Esme." The Raven stepped out of the shadows. "Welcome to Black Manor. I rarely get visitors, so this is a treat."

She turned to face him. "How did you know I'd be in the park today?"

The expression that crossed his features was one of sheer disappointment. He turned his back to her and made his way to the brandy tray.

"It's been you all along. You're Mr. Brown." She sank back into the tightly padded chair. "That's how you knew I had the key."

"Because you told me," he said, pointing his brandy snifter in her direction. "And there was that time in the library. You told me all about your pendant."

It *had* been him and she'd simply forgotten his face. She'd been a fool.

"I admit it did take some doing to uncover your true identity," the Raven said. "Mr. Spencer only got me so far; clever of you to use your father's first name like that."

"You killed Mr. Nichols," she said. Her stomach turned over as she said it. This was her fault. All her fault.

"I'm afraid I did," he said casually, as if he were admitting that he'd stolen the last biscuit.

"Are you to kill me as well?" She did her best to keep her tone even but knew she failed, knew he could smell her fear as a predator sniffed out its prey. She shuddered.

"It is always a possibility, but I suspect it won't come to that. Fielding does seem rather fond of you. Perhaps he'll rescue you." He sipped his brandy, rolling it around on his tongue with obvious relish. "Yes, you'd make a tasty bit of cheese with which to set my trap."

"Is that what you're counting on?" she asked. "That he'll come here and make some sort of bargain with you to save me? I can assure you that despite what you must believe, Fielding harbors no tender feelings toward me."

"Well, then, perhaps I will have to kill you." He stepped into the hall. She could hear him murmuring but could not decipher any of his words. A moment later he reentered, this time with a familiar man following behind him.

"Ah, Miss Worthington, I believe you've met Thatcher."

"Unfortunately, yes."

Thatcher looked much as he had the night he'd kidnapped her. Dressed head to toe in black; long, unkempt hair tied at the base of his neck. He winked at her lasciviously as he passed by.

How was she to get herself out of this mess? Panic began to claw its way through her belly, but she forced herself to calm down. Hysterics had never solved anything. She needed her wits about her if she was to survive this. If the Raven had wanted her dead, wouldn't he have already killed her? Hoping that thought would soothe her nerves, Esme tried to lean back into the vulgar chair.

The two men stood over by the sizable desk and talked

quietly. She strained to hear what they were saying but couldn't make out their conversation.

The Raven bent down and retrieved a large rolled-up piece of parchment, perhaps a map of some sort, which he let spread across the desk. Both men motioned to different places on the paper, but only the Raven spoke. Though she did her best to eavesdrop, Esme was able to make out only the words *guards* and *majesty*.

Thatcher put both hands down and leaned forward casually. The gold band shimmered against his tan skin. She longed to get close to it, read the inscription, but she didn't dare move.

She wasn't the only one who'd noticed. The Raven stopped talking and stared intently at the bracelet.

"Take it off," he muttered.

Thatcher's face pinched with confusion.

The Raven reached over and grabbed Thatcher's arm; he tugged on the bracelet. "Why won't it come off?"

"I told you, I've tried everything," Thatcher said. He pulled his arm back.

Esme momentarily thought about volunteering the information Fielding had uncovered about the curse's effect, but she decided to keep it to herself.

"What are you planning to do?" Esme asked, still curious about the map.

"We have a brilliant plan," Thatcher said. "We are going to—"

"Careful, Thatcher," the Raven warned. The man's eyes again were drawn to the bracelet.

It had to be greed, Esme realized. Every time the Raven saw the band, he couldn't help looking at it. In the carriage, with her own band, he hadn't tried to take it off her, but he had touched her, more than once, perhaps afflicted with a touch of lust in that short amount of time. And in the previous meeting with her, he'd seemed calm, as if he was utterly in control of not only himself, but her as well. And now, it was the greed bracelet that was seducing him.

"You'll have to wait and see what we're going to do," Thatcher continued. "We've got it all figured out, though. We—"

"*We?*" the Raven roared. "We? There is no we. This is my plan. And you work for me." With the last word, he pulled the sword off the wall and in one clean stroke brought it down onto Thatcher's hand. Blood sprayed over the desk, creating a red-splotched pattern across the map.

Thatcher howled in pain and fell to the floor, holding a bloody stump where his hand had been. Esme caught her own scream as she pressed both hands to her mouth. Her heart raced to a degree she wasn't certain would allow it to ever slow again.

"No we," the Raven repeated. He plucked Thatcher's hand from his desk. "I don't know why I didn't think of this before."

Esme watched in horror as the Raven tried to pull the bracelet off the severed hand, but as if there were an unseen barrier, it would not budge.

Thatcher continued to scream in pain.

"Quiet!" the Raven growled.

Tears streaming down his face, Thatcher cradled his bloody arm to his chest and rocked back and forth against the desk.

The Raven swore loudly. "The bloody thing still won't come off." He stepped around the desk to loom over

Thatcher. "You are worthless," he said. With one quick thrust, he sank the sword into Thatcher's chest.

This time Esme was not able to silence her own scream.

"I suppose his hand will work just as well. I need only the band," the Raven said. He took several steps toward Esme.

She swallowed the fear choking her as fast as she could, yet she was unable to get it all down.

"Do you have something to say, Miss Worthington?"

She shook her head fervently.

"Good." He pulled a bell cord hanging in the corner. The butler reappeared in the doorway. He silently eyed Thatcher's body, maimed and bloody. "Take Miss Worthington to the north tower. I have no further use for her at the moment. Then clean this up while I ready us to leave."

Fielding leaned against the closed door and exhaled slowly. He'd been a complete ass. He should go and apologize. Tell her he'd returned the diary. But he knew he wouldn't. This was for Esme's own good.

As long as she was in his life, she was in danger. The Raven would use her against Fielding, and he wouldn't always be able to protect her.

Pandora's box lay hidden in the bottom of a travel chest in his room. He pulled it out to examine it. The ornate carvings of the gods and goddesses were so intricate and detailed, it seemed unlikely they were made with human hands.

Every turn they'd taken since finding the box seemed to lead to the unbelievable. The stuff of novels and fairy tales, not modern-day England. Yet, there was part of him that very much felt as if he'd been under some sort of curse. Only it wasn't lust he'd been afflicted with, but rather love for a woman he couldn't truly have because he didn't deserve her.

And in the end the Raven would do what he could to retrieve the box. Not only that, but they were now only one day away from the lunar eclipse. Fielding couldn't allow Esme to face her fate alone.

He withdrew the key from his pocket. Esme had not noticed him swipe it from her bedside table yesterday after their argument. With a click, the box opened, and Fielding reached inside.

He felt the final bracelet latch onto his wrist. Now they were in this together. The Raven couldn't get any of the bracelets off without Fielding present. And if worse came to worst, he and Esme would face the end together.

Chapter Twenty-two

A knock sounded on his bedchamber door the following morning. Fielding rose, and upon opening the door found Thea standing there, her hands knotted in an old handkerchief.

"Is Esme with you?" she asked.

"No, I haven't seen her all day. I went out for a while earlier and thought she was still abed." Actually, he'd assumed she was still in her room avoiding him.

"She's not in her room," Thea said with a choked sob. "And her maid hasn't seen her since yesterday morning. I think something dreadful has happened."

Alarm spread through Fielding. "You know Esme; she probably went for a walk on the grounds," he said, trying to soothe the older woman.

"You have to do something," Thea pleaded.

He squeezed the woman's arm, then stepped around her and into the hall. "I'll take care of it."

Twenty minutes later he'd scoured the house and found no sign of Esme. Only one servant, a footman, remembered seeing her leave the house in her cloak around eleven-thirty the previous morning. Fielding had already left for the museum by then.

He glanced at the clock in the hall, quarter of seven. The Raven had her; it was the only explanation. He climbed the stairs back to his room and threw open the packing trunk. There was only one way to get her back. He pulled out the box and dropped it into a bag. Five minutes later he was in a borrowed coach on his way to Black Manor.

He'd never known his uncle to harm a woman. The man had done his share of wretched things, the least of which might include murdering Mr. Nichols, but Fielding had never seen him take advantage of a lady. Once upon a time his own mother had loved the Raven; surely that meant a heart beat inside the man's chest.

The carriage had not even rolled to a complete stop before Fielding had jumped down and scaled the steps. A quick pound on the door, and the butler had given him entrance. "Where are they?" he demanded.

"The master of the house is out," the butler said.

Fielding grabbed the old man by his jacket and held him up to his face; the servant's breath was sour with age. "Tell me where they are."

The only sign that the butler felt threatened was the slow swallow he made before he spoke. "I do not know where he went."

With one last look, Fielding shoved the old man away from him and left the house. Where the hell would the Raven take her?

"I trust you're comfortable," the Raven asked, though he couldn't have expected an answer considering he'd gagged Esme before they'd left his estate. She was crouched on a dirty wooden floor in an old house with no fire and only two lamps to light the room. The Raven eyed her as if he did in fact want her to answer. So she merely nodded.

She had no idea where they were. At some point after he'd ordered her held in the tower room, that old butler had brought her back downstairs, and the Raven had tied her up and tossed her into the back of a carriage. The room they were in now was not large and sparsely furnished, holding only the small wooden table the Raven currently sat near, and two chairs.

"Do you know what this place is?" he asked. He came to his feet then and spread his arms out to encompass the room. "This was my home at one time." He looked down at her. "I know it's hard to imagine, considering the house I live in now. But there was a time when I'd lost my inheritance at the tables playing cards, and my brother wouldn't give me another dime." He shook his head. "No, he had a family to care for."

Esme eyed the door and momentarily considered attempting to run while he was distracted, but with her ankles strapped together, she doubted she would get far.

"Without my brother's aid, I had to move here and start over. But I did it." He pointed at her. "First I acquired and sold one antiquity, and then another, and the fees I earned impressed even me. In less than a year I was able to move out of this hovel, but I never sold it. No, I wanted a reminder of where I'd come from." He smiled broadly at her. "Impressive, isn't it?"

She nodded fervently.

He stood above her and pulled her to her feet. "You are most agreeable, Miss Worthington. I like that in a woman." He pulled her into the next room and tossed her down on a dirty feather mattress. "You need to get your rest. I have plans for you later."

Fielding was trying, in vain, not to panic. The Raven was simply toying with him, sending him on a chase just to remind Fielding who had the upper hand. He'd searched his mind, trying to think of anywhere the man would take Esme. At the moment he'd stopped at Thatcher's house, a two-story brick townhome near Piccadilly Square.

Fielding tore through the front door. "Thatcher!" But there was no answer. He checked every room on both floors, but he found no sign of Esme. Fielding picked up a lamp and slammed it into a wall, the glass shattering and oil spilling all over the floor.

He swore loudly, then raked his fingers through his hair. *Think*. Where could he have taken her?

Waters's place was out of the question as the man never stayed in one place for very long. He was content to rent rooms here and there and spend his money on women and ale.

Then an idea hit him. It would fit in with the Raven's desire to taunt him. Fielding jumped back onto the rig and grabbed the reins from the startled driver. The chilled night wind bit at his face and made him wish he'd thought to bring his greatcoat, but his own comfort didn't matter right now. He'd promised Thea he'd bring Esme back safely, and he'd be damned if he wouldn't make good on that vow.

Fifteen minutes later he pulled the horses to a stop in front of his own townhome. Not a single light shone through any of the windows; still, they could be in there. The Raven would likely move here to Fielding's house for his own amusement, see how long it took Fielding to locate them. But as he searched through the darkened rooms, he found no sign of life.

His every nerve was on alert, waiting for any indication that Esme was nearby. He knew he'd smell her lilac-scented hair or hear the melodic tone of her voice. If she was here, wouldn't he be able to feel her, sense her somehow?

Fielding swore loudly, his voice echoing through the empty halls of his home. "Esme," he whispered. He fell to his knees. For several moments he stayed in that position. And then, as if the answer had been whispered in his ear, he knew immediately where the Raven had taken her.

He only prayed he wasn't too late.

Fielding slowed the carriage to a halt two blocks from the house. The element of surprise might give him an edge he desperately needed. He hopped down and snuck quietly through the darkness toward the small wooden structure at the edge of the pier. In the distance waves from the Thames lapped softly against the shoreline.

Boats creaked, rocking against the piers in a rhythmic beat. The moon hung heavy and low in the sky, lighting his path but also reminding him of the ticking clock he and Esme were facing. The eclipse was only one day away. They were running out of time.

Fielding made it to the small house and pressed himself against the outer wall. Inside he could see the flickering of an oil lamp. They were here. He felt sure of it.

He pulled the pistol from the back of his pants as he crept to the entrance. One, two, three, then he slammed his shoulder against the door. It crashed to the floor, and he held his arms steady as he let his gun lead the way inside.

"I told Miss Worthington you would come for her." The Raven's slick voice came from the dimly lit room.

"Where the hell is she?" Fielding grounded out.

"She didn't believe me, though," he continued. "Claimed you had no tender feelings for her."

Guilt stabbed at Fielding's gut. She'd been abducted yet again, brought to this tiny home where she probably thought she was going to die, and she didn't know how Fielding felt about her. In his mad desire for her, he had used her body but offered no solace to her heart.

The Raven stepped out of the shadows, and Fielding was faced with the image of his lineage for the first time since discovering the truth. For years Fielding had noted physical similarities between himself and the Raven—their height, for one. Though Fielding had always thought he got his eyes from the man he'd believed to be his father, the rest of his facial features were quite similar to those of the man standing before him.

"She's safe," the Raven said. Fielding noted a bloodied rag encased in his uncle's hand.

"What the hell is that?" he asked, pointing.

An unnatural laugh came from the Raven's throat. "What's left of your old friend Thatcher."

He'd killed him. Just as he'd killed Mr. Nichols. Had he done the same to Esme? Nausea crashed through Fielding. "I want to see Esme," he said. This was his father, Fielding reminded himself. It was on his tongue to tell the Raven, to let him know that Fielding knew. But that would give him too much pleasure. Had the man not destroyed his family simply by holding that secret over their heads? No, there was no reason for him to know that Fielding knew the truth.

"In due time. Tell me, did you reconsider my offer?

Have you come back to work? Because as you can see"—he held out the offensive mass, and Fielding finally realized it was a severed hand—"I'm down to one employee." Again he laughed.

Fear ate at his stomach, but he refused to let the Raven see it. "There is nothing in this world that would make me work for you again," Fielding said.

"Pity." He leaned against the doorjamb of a connecting room. "Still, you must know I'm not going to hand her over for nothing. You must know me better than that, boy."

"I have what you want. It's yours, once I have Esme safe with me."

The Raven stood straight. "Pandora's box? You will trade the box for the girl?" His eyebrows arched. "And she was so certain you wouldn't. Interesting."

"The condition being that you will never again go anywhere near her. Is that understood?" Fielding asked.

"You are becoming quite the romantic." The Raven exhaled slowly. "I do believe you've got yourself a bargain. Show me the box."

"First, bring me Esme." And just to prove to the Raven that Fielding was serious, he cocked the gun, allowing the bullet to roll into the barrel.

Both eyebrows rose. "You intend to shoot me?" the Raven asked.

"Merely a precaution," Fielding said. "I don't precisely trust your word."

"Suit yourself." He stepped out of the room for a moment, then returned pulling Esme by her elbow.

Aside from her red-rimmed eyes, she looked unscathed. And she held her head high with an inherent dignity that made Fielding proud, despite the gag and her tied limbs.

Relief washed over him so forcefully he came close to dropping the gun. But he couldn't afford to lose his concentration; he needed to get her out of here first. "Untie her," Fielding demanded.

The Raven did as he was told.

"Fielding," she said.

Fielding held out his hand. "Esme, come here."

He didn't have to ask twice, and she was there close to his side. Her scent of lilac permeated his senses, and he sent up a silent prayer, thankful she was in one piece.

Once she was safely behind him, he turned his attention back to the Raven. "Catch," he said, then he tossed the bag into the air.

Once they were rolling down the street, Fielding pulled Esme close to him.

"You scared me," he whispered.

"I was rather terrified myself." She looked up into his eyes. "Not initially. I didn't think he would harm me." A frown shrouded her face. "But then he got so angry with Thatcher. He just pulled that sword off the wall"—her voice hitched—"and cut Thatcher's hand off." She snuggled closer. "The bracelet still wouldn't come off. That's when he killed him."

"I fear the Raven has lost his mind," Fielding said.

"I believe he's going after Her Majesty," Esme said.

"The queen? He'd have to be mad. He'll be killed if he tries to get anywhere near her," Fielding said.

"Fielding, he is mad." She shook her head. "That bracelet, the one Thatcher was wearing, it carries the curse of greed. You should have seen him. He was out of control. I realize I'd only met him once before, but that night in the carriage, he was cold, yes, but calm, completely steady.

Earlier tonight, though, he was erratic, impulsive; it had to have been the effect of the bracelet. He's already killed two people; what would stop him from aiming for the queen?"

"I don't know, but something doesn't fit. There would be no purpose in killing her. That would get him nothing. He only pursues things that will bring him something in return—wealth, power."

The Raven had gone after one of his own men, shown him no mercy, and brutally murdered him. Had Fielding not arrived, what would have happened to Esme? He squeezed her tight to his side.

"You gave him the box, didn't you?" she asked. "Traded it for my safety."

"I couldn't risk him harming you," Fielding said, his own voice sounding fierce and raw. "Esme, he will always be able to use you to get to me. I can't allow that. You'll never be safe."

She leaned over and kissed his cheek, then his mouth. "I'm safe now," she murmured. Then she kissed him again, holding nothing back.

God, how he wanted this woman. And he'd almost lost her. The thought squeezed at his throat, threatening to steal his breath. He cradled her face in his palms and deepened the kiss.

She broke it off and met his eyes. "When this curse is removed"—she gripped the bracelet—"if we can get it off in time, you will finally be able to see me as the woman I truly am. I want—"

"I know you believe I've been under some kind of spell," he interrupted. "Esme, there is nothing false about the desire I feel for you."

He pulled her to him. His mouth met hers in a hungry

kiss, and he forgot all about curses and bracelets and quests. In that moment there was only Esme. Pure, sweet, hot, lovely Esme.

His hand dipped into the front of her bodice and found her nipple. She was safe, and in this moment, she was his.

She cried out and arched against him. "Oh, Fielding."

His hand continued to rub at the aching nub all the while he nibbled on her collarbone. Her bodice dipped low, and in an instant his mouth was on her breast, soft, round, and sinful. There was no time to think. He wanted only to touch, to feel.

While his lips and teeth made love to her left breast, his hand weighed her right carefully, his thumb rubbing back and forth over the nipple. She bucked against him. He knew she was looking for her release, trying to feel him through the layers of her skirts.

"Easy, love. We'll get there. I know what you need."

"Touch me, please." He pulled her to him and suckled hard on her breast. Her cry nearly pulled him right over the edge.

Then his hand was on her thigh, warm and strong. His finger slid up inside her and she bucked against him. His mouth returned to her breast, and again he suckled, all the while moving his finger inside her.

"You are the most beautiful woman in the world," he whispered.

She parted her legs, further opening herself to him, and the last shred of his restraint dissolved. He had to have her right then. In one swift movement, he'd unfastened his trousers and positioned himself at her opening. She didn't give him warning or time to think before she'd slid herself down on top of him. She was slick for him, and sitting atop him drove him deep inside her.

His control had disappeared, but she didn't seem to notice or care. Instead she took the reins and set her own pace as she rocked herself over him again and again. She fit him so tightly, and the friction built his climax so quickly he could scarcely breathe.

"Oh, God, Esme," he panted.

Faster and harder she rode him, until she tossed her head back and yelled his name. Her body shook with her release. It took only one more thrust before he spilled his seed.

Their labored breathing filled the interior of the coach. He held her tight, not yet wanting to relinquish the moment. Right here in his arms, she could be his.

She put her hand over his wrist, directly on the band. "When did you do this?" she whispered.

"It doesn't matter."

"Why, Fielding? Why would you risk your life like this?" Her green eyes searched his.

"I won't allow you to face this alone. I'm with you in this, Esme, until the end."

Later that night there had been no argument about whether or not Esme would go with Fielding to find Waters. Since they'd left the Raven's earlier, Fielding had not let her out of his sight. Even when she'd taken a warm bath to wash off the filth and to try, for a moment, to forget the horrors she'd seen, Fielding had been right by her side.

Despite her longing to curl up in her bed and forget all about what had happened, finding Waters couldn't wait any longer. The eclipse was tomorrow, and without him by their side, they wouldn't have a chance at breaking the curse. They hadn't talked about Thatcher's bracelet and the fact that they'd need his hand to complete the task.

It was understood that they needed to steal the box back from the Raven, and they'd need that fourth band.

"We are getting rather accomplished at skulking around in the dark," Esme whispered.

"Shhhh." Fielding pulled her closer to his body, closer to the brick wall they were leaning against.

They'd found Waters at the same little pub and had followed him into another one. At the moment, though, Waters stood on the street, relieving himself in a drunken stupor.

Their plan was simple: follow Waters back to his place of residence where they could get him alone, and then take him captive. Esme thought it quite fitting that she be the kidnapper for a change. She'd had about enough of being abducted herself.

The stench from the streets was enough to churn Esme's stomach. Bodily fluids mixed with garbage and who knew what else floated past them. She pressed her nose to Fielding's back, hoping his pleasant scent would detract from the horrid smell. The wool of his coat tickled her nose.

Waters was on the move again, swaying widely and humming off-key. She and Fielding kept their distance, staying in the darkness. Wrapped in her darkest cloak, it seemed unlikely that she would be seen. Still, her heart seemed to be hammering in her chest and her nerves were frazzled.

Waters turned down an alley and they followed. The man staggered and practically fell down the steps that took him into what they could only assume was his residence. They waited a few seconds before entering through the same door.

"Esme, you must keep your distance. Whatever you do, don't touch the man."

Esme swallowed her fear. "What about you?"

Fielding's eyes softened. "I'll be careful. I'll be *fine*."

Footsteps sounded overhead. It took a while, but they were finally able to locate the stairs. Boards moaned beneath their weight as they climbed. Still, Waters kept humming and didn't seem alerted to their presence.

The staircase led them, not to a landing, but rather a large loft area that served as Waters's bedroom. A sagging mattress lay directly on the floor, with blankets strewn haphazardly over it. Scattered pieces of clothing littered the floor as well as half-eaten chunks of food. By the time Esme had finished surveying their surroundings, she'd realized there was no time for them to hide from plain view.

"Fielding?" Waters said in drunken surprise.

"Hello, Waters," Fielding said.

Waters frowned in confusion, and his long, thin body wavered. Then he pointed at them, his arm shaking. "Did you follow me?"

"I did." Fielding's voice was strong, yet lined with something else. Amusement, perhaps.

Esme waited, still standing with one foot on the stairs, one in the room. She was unsure of her role in this scheme, but she was prepared to strike should Fielding require her assistance.

"The Raven must be furious," Waters said. "He hasn't found me yet."

Esme doubted that was true. Had the Raven wanted Waters, he would have captured him by now.

Fielding took several steps toward his drunken foe.

"Why haven't you returned to the Raven since the monastery?"

Waters blinked rapidly. "I stole from him. I figured that would do me in for good. Thatcher didn't think we were in danger, but . . ." Waters just shook his head. "Bloody 'ell."

Esme wondered for a moment if Fielding would tell Waters that he'd been right, that Thatcher was dead, but Fielding said nothing.

Waters gave a toothy grin, and it seemed then he first saw Esme standing there. "Hey." He pointed at her. "You're that lady."

It was at that moment Fielding grabbed Waters's shoulders. "You need to come with us."

"I don't think I should." He shook his head and tried to stumble away from Fielding. But his inebriation robbed his coordination. Fielding grabbed Waters by the shirt and, careful not to touch the man's skin, dragged him down the stairs.

It took them another fifteen minutes to make it back to their carriage. All the while, Waters sputtered about how the Raven was going to find them.

Fielding boxed the drunk man's ears. "Quiet! You're giving me a headache."

"Where are you taking me?" he asked once they'd tossed him into the confines of the rig.

"We need your sorry arse to save my life. And perhaps the queen's," Esme said.

Waters hiccuped, and then he promptly passed out.

Chapter Twenty-three

Fielding knew he could not do this alone. As much as he didn't want to, he knew it was time to ask for help. He'd spent so much of his adult life hating the men of Solomon's and what they stood for because he'd blamed them for his father's death. But he'd seen the way they'd come to Mr. Nichols's side, the way they'd taken care of his affairs.

It was time to accept the truth. They had not led his father to his death. It had been an accident, just as his mother had said.

There was only one person to blame. The Raven. His blackmail had driven his father to chase a foolish dream, to go after the treasure himself instead of hiring someone more qualified. And that was why Solomon's had sent those other two men with him—they'd only been trying to protect him.

Even knowing that, even having accepted that the men of Solomon's were honorable, he was still reluctant to ask them for assistance. He'd worked alone for the past seven years. It suited him. But to protect Esme, he'd deal with the devil himself.

Fielding tapped two knuckles on Max's study door.

"Come in," Max said. "Where did you put your cursed friend?"

"In an empty room below the servant's quarters," Fielding replied. "There aren't any windows and I bolted the door, so no chance of him escaping."

"How is Esme?" Max asked when Fielding fell into a chair.

"Sleeping," Fielding said.

"She won't go out again without you?" Max asked with a frown.

"I doubt it, but to be on the safe side, I put a bell on her door." When Max laughed, Fielding explained. "It was something my mother used to do when I was a boy. I had this nasty habit of digging up her flowers."

"Looking for treasure?" Max asked.

Fielding nodded.

"I suppose you've inherited your father's sense of adventure," Max said.

Ah, but which father? The murderer whose blood flowed through his veins, or the scholar who'd raised him? Fielding had a sinking feeling he was more similar to the former. "I suppose," he said.

"What can we do to help?" Max asked.

"We" meaning Solomon's. It was time, he reminded himself, time to forgive and time to ask for help. "You've done plenty for us already," Fielding said.

Max waved him off. "Your father was one of us, and we take care of our own."

And that courtesy evidently extended to him. "The Raven is planning something," Fielding said. "All Esme knows is she saw him studying a map of some sort, and she heard mention of guards and Her Majesty."

"You think he's going after the queen?" Max asked.

"That's just it; I can't see his reasoning for killing Victoria." He leaned forward, bracing his elbows on his knees. "We don't have much time left. The lunar eclipse is tomorrow night, and we have until then to get the bracelet off Esme's wrist." He held his arm up with a shallow laugh. "And my own. Before we—"

"We won't allow that to happen," Max said firmly. "I do believe I know what your uncle's plans might be."

Fielding threaded his fingers through his hair. "I'm glad one of us is able to think clearly. What's your theory?"

Max unfolded the newspaper from his desk and turned it so that Fielding could read it. He tapped on the printed type.

"The Golden Jubilee?" Fielding asked. "That's still two days away."

"Yes, but the celebrations begin tomorrow. Evidently a large number of monarchies and rulers from other nations have come here to join Victoria in the festivities. Tomorrow is their private ceremony at Buckingham Palace."

Fielding sat straighter. "Which will require a greater number of guards," Fielding said. "They'll likely pull the extras from the Tower."

"Precisely. I think he might try to break into the Tower." Max leaned back. "The jewels housed there are worth millions."

"Do you have friends you can trust?" Fielding asked.

Max nodded. "With my life."

Fielding stood. "Gather them tomorrow evening, and then I suppose it will be time to storm the Tower."

*   *   *

"What makes you so certain the Raven will have the box with him?" Esme asked.

"Now that he has it in his possession, he'll not allow it out of his sight," Fielding said. He pulled back the curtain and peered out the carriage window. He and Esme, as well as a bound Waters, were parked a block away from the Tower of London, next to a thick line of laurel bushes.

Esme nodded. It was dusk now and the moon would start rising soon, expanding to its full rounded size before the earth would create a shadow. They had a few hours, but her heart thudded loudly in her ears, like a clock ticking off her remaining minutes.

Fielding flipped open his pocket watch. "They'll be there soon." He put his hand on Esme's knee. "Do you have the pistol I gave you?"

Reaching up under her dress, she untied the small pistol and set it in her lap. Waters's eyes grew round. Good, it was about time she struck fear in someone.

"Do you see how you've driven me to a life of crime?" she asked him in her best chastising tone. She raised both of her eyebrows. "Had you not kidnapped me, I could have been left alone with my studies, minding my own concerns."

Waters shrugged and tried to speak, but the gag muffled his words.

"But no," she continued, "you dreadful men had to include me in your nefarious plans, and now look at us." She picked up the pistol and shook it at him. "I have a weapon, for goodness' sake."

Their captive's eyes rounded even further, and he nodded fervently.

"I should hope you'll know better than to provoke me into using it. You never know how dangerous a woman can be." It occurred to her then she didn't even know if the weapon was loaded. It was on her tongue to ask Fielding, but she thought better of it so as not to alert Waters should her gun be functionally worthless.

"Easy." Fielding put his hand over hers and pressed the gun into her lap. "Stay here. I'll be right back." Fielding exited their carriage and then stuck his head back inside. "And whatever you do, don't touch him!"

Esme nodded at Fielding, then turned back to her captive. "Now listen," she said, jabbing the gun into Waters's knee. "You follow our instructions, and this will all go smoothly." At least she hoped it would. Her insides were shaking so violently it was a wonder she could form complete sentences.

"It's time," Fielding said as he poked his head in. "Esme, do you have the key?"

She reached up and fingered the chain at her neck, then nodded.

The walk down the block didn't take long, and thankfully the streets were virtually empty. Banners hung from streetlamps announcing tomorrow's festivities for the Golden Jubilee. Her Majesty had planned a long and winding parade through the streets of London, and the entire city was expectant and encouraged, longing to see their queen after her extended period of mourning her husband, Albert.

Everyone with the exception of Esme. She couldn't afford to feel excitement about celebrations, not until she knew she would be here to enjoy them.

Esme and Fielding huddled against the outer wall of the Tower with their captive and waited for the rest of the men to arrive. Esme scanned the street, taking note of the scaffolding that had been built as makeshift seating for the parade. Down the way she saw a gardener putting finishing touches on a bed of flowers laid out like a jewel-toned carpet.

And then she caught sight of Max approaching with two men behind him.

"Grey," one man said with a smile and an outstretched hand. "It's been a while." Nick Callum was startlingly handsome, with thick wavy black hair and equally dark eyes.

They shook hands. "Yes, it has been," Fielding agreed.

The second man held his hand out to Fielding.

"Fielding," Max said, "this is Graeme Langford."

Graeme's unfashionably long hair gave him a wild appearance, but his mossy green eyes softened the look. When he spoke, he hid a hint of a Scottish brogue. "Max's told us about your current predicament." He looked to be a serious sort but seemed ready to assist.

"Gentlemen," Max said, "this is Esme Worthington."

"Ah, the lady with that awful curse," Nick said with a flash of a smile. "The Raven has caused problems for us in the past. We've been looking for a little retribution."

"Who exactly are we looking for?" Graeme asked. "I'm not sure I know what this Raven looks like." His brogue thickened as he spoke.

"He looks a lot like me," Fielding said, his jaw tensing. "Only he's older, and he has silver hair." Fielding took a moment to peer over the wall. "I suspect he's already inside."

"It's obviously important that we save Her Majesty's crowns and whatnot," Esme said, "but we also need to get that box back from the Raven. You can see the mischief the box has caused already. It must be retrieved and dealt with."

"And we need Thatcher's hand," Fielding said.

"His hand?" Nick asked.

Fielding shook his head. "It's a long story. Suffice it to say, we need the box and all four bands. Someone will have to watch Waters here to make certain he behaves."

"I'll do it," Graeme said. He wrapped his large hand around Waters's throat and pinned him against the stone wall. Two open wounds appeared along Graeme's forearm, but he ignored them.

"Are you certain?" Fielding asked, noting the sores on Graeme's arm.

"Had worse. You and your lass go and get that box."

"We'll occupy the guards after you get inside," Max suggested.

Fielding peered over the wall again. From this angle he could see four beefeaters pacing slowly outside the Jewel House. He looked at the courtyard surrounding the wardens, trying to find some way around them. He wished he'd paid more attention to the rumors at school of hidden tunnels in and out of the Tower.

"How are we to get past the guards?" Esme asked.

Fielding looked back at the beefeaters and recognized one of them as another of the Raven's men.

He crouched back down. "I have an idea." He reached over and grabbed the hem of Esme's dress and ripped.

"What has gotten into you?" she asked, frowning. She tried to stop him from continuing, but he shoved her hands aside.

"Trust me." He cupped her cheek.

She allowed him to continue until he'd torn away the hem so that her dress hit her right at mid-calf.

Then he grabbed her bodice and pulled it down low.

Nick whistled.

Fielding narrowed his eyes at the man. "Keep your eyes to yourself." Then he said to Esme, "I need for you to walk to those men and flirt with them."

"I beg your pardon?"

"This will work, Esme. You distract them, and the three of us can sneak behind them."

She glanced at the men around them, her features tightening. "I don't know how to flirt," she hissed.

"Esme, love, of course you do." He nodded toward the bracelet. "At least one of the beefeaters over there works for the Raven. I don't know about the others. While you distract them, we should be able to manage the rest."

Her insecurity about her flirtation skills was charming, but they didn't have much time to dawdle. He gave her a pointed look, and she marched off in the direction of the guards.

Then he motioned to the other men to follow him as he ran the length of the wall to their right. They would have to climb over and wait for her distraction to move behind the counterfeit guards.

Fielding could hear Esme's voice as he maneuvered himself into position. Retrieving the pistol from his waistband, he inched closer.

"Well, hello," Esme said as she rounded the corner to face the beefeaters. "It's a lovely evening." Her hand trailed down her neck to her cleavage. "Although I'm afraid I'm a little chilled and I left my cloak at home."

"Come a little closer," one of the guards told Esme. "We'll warm you up."

"Why don't you come and get me," she suggested.

Fielding smiled.

One man took her bait and stepped forward, which enabled Fielding and the others to jump over the wall and take down the guards. One guard, the man Fielding had recognized, turned around. He took one look at Fielding and went for a whistle he had hanging around his neck.

But Fielding leveled the gun at him and dropped the bullet into the chamber. "I wouldn't if I were you."

The man let go of his whistle.

"How many are in there with him?" he asked.

"He's alone. He went in alone," the man said, his voice trembling.

"Good." And with that Fielding slammed the butt of his gun against the man's temple.

"We can hold them," Max said.

"Go," Nick urged.

"Let's go find the Raven," Fielding said as he held his hand out to Esme.

Before they left the courtyard, Esme turned to look at the moon, slowly climbing the night sky.

"Come, Esme."

She nodded and together they slid into the Jewel House. They stood still a moment, allowing their eyes to adjust to the limited light. Someone had taken the torches out of the hallway, shrouding it in near darkness. Thin shafts of light from the moon slipped in through the narrow slits in the wall and gave them a small measure of visibility.

"Do you know where they are?" Esme whispered. "The jewels, I mean."

"We have to get down to the lowest spot in this tower. There is a room at the end of a long hallway. They should be in there."

Together Esme and Fielding wound down the spiral stone steps, keeping close to the wall until they came to the hallway at the bottom. The cold stone acted as an anchor, like a shrubbery wall in a garden maze. They followed the hall to the right and there found a relatively well-lit corridor. Two wall torches remained in their sconces.

Esme nearly screamed when they came across a guard who had met an untimely demise. There was a bullet hole in the middle of his forehead; blood pooled beneath his lifeless body.

Fielding pulled her tighter to him and ran his hand across her back in a vain attempt to soothe her. "Shhh," he whispered.

The familiar scent of the Raven's tobacco filled the air. They were getting close.

Farther down the hall, glass shattered. One of the display cases, Fielding guessed. They quickened their pace. Then he held out his hand, stopping just short of the passageway that led to the room where the jewels were stored.

"Stay behind me," Fielding said. "And try to hold your pistol steady."

She nodded.

Meeting her eyes, he leaned in for a quick kiss.

"Be safe," he told her.

He held up his own pistol, and together they stepped into the room.

The Raven stood amid broken glass cases, holding a large sack already half full of the royal jewels. A large sapphire necklace dangled from his hand. Behind him another guard lay slumped against the wall, two bullet wounds in his chest.

"You know I'm not going to let you out of here with that," Fielding said as he pointed the gun at his uncle.

They had him trapped; there was no way out of the room except around them.

The Raven tilted his head back and laughed. "Fielding, my boy, you always did know precisely how to ruin my fun."

"We'll take the box now," Fielding said, moving toward the golden artifact lying by the Raven's boot. Along with Thatcher's hand. He took three steps forward, aiming his gun right at the Raven's heart.

"What are you going to do, Fielding? Shoot me?" the Raven asked.

It was a fair question, one he'd been asking himself all day. If given the chance, would he be able to do it? Perhaps he might have been prepared to kill the Raven, but his own father? He wasn't certain he'd be able to pull the trigger.

The Raven took a step forward, and in doing so stepped right up to the gun so that it pressed into his shirt. "One shot, that's all it would take."

"We only want the box," Fielding repeated.

"I don't see how that benefits me," the Raven said. He toed the box closer to him but did not release the bag of jewels.

"It allows you to live," Fielding said.

The Raven shrugged. "Either you're going to shoot me or you're not. The box is irrelevant."

"And drop the bag," Esme said. "You're not leaving here with the monarchy's treasure."

The Raven stood there, his eyes moving from Fielding to Esme and back again. Then, suddenly, the bag fell to the floor.

"Esme, very carefully pick up the box."

"What about Thatcher's hand?" she asked with a wince.

He nodded. "We'll need that too."

She stepped over and quickly grabbed the box, which she clutched to her chest. With two fingers, she picked up Thatcher's hand, then coughed into her shoulder to get away from the stench.

"We're going to walk out of here together," Fielding said, the gun still tight against the Raven's chest. "Esme, you walk in front of us, back the same way we came in."

She nodded and started walking.

They were halfway down the hall when something went wrong. The Raven jerked away from Fielding and with one move had Esme pressed against his side, the pistol Fielding had given her held up to her throat.

Fielding's mouth went dry. He kept his gun aimed, but he dared not shoot with Esme so close.

"I'd rather not take her with me, but I will if you insist on taking me to the authorities." With his other hand the Raven yanked the necklace from Esme's neck.

"What do you want?" Fielding asked.

"To leave here. Alone."

Esme's green eyes pleaded with Fielding, and she grimaced when the gun bit into her tender flesh. She squirmed as the Raven tightened his grip on her.

"You have to keep still," the Raven said, his mouth pressed against her cheek. "Though I can see why my nephew favors you so much. Plump in all the right places and just enough fight to make things interesting."

Fielding was going to have to shoot; he had no other choice. Anger surged through Fielding as he aimed for the Raven's shoulder and pulled the trigger. Surprise etched across the man's features as the bullet hit its mark and blood spattered the wall behind them.

Esme screamed and pulled away from the Raven, quickly making her way to Fielding's side.

The Raven turned and ran as best he could while clutching his shoulder.

Fielding grabbed Esme and together they ran after the Raven.

"We still need the key," Esme said.

"We'll get him," Fielding said.

They followed the Raven's bloody trail down the hall-way, then up the flight of stairs and across the battlement to another tower. The wind howled around them, and Fielding caught a flash of the Raven's black cape as he rounded a corner.

"He's getting away," Esme cried.

Fielding sprinted after the Raven and followed the madman's leap to the top of the tower wall. The Raven stopped, looking down at the Thames far below them. There was nowhere else for him to run. Fielding had him trapped.

"Come to finish me off, have you?" The Raven's voice was gravelly with pain.

"I just want the key."

With his good arm, the Raven reached into his shirt collar and withdrew the necklace. "I want the box."

"You have nothing left to bargain with. You're losing blood," Fielding said. "But we can still get you to a doc-tor; they can remove the bullet and you'd survive."

He reached out for the necklace at the same moment the Raven looked over his shoulder at the water below.

"David, don't," Fielding said.

The Raven's face tightened. He inched his feet back.

"That's Traitor's Gate below," he growled. "Fitting, I suppose."

Fielding closed the distance between him and the wall and grabbed the Raven's shirt. "Get down."

But the man wouldn't budge.

"David," Fielding said. "I know the truth. I know you're my father." Fielding knew Esme was behind him, knew she'd hear the truth, but none of that mattered.

The Raven's features softened and he almost smiled. "Beatrice finally told you." It was not a question. And for a moment it looked as if the man might climb down, but then his foot slipped. "It's too late."

Fielding reached up and put his hand around Esme's pendant right as the Raven pushed off the wall. The necklace broke off in Fielding's hand.

"David!" Fielding yelled.

He looked over the edge in time to see the splash below. Esme ran to his side and peered over the wall into the river. Still he saw nothing. He pushed himself away from the wall.

"Fielding, look," she said, pointing to the splashing in the middle of the river. The splashing settled into a rhythm and became strokes as the Raven swam to the opposite bank. "He made it," Esme whispered.

Fielding turned to her. "I know you heard everything. And I wanted to tell you." He sighed. "I didn't know how—"

"You were afraid I'd believe you to be the same as the Raven."

"I am," he said. "I'm his son; his blood is my blood."

She shook her head. "That doesn't matter. You are nothing like him. You are kind and gentle and brave.

Family only determines where we come from; it doesn't mandate who we become."

And in that moment, he knew she truly loved him.

"Are you all right?" he asked, gripping both her arms.

"I think so," Esme said.

He looked up at the sky. The moon was only partially covered. "We don't have much time."

Fielding took her hand, and together they ran until they reached Max and the rest of the men.

They'd taken the liberty of notifying the police, and several officers were just coming out of the Jewel House.

"The jewels were put back in their appropriate place," the lead investigator said. He held his hand out to Max. "Your country thanks you."

Max shook his hand. "I'm afraid I'm not the one to thank." He nodded toward Fielding.

"No time," Fielding said as he dragged Esme over to where Graeme still held Waters prisoner.

Fielding pressed the key into Esme's hand, then held the box out for her. With shaking hands, she pressed the key to the engraving. The box opened and her bracelet immediately fell to the ground. Fielding's and the one from Thatcher's hand also dropped.

"I've got this one," Graeme said.

Fielding grabbed Esme and pulled her tightly into his arms. "We did it," he whispered.

She leaned into him and exhaled. "I didn't think I was going to survive."

"I told you I'd make certain you did," Fielding said.

"Yes, you did." She smiled.

Max bent to pick up the band that had fallen at Esme's feet. "Hope," he said. He smiled at Esme. "That seems fitting for you."

Her head snapped up. "What?"

"Your bracelet—the engraving." He pointed to the word scrawled across the gold band. "This says 'hope.' "

"But that's impossible," she said, shaking her head.

"I thought you said it was lust," Fielding said, then he handed the other three bands to Max. "And these?"

Max looked down at them. "Lust, greed, and disease," he read.

"All this time," Fielding said, shaking his head. "You can read ancient Greek?" he asked Max.

"Atlantis," Max said with a smile. "Greek is a necessity if you want to read about the lost continent. Well, at least some think it's lost. I happen to believe . . ."

"Ahem." Graeme cleared his throat with a gravelly cough. "I think the lady's more interested in her bracelet."

Max looked sheepish as he ducked his head to once again inspect the bands. "Ah, yes . . . I can see how you might have misinterpreted the engraving." He lined up two of the bands and handed them to Esme. "See how similar the two words are?" He pointed to the third letter of each word. "If you mistake this theta for an omicron and this psi"—he pointed to another letter—"for an up-silon, both perfectly natural mistakes . . . and of course they both come from the same root word. For what is hope, but desire in its purest form?"

Chapter Twenty-four

~~~⋙∽∻∽⋘~~~

"Come," Max said. "Everyone is waiting for you."

"Where are we going now?" Esme asked. Fielding still had his arm wrapped securely around her shoulders. "I'm rather tired."

"I'm certain you are," Max said. "But there is some last-minute business to attend to. At Solomon's." He winked at her.

"Solomon's? Truly?" She took a cleansing breath; Fielding guessed it was an effort to settle her nerves. "Do you suppose they'll let me in?" Then she looked down and clearly remembered what he had done to her dress. She tugged on the bodice, trying to pull it back into a more modest position.

"Here." Fielding took off his jacket and wrapped it around her shoulders. "I won't go in without you."

With three Solomon's members among them, they had no problem gaining entrance. They were immediately led back into that same meeting room. Fielding held tightly to Esme's hand. She looked so small wrapped in his greatcoat, but despite her ordeal, her eyes were bright with curiosity.

The room was full of men and roared with noise until they stepped inside, then everything fell quiet.

"Mr. Grey." Jensen rose to his feet. "And Miss Worthington. We are pleased to see you both."

The other men around the table said nothing, just eyed them as they entered the room.

"Please, sit," Jensen said.

Esme placed the bag on the table and withdrew the box. "I believe this belongs to you," she said. She eyed Fielding, and when he nodded she slid the box across the table to Jensen.

Jensen caught the box and kept his hand resting on top. "We have a place to keep dangerous antiquities such as this."

They passed an envelope to Fielding. He opened it and found his payment. He set the envelope on the table. "I believe Miss Worthington would prefer to keep the key in her possession. It was a gift from her father and is rather special," Fielding said.

"That shouldn't be a problem," Jensen said. "But before you go, we have another proposition for you."

"I believe I've retired. For good this time," Fielding said. He had a different sort of life in mind now. One he hoped would involve Esme, but he hadn't yet had the courage or the opportunity to ask her.

"We do not wish to hire you again, but rather have an offer for both you and Miss Worthington."

At that Esme raised her head. "Me, sir?"

"Indeed. Not only have the two of you saved Pandora's box, but I believe it is safe to say you saved our country's prized possessions. Because of your great risk," Jensen continued, "and your heroism, we would like to officially extend an invitation to both of you for membership into Solomon's."

A round of applause sounded around them, and Fielding nearly forgot where he was.

"Join? Solomon's?" Esme's hand moved to her heart. "But you do not allow women," she said softly.

"There is, on occasion, opportunity to make exceptions," Jensen said.

"Then we accept," Esme said, coming to her feet. "Thank you."

Fielding stood and put his hand on Esme's shoulder, giving it a gentle squeeze.

"Hope," she said as she looked up into his eyes.

His heart swelled with love. He'd come close to losing her too many times. He'd never make that mistake again. If he had to spend the rest of his life proving to her that he loved her, he would do precisely that.

Jensen stood and left the room momentarily, then came back with a tattered brown book. "The butler will explain to both of you the layout of the building and all the rooms within. You will be given the password, which changes weekly. You may return any time you like. This is your club now."

"Thank you," Fielding said. He held the envelope out to Jensen. "I believe the previous payment more than covered my expenses."

Jensen nodded and took the money. "Mr. Grey, one more thing. I do believe this belongs to you," Jensen said, holding out the book.

Fielding flipped it open. There within the ratty pages were notes and drawings and diagrams and equations, all in his father's pen. "My father's journal. I thought it was lost in the cave-in."

"Our men recovered it," Jensen said. "We'd been saving it for you, for the appropriate time. I know you said you were retired, but in case someday you want to finish his work . . . He had gotten very close to unearthing the Templar's gold."

For the second time that day, Fielding was at a loss for words.

They were seated in the carriage on the way back to Max's house. They'd spend one more night there, and then she could return home. A hint of wistfulness passed over her. Would it be the last night she'd see Fielding?

Hope. She had worn the band of hope. So the desire they'd felt couldn't have been part of any curse. It had been real. Authentic need. And it was finally time to tell Fielding how she felt.

"Perhaps that's why we were able to succeed," she offered. "The hope from my band."

"You were so worried that my desire for you was manufactured by the curse. I told you I wanted you. Honestly wanted you." He pulled her to his lap. "I still do."

She felt the proof of his desire pressing into her bottom.

"I don't want to lose you," he said, his voice raw with honesty. "I thought I'd lost you yesterday, and I can't face that again."

She didn't want to lose him either, but it was time for her to have what she truly longed for. "I don't want to be your mistress, Fielding," she said. "I might have once believed that was enough for me, but not any longer. I love you; I want you to love me. Anything short of that, I can't accept." She ran her hand down his cheek. "It's all right, though. We had a lovely time together, and I'll cherish the memories forever. But you've changed me; this experience changed me."

He nodded gravely. "You deserve everything you want, everything that has been denied you."

Pain knotted in her stomach. He wasn't arguing with her. Let her leave the carriage without crying, that's all she asked. If she stayed cradled in his arms much longer, she'd end up back in his bed, and it would be even more difficult to walk away. She tried to remove herself from his lap, but his arms stayed tightly wrapped around her.

"You need to let me go," she said.

"No doubt I'll be a wretched husband."

"Precisely," she said, and then his words penetrated. "Husband?"

He smiled, those dimples of his piercing his scruffy cheeks, and she thought her heart might explode.

"Esme, I love you. I have no doubt you'll drive me to Bedlam, but it will be a hell of a ride. Marry me."

The tears she'd tried to keep at bay came despite her best efforts. "Do you mean it? Truly, you want me to marry you?"

"I'm quite serious. Be my wife." His expression was so gentle, his eyes so full of love for her. "I can't offer you much in the way of name and reputation, since I am a bastard"—he gave her a wry smile—"but I have plenty of money. Will you still have me?"

"I don't need a reputation. I only need you."

"Do you worry that someday"—he paused—"I might change? Become more like him?"

"The Raven? Of course not," she said.

"But he loved my mother once, and losing her drove him to—" He shook his head, unable to finish the thought.

"You're not going to lose me. Even still, you aren't your father. Now the man who raised you, I suspect there are probably similarities there. I love you—Fielding, the man you are right now, and the man you'll be tomorrow." She flung herself against him, wrapping her arms around his neck. "Say it again."

"What?" he asked.

"That you love me."

"I love you, I love you, I love you."

THE DISH

Where authors give you the inside scoop!

♥ ♥ ♥ ♥ ♥ ♥ ♥ ♥ ♥ ♥ ♥ ♥ ♥ ♥ ♥

From the desk of Rita Herron

Dear Reader,

I have to admit that I'm a TV junkie. I love comedies, dramas, crime shows, and paranormal series, especially those with a romance in them. Of course, I always find myself drawn to the strong heroes.

Two of my favorites are Jack Bauer from *24* and Cole Turner from *Charmed*. Both are charismatic, tough, sexy, dark tortured guys with tons of emotional baggage. In fact, my husband, who is also a huge *24* fan, named our cat Jack Bauer.

When I first decided to write about demons, I wanted my heroes to have the same qualities as Jack and Cole, to be larger-than-life men who risked their lives to save the world—and of course, the women they love.

In DARK HUNGER, the second book in my paranormal romantic suspense trilogy *The Demonborn*, (out now!), I combined Jack and Cole and created Quinton Valtrez, Vincent's lost long brother.

Quinton is a loner, a government assassin, and a man determined to keep his job and supernatural powers secret. Like Jack, he fights terrorists. Like Cole, he battles demons—as well as the pull of evil inside him.

Pit him against a sassy, tenacious, struggling reporter named Annabelle Armstrong who is determined to unravel his secrets, and the sparks immediately fly. Quinton doesn't know whether to kill her or love her.

Quinton also faces a new kind of terrorist—a demon who has the ability to exert mind control over innocents and turn them into killers. Soon he and Annabelle realize they must work together in a race against time to stop this demon. But Annabelle isn't quite prepared to be thrust into this terrifying demonic world, or to face Quinton's father Zion, the leader of the underworld, who will use her to get to Quinton.

For any paranormal story, setting and world-building is important. Blending the real world with paranormal elements makes the stories more frightening. In DARK HUNGER, I also take you to three of my favorite southern cities: Savannah, Charleston, and New Orleans. All three are steeped with folklore, ghost legends, history, and a spooky ambience that adds flavor to the world of *The Demonborn*. If you haven't visited those cities, put them on your TO DO list. And don't forget to take one of the ghost tours and be on the lookout for demons!

Enjoy!

Rita Herron

♥ ♥ ♥ ♥ ♥ ♥ ♥ ♥ ♥ ♥ ♥ ♥ ♥ ♥ ♥

From the desk of Robyn DeHart

Dear Reader,

I've always been a huge movie buff and my very favorite genre is romantic action adventure; think Indiana Jones and *The Mummy*. Toss together some archeology, a dash of history, and a nasty curse, add in two protagonists with lots of sizzle and I'm one happy woman. I suppose it's this love that brought me to my Legend Hunters and the first book in that series, SEDUCE ME (on sale now).

I admit I'm a geek at heart, but there's something so compelling about old things: ancient texts, antiques, dusty old tombs. I mean, who hasn't dreamt of going on a dig and unearthing something so amazing it changes your life? Well, this is precisely what happens to our heroine Esme Worthington. She ends up getting herself kidnapped, but in doing so she comes face-to-face with the object of her lifelong obsession, Pandora's box.

Enter our hero, Fielding Grey, a treasure finder-for-hire who is none too happy that his latest assignment comes with a damsel in distress. But he can't walk away from her while she's literally chained to a wall. So he snags Esme and the fabled box and thus begins an adventure neither could have imagined. Not only does the box come with a unique curse that has Esme acting the wanton, but a nefarious villain is hot on their trail and will stop at nothing until he possesses Pandora's treasure.

This new series is about Solomon's, a luxurious gentleman's club equipped with all the accoutrements one would expect from such a fine establishment. Membership is by invitation only, because in this club there's a hidden room where secret meetings occur. In these secret meetings some of London's finest gentlemen gather to discuss their passions; their obsessions. Some are scholars, some collectors, some treasure-hunters, but each of them is after the find of the century. I can't wait for you to meet the Legend Hunters . . .

Visit my Web site, www.RobynDeHart.com for contests, excerpts, and more.

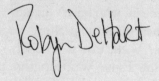

♥ ♥ ♥ ♥ ♥ ♥ ♥ ♥ ♥ ♥ ♥ ♥ ♥ ♥ ♥

From the desk of Diana Holquist

Dear Readers,

When my family moved from the big city to a tiny rural town for my husband's work, there were no jobs for me. I wept for about a week. Okay, maybe two weeks. Then I realized that this was the perfect time to start something new. Because I was incredibly naive, I opened a file on my computer and typed, "Chapter One."

Uh-oh. Now what? I needed a story. But what? What did I care about enough to pour my heart and soul into? Later, I learned that what a book is about—what it's *really* about—is called a premise, and every good book has one. What was my premise?

I started lurking on the Web site of a woman who was looking for her soul mate. She wanted him to be a certain height and make a specified income and on and on. But no matter how hard she looked, she couldn't find her "one true love."

What if there was a soul mate put here on this earth just for this woman, but he wasn't tall and rich? This woman needed a guide to the world of love.

Thus, Amy Burns was born, the psychic gypsy who can tell you the name of your One True Love. She starred in my first three books, creating chaos, love, and a premise I could believe in: only when we face our true desires can we find happiness.

In my first book, MAKE ME A MATCH, Cecelia Burns is a doctor about to marry the "perfect" man: a rich, successful, handsome, charming lawyer. Along comes her psychic sister Amy, to announce that Cecelia's one true love as destined by fate is not only an underemployed single father, but that he might be dying. If she wants her one shot at experiencing true love, she's got to act fast.

In SEXIEST MAN ALIVE, Jasmine Burns, the shyest woman alive, learns that her one true love as destined by fate is Josh Toby, *People* magazine's Sexiest Man Alive. Uh-oh. She can't talk to a regular man; how will she ever get near this one?

HUNGRY FOR MORE is Amy's book. She has to choose between learning the name of her own one true love or keeping her psychic powers. When she meets a sexy French chef, she realizes that accepting true love is harder than she thought it would be.

The One True Love series got great reviews, a RITA nomination, and won awards like the New York Book Festival romance award. But more important, this series introduced me to so many wonderful readers, some of whom I now count among my friends. When I look back on those first days of moving away from the city, I laugh when I think about how what I thought was the end was actually a new beginning. I didn't realize then that I was living my own premise: be careful what you wish for. Because when you try something new, open your mind to the possibilities that life offers, and focus on your true desires, good things happen.

Happy reading!

Diana Holquist

Want to know more about romances at Grand Central Publishing and Forever? Get the scoop online!

GRAND CENTRAL PUBLISHING'S ROMANCE HOME PAGE

Visit us at www.hachettebookgroup.com/romance for all the latest news, reviews, and chapter excerpts!

NEW AND UPCOMING TITLES

Each month we feature our new titles and reader favorites.

CONTESTS AND GIVEAWAYS

We give away galleys, autographed copies, and all kinds of fun stuff.

AUTHOR INFO

You'll find bios, articles, and links to personal Web sites for all your favorite authors—and so much more!

THE BUZZ

Sign up for our monthly romance newsletter, and be the first to read all about it!

VISIT US ONLINE

@ WWW.HACHETTEBOOKGROUP.COM.

AT THE HACHETTE BOOK GROUP WEB SITE YOU'LL FIND:

CHAPTER EXCERPTS FROM SELECTED NEW RELEASES

•

ORIGINAL AUTHOR AND EDITOR ARTICLES

•

AUDIO EXCERPTS

•

BESTSELLER NEWS

•

ELECTRONIC NEWSLETTERS

•

AUTHOR TOUR INFORMATION

•

CONTESTS, QUIZZES, AND POLLS

•

FUN, QUIRKY RECOMMENDATION CENTER

•

PLUS MUCH MORE!

Bookmark Hachette Book Group
@ www.HachetteBookGroup.com.